Phoenix Rising

By
Stan Daneman

Published by and available from
theendlessbookcase.com

The Endless Bookcase Ltd
71 Castle Road, St Albans,
Hertfordshire, England, UK, AL1 5DQ.

Printed in the United Kingdom
Also available in multiple e-book formats.
First Printing, 2017

Front cover image is provided under license from Adobe.
stock.adobe.com/uk/

ISBN: 978-1-912243-09-9

Dedicated to my wife and daughters,
Anita, Taryn and Lauren
With all my love

Acknowledgement

No one can write a book in isolation. Whether the support is direct or indirect, the encouragement and advice of family and friends is paramount.

My family supports me in my desire to write and has always encouraged that interest in writing – be it poetry or novels. Without them I would not have the motivation, drive or desire to write. My books are dedicated to my wife Anita, and our daughters, Taryn and Lauren. My appreciation is expressed to Lauren for the final editing and critique.

When I completed my novel, I was fortunate enough to have three friends who read it, provided advice and edited the manuscript;

To Kunal Shah in Toronto – thank you so much for reading my raw material! Your input is greatly appreciated. You are a dear friend.

To John Hourigan in Sydney, Australia – your tireless editing of the manuscript of 'Phoenix Rising' has significantly enhanced the structure and quality of the storyline. Thank you my friend!

To Bob Little – my friend, and rugby and cricket mate from the UK! Thank you for reviewing my three previous books and for your substantial contribution to Phoenix Rising.

My most sincere thanks to Kunal, John, Bob, and Lauren for their contribution to bringing 'Phoenix Rising' to fruition!

Also, my sincere thanks to the Delheim wine estate, Stellenbosch, South Africa, for providing me with written permission to mention the estate and the owners in the book. A gem winery in South Africa!

About the Author

Stan Daneman was born in South Africa. He is a graduate of the University of South Africa obtaining a B.Com (Accounting) and a postgraduate Hon. B.Com (Business Economics). He also holds a diploma in Organization and Methods and is a certified management consultant.

He is a past president of the Institute of Management Consultants of South Africa and was awarded fellowship of the institute.

During his business career, he held senior positions as a management consultant with professional firms and Director of Education positions in the IT industry.

Mr. Daneman has published six previous books. His three books of poetry were published in 1987, 2002 and 2013. In 2009, he published a book on positioning and measuring learning in an organization. His three previous books through The Endless bookcase were: 'From my hilltop – a living history of South Africa' (a unique look at the changes in the country as narrated by a tree), 'Reflections of heaven' published in 2013, and Stan's first novel, 'The Solar Murder', which was published in 2014.

Mr. Daneman immigrated to Canada in 1995 and resides in Richmond Hill, Ontario. He is married with two adult daughters, and has been involved in sport management and volunteer activities for over forty years. This book is dedicated to his wife and daughters.

This book is Stan's second novel, and is a spin-off from 'The Solar Murder'.

Part 1

Chapter 1

Elizabeth McKenzie was not one for the limelight. She did not enjoy speaking in front of people. She had a quiet demeanor. She was short and to the point. That is the way the lawyers whom she had worked for preferred her to be – to get the message across without being flowery.

She had thrived in the legal firm environment. Over the years very few people knew much about her – she kept her private life to herself. However, on a scale of one to ten in regard to being efficient and professional in her job, she was a twelve.

After joining the law firm of Greg Winters, she felt that she had developed even further. She ran the office administration, kept everyone to his or her deadlines and made sure that the law firm functioned as smoothly as possible. She succeeded!

She knew that Greg and his associates teased her – in particular Greg, but right to the very end she knew that Greg respected her and loved her. After all, when he died just after his retirement, he left her two million dollars and his cabin in Alpine Meadows.

Elizabeth had never cured Greg of his habit of eating greasy burgers and drinking too much coffee. She could only reprimand her boss to a certain extent! As a top-class defense lawyer he seldom found time to eat properly. Coffee provided the adrenalin when his tank was truly empty. Deep down he knew that he had to pay more attention to his work-based life style. Even before his beloved Mary passed away he had poor eating habits. But at least Mary would cook him meals and keep his mind off work on weekends.

When Elizabeth resigned from the law firm and moved into Greg's cabin she thought that she would be happy in retirement. She expected the setting of the cabin in the woods would bring her comfort and a quiet life style. The small lake just off to the left of the cabin and the tall trees surrounding most of the area nearby presented a very tranquil setting.

After all of Greg's electronic equipment had been removed and the cabin refurnished, Elizabeth settled down into her new environment. The drive to town was only seven miles, and she spent most days there. Maybe she was looking for something to do. From being a high energy Office Manager and Assistant to the most famous lawyer in the state, to being retired to a cabin in the woods was a gigantic change. Maybe too big a change!

Elizabeth never did feel very safe in the cabin, especially alone at night. Even during the day, it was so secluded that she wondered if anyone would hear her scream if something should happen. The setting of the cabin was a touch of heaven on earth but somehow, she felt uneasy about her new abode. She had installed a high-tech security system and had replaced all the windows with shatterproof glass but still she felt vulnerable at night.

It was a hot Tuesday afternoon when Sheriff Norman Wilson walked past the diner where he saw Elizabeth sitting at a table by herself. It was the best place in town to have tea or coffee and something to eat. He stopped for a second and then decided to walk into the diner. He had only met Elizabeth briefly at Greg's funeral and he thought it right that he make himself known to the town's new resident.

"Hello" said Norman, "It is Ms. McKenzie, right?"

Elizabeth had not seen the sheriff enter the diner nor walk up to her table. She was a little taken aback as she heard her name.

"Oh, hello Sheriff, I didn't see you come in. I must've been deep in thought. How are you?"

"Sorry if I startled you!" he said.

"No need to apologize, I was a thousand miles away!"

"How is our newest resident doing? Are you finding your way around our bustling metropolis?"

"I'm fine thank you, and yes, I'm finding my way around town. It is a lovely town, and so different from living in the city."

"Well, if you need any help you know where to find your friendly police department."

Norman Wilson was a big man but he had such a gentle smile, it made his whole face light up.

Elizabeth thought for a moment then said, "Sheriff if you have a moment would you like to join me for tea?"

"Yes, that would be great but could I trade it for a coffee?"

"Sure, whatever you like."

As the sheriff sat down the waiter was already pouring a coffee for him. This was only another of the thousands that Norm Wilson had consumed in the diner over the years. Regulars have a way of not requiring communication when they enter their local coffee shop or bar.

"So how are you settling down?" he asked.

"Well, it's so different from the city. It is much more relaxed and stress free. Working for Greg was totally consuming. We had hardly any time to think about anything else but the case that we were working on. I can see why he wanted to get away from San Francisco and visit Alpine Meadows whenever he could."

The two chatted about Greg for the next minute or two before the waiter came back with a burger and fries and fresh coffee for the sheriff.

Norm Wilson did not know if he should be embarrassed or not. His standard fare was a burger and coffee whenever he came into the diner.

Elizabeth came to his rescue, “He must have known that you looked hungry!” She smiled at the sheriff and they laughed.

“Please, go ahead and enjoy your burger”. She could not comprehend how one could eat so much meat and fries. A while back she would have scolded Greg for eating a meal like this but she could not say anything like that to the sheriff of Alpine Meadows.

When Norm Wilson had finished his meal, he insisted on paying for the herbal tea that Elizabeth had ordered.

Chapter 2

Madelyn Wilson developed an early interest in the arts – in particular in painting. After graduating high school she obtained a Bachelor of Fine Arts degree. Her further academic ambitions were curtailed, however, by a lack of finances and a developing relationship with Fred Nelson. They moved in together once they had graduated with their Bachelor degrees. Living together was frowned upon in those days.

Madelyn chose to become an arts teacher while Fred furthered his academic career. It seemed almost natural for her to fund Fred's future studies. They planned to marry as soon as Fred obtained his Doctorate in early childhood education.

After loyally being the breadwinner for over three years, Maddy was shattered when Fred called off their relationship straight after he graduated. She had poured all of her income, her body and soul into funding Fred. Each month had been a financial struggle but somehow they had made ends meet. When Fred walked out on her, she lost all faith in the male form of the human species. Maddy could not bring herself to go home to see her family for almost a year after Fred left her.

Over the next thirty years she taught painting in Reno. Her studio was well known and her income was good. She lived a simple life style and over the years she had accumulated a respectable bank balance.

Just like her much younger brother Norman, Maddy had never married.

Norman was the result of an unexpected pregnancy for his parents. Maddy was in high school when Norman arrived as an addition to the family. Just as *Sis* was dedicated to painting so Norman was dedicated to police work.

After many years of loyal service he was appointed as chief of police for Alpine Meadows. He stood just over six feet one inch tall but he had put on a great deal of weight since first joining the police department. Meeting the physical examinations was becoming more difficult for Norman. To the surprise of the review board he was still agile and fit for his size. The question was for how much longer could he pass the grueling police testing.

Norman Wilson had lived with his mother in their long-time family home in Alpine Meadows. When she passed away, Norm felt very lonely. He struggled to care for himself.

It was about this time that Maddy started to develop arthritis in her hands and painting became more and more difficult. When her mother died, Maddy asked Norman if she should move back to Alpine Meadows and live with him. He was delighted to have her home. Maddy was a strong and determined woman and, with the substantial age difference between them, she often came across as the mother figure. In truth, Norm did not mind it too much – but sometimes she was difficult to deal with once she got an idea in her mind.

Norm was now in his early fifties and Maddy Wilson in her late sixties.

Chapter 3

Maddy Wilson was never one for mincing her words. She was direct, even more so with men. Deep down, she had never really recovered from the hurt that Fred had inflicted on her all of those years ago.

One evening after work, Norman was to again experience the unrelenting personality of his older sister.

Maddy was in the kitchen when Norman arrived home.

The greeting was always the same.

"Hi Maddy, how are you?"

"Hello Norm, I'm good thanks, and you?"

"Good thanks. I'll wash up and be ready for dinner soon."

"Don't be too long, dinner will be ready in a few minutes."

Norman would change out of his police uniform, wash up and throw on some casual clothes all in about ten minutes.

When he came down stairs he kissed his sister on the cheek and she gave him a hug. She could never put her arms fully around him, as he was too big.

"I could eat a horse I'm so hungry."

"Knowing you, you've already eaten one today." she replied.

Norman refused to be baited. He just walked over to the fridge and took out a beer for himself and a strawberry cooler for Maddy. This was the same routine every evening.

Norman would devour his first plate of food and then have to sit patiently until Maddy finished her meal. Only then would she offer him seconds. It was as she completed her meal – and with Norman almost ready for his seconds – when she dropped the bombshell.

"So why don't you invite her over for dinner? I'd like to meet her".

Norman almost gagged. Maddy' s timing was perfect!

After he composed himself he said, "Whom are you talking about?" He put on a puzzled look on his face. It did not work. He looked more like a kid caught with his hand in the cookie jar.

"Norman Wilson, do you take me for a fool? Really, who do you think that I am talking about – Snow White?" She gave Norman a very disgusted look. She continued before Norman could answer her.

"The city lady, the one that used to work for Greg Winters, the one he left his cabin to, the one that you've had coffee with several times this month. Does that jog your memory?"

Norman had no way out.

"Oh, you mean Ms. McKenzie? Sure we've met for coffee several times. But what business is it of yours anyway?" Maddy looked at him without replying and he had no choice but to elaborate.

"I introduced myself as sheriff one day in the diner and we started to chat. She was very polite and offered to buy me tea. She is very formal – and rather icy I might say."

Norman paused.

Very calmly she prodded, "And the other times that you've met?"

"Gee, are you spying on me? Sure we've met when she comes into town. I think that she's pretty nervous being out at the cabin by herself. And what business is it of yours anyway?"

"What did you talk about?"

"It is not a big deal. If you must know, we spoke about Greg Winters. I knew Greg for many years but only really the person who came to Alpine Meadows. I knew very little about Greg, the famous and successful lawyer. Ms. McKenzie knew him as that lawyer and how he operated in the legal world. We spent time chatting about him and exchanging stories. Does that satisfy your interest in who I talk with in town?"

Maddy continued as if she had not heard a word that Norman had said.

"So, you call her Ms. McKenzie? Does she have a first name?"

"My God woman, what's the matter with you? She introduced herself as "Elizabeth McKenzie". I address her as Ms. McKenzie and she has never said that I should call her by her first name. She addresses me as Sheriff Wilson. Are you satisfied?"

The answer to that question was obvious. Maddy Wilson was not satisfied.

"Are you telling me that all that you have ever discussed is Greg Winters? Have you ever asked her about her background, where she was raised? Nothing about her?"

"Let me put it simply and clearly for you - 90% of what we have ever discussed has been about Greg, the rest has been about how she has settled into town. Can we move on now – I'm hungry!"

So many times in his life Norm had under-estimated his older sister – this was again one of them. Maddy Wilson was not satisfied.

"So, when are you going to invite her for dinner – how about this Saturday? We could have drinks outside before dinner. You should offer to fetch her and take her home afterwards – it's too dark to drive home alone."

To say that Norm Wilson was frustrated with the conversation would be an understatement. He was angry. This for him was very unusual. He normally had a very level personality. But here he was dealing with his older and determined sister.

"Tell me why you want to have her over for dinner? We don't owe her anything. I don't understand why you are so hell bent on meeting her."

She thought for a moment and then lied with a straight face, "Because I need company. My friends are so boring. There's never anything new to talk about in this small town. I thought that Ms. McKenzie could be an interesting person for me to meet. Besides, you are the most respected person in town and showing a newcomer some hospitality might encourage others to accept her. So, what is wrong with inviting her for dinner?"

Norm thought for a long time before he answered. In reality it might only have been thirty seconds but the silence at the dinner table seemed like an eternity. When he spoke it was both with a sense of acceptance of Maddy's logic and, to a degree, knowing he could not win.

"Alright, I will phone and invite her for dinner on Saturday."

"Will you call her in the morning?"

"Don't push it – I said that I'll phone her."

She smiled and said, "Norm, would you like seconds?"

Chapter 4

Elizabeth was washing up her breakfast dishes when the telephone rang. The sound startled her. Sometimes a week or more would go by without a telephone call. This was so different from working in a law firm where everything was push-push to get done.

Elizabeth would not accumulate her dishes and do them only once a day. After every meal her home in the woods was tidy and clean.

"Hello, can I help you?"

"Ms. McKenzie this is Sheriff Wilson, how are you? Is this a good time to talk?"

Elizabeth was taken aback by receiving a telephone call from the sheriff.

"Oh, hello sheriff, is anything the matter?"

"No, nothing the matter. I just have a question for you. My sister and I would like to invite you over for dinner at our home this coming Saturday evening, so, I'm calling to check if you can make it".

Elizabeth was stunned by what she had just heard. Her first reaction was *"why would the sheriff and his sister want to invite me over?"*

"Hello, are you still there?" asked Norman.

"Yes, I am still here. I - I was just thinking about what you said, sorry; it took a minute to register. Is there a special occasion or something?"

"No, nothing special, it will be the three of us. Madelyn loves to cook and she thought that it would be nice to show some local hospitality. We hope that you can make it. If you're available then I'll drive out to fetch you."

"Actually, that would be very nice – can I bring anything?"

"Great! And there's no need to bring anything. We'll have drinks before dinner and then we'll eat a little later. Should I collect you around six?"

"Yes, that will be fine, thank you. I look forward to seeing you on Saturday."

When Elizabeth put the telephone down she sat in the kitchen and thought about what had just happened. She was certainly not the social type. She was very tempted to telephone the sheriff and cancel the arrangement but she thought that it would not be professional.

Once she had got her mind around the invitation then she thought *"Oh, what would I wear? I haven't been to many home dinners before. Most of my clothes are business formal."*

Over the next few days Elizabeth was riddled with doubt about the upcoming dinner invitation and what to wear.

When Norman put the telephone down after his conversation with Elizabeth he too felt as if this was a mistake. He was still thinking about the call when his cell phone rang; it was his beloved sister making sure that he had telephoned Elizabeth.

Finally on the Friday Elizabeth drove into town and found a dress shop. She bought a skirt and blouse that looked respectable on her. She decided to wear her hair in her favorite style for the dinner.

On the Saturday, Norman pulled up at the cabin just on 6 p.m. The buzzer in the cabin had gone off as Norman had crossed onto the property. Some of Greg's security gadgets were very practical.

Elizabeth was locking her front door when Norman reached the cabin. He took a deep breath when he saw Elizabeth. She looked so different and ten years younger. He noticed her hair and what she was wearing. A smile came to his face.

"Good evening Ms. McKenzie how are you?"

"Good evening sheriff, I'm well, thank you. How are you? Please, call me Elizabeth."

"I'm fine thank you Elizabeth, please call me Norman – I'm off duty now!" He smiled.

They had a pleasant but somewhat tense ride into town.

Maddy either wore her hair up in a bun or loose over her shoulders. When preparing for the evening with Ms. McKenzie she decided that it had been a long time since she had a reason to do something special with her hair. She used to wear her hair in a special way many years before. It took her several hours to get the house in order and prepare dinner but she seemed to be able to do her long hair in lightening quick time.

Norman had left to fetch their guest after 5:40 p.m. She expected them back just before 6:20 p.m. This time gave Maddy the chance to recheck the house, finalize the dinner and peek at herself in the mirror.

As per her calculations, Norman and Elizabeth arrived at the home just after 6:20 p.m.

Norman could not wait for the two ladies to meet face to face!

Maddy walked down from the porch as Norman and Elizabeth climbed out of the vehicle and walked towards her.

"Hello Ms. McKenzie, I'm Madelyn – everyone calls me Maddy. It's so nice to meet you."

"It's a pleasure to meet you Maddy – and please call me Elizabeth."

It was then that the two women looked more closely at each other.

Not only were they wearing the same skirts and blouses but also both women had decided to do their hair in French plaits. Norman could not believe his eyes when he had seen Elizabeth at her home.

The initial stare of embarrassment gave way to a roar of laughter from Maddy. Elizabeth felt her knees knocking and her legs shaking as she realized that they were dressed identically. She could have fallen through the floor if there was one. It was within the next ten seconds that she began to like Madelyn Wilson.

"Elizabeth, we have such good taste in clothing!" She smiled at Elizabeth and that spark of friendship ignited.

"Norman, why didn't you say anything when you picked me up? I feel so foolish! I could have changed."

"What could I say?" He thought for a moment then said, "Besides you both look great! Just like twin sisters." Both women smiled at him.

"That was very diplomatic Norman, thank you!" Elizabeth smiled at him.

"Elizabeth, let me see your hair"

Maddy entered into a conversation as she took Elizabeth by the arm and walked with her towards the steps leading up to the porch. Norman followed them up the steps and finally found an opportunity to indicate that they should sit down.

Norman sat in silence listening to the conversation. It must have been at least five minutes before Maddy said, "Norman, you are a very bad host, you haven't offered Elizabeth something to drink!"

In reality he had not had an opportunity to say a word!

"Of course, of course, Elizabeth what can I get you?"

"Well, I'm not much of a drinker actually – what would you suggest?"

Before Norman could answer Maddy interjected, "Norman makes a wonderful sherry brandy, would you like to try one?"

"I haven't had that before. Yes, I'll try it but only a small one if you don't mind."

Norman smiled and said, "Sure, two sherry brandies coming right up." He unfolded his large frame from his chair and walked into the house.

Maddy did not waste a second to continue their discussion. She asked Elizabeth about how she was fitting into town, if she found any shops that she liked – including the dress shop where they had both purchased their skirts and blouses – only that Maddy had acquired hers many years before. She kept up the polite questioning.

Elizabeth felt as if she was being questioned on so many things but at least she did not have to make the conversation. Maddy was doing an excellent job at that.

Norman returned with a tray of drinks.

"There you are Elizabeth, one small sherry brandy." He placed the drink on a side table next to her.

"Thank you Norman."

He handed his sister her drink and then sat down with his beer in hand.

After some idle chatter – mostly that excluded Norman – Maddy went inside to put the dinner out. When she was out of earshot Norman said, "Maddy does like to chat, sorry if she just climbed in!"

"Oh, I didn't mind at all, I'm not a great conversationalist and I prefer it when someone else is keeping things going. Your sister seems very nice."

They chatted for another minute or two before Maddy returned.

"We can eat in just a few minutes. Norman your bar duties are required again."

"Yes! I am reporting for duty." He smiled as he stood up.

"Elizabeth what would you like to drink with dinner? Red or white wine, or a cooler, or another sherry brandy?"

"Well, to be honest I don't drink very much – I'm not sure, maybe a half glass of red wine."

"Coming right up!" Norman walked into the house without asking Maddy what she would like to drink with dinner. She always had red wine.

"Come Elizabeth let's get settled at the table while Norman pours the wine". As they rose she took Elizabeth by the arm and walked her into the home. Elizabeth was not a touchy feely person and she was a little uncomfortable by being held.

Over time she would get used to her new friend and not mind the occasional pat on the hand or the arm. It was just her way of communicating. All things take time and some adjustment.

The Wilson home was old and furnished out of a bygone era. It looked very 19th century inside. Display cases were large and made of dark and heavy wood. The living room that Elizabeth walked through on the way to the dining room was dim even at this early evening time. Elizabeth was no connoisseur of old furniture so she could not date anything in the fleeting moment as she walked through the house but what did strike her immediately was how sophisticated and smart the house looked. Maddy was obviously very proud of their home. As Elizabeth would find out later, the home had been in the family for over ninety years.

The dining room was beautifully decorated. The large display case and dining room table dominated the room. The table settings were a work of art. As Elizabeth took her seat she felt as if she was on a movie set. The layout of the cutlery was as prescribed by etiquette professionals.

Maddy and Norman excelled as hosts and the evening flitted by in an instant. Elizabeth told her hosts how she used to shop in her local village market on a Saturday. She was always on the lookout for homemade products. While describing her Saturday morning adventures to buy fresh produce Elizabeth stopped in mid-sentence.

"Elizabeth, are you unwell? Is something the matter?" asked Norman.

Elizabeth felt her cheeks go red and then she felt as if she was going to faint. She took a deep breath as her hosts looked on with concern. She raised her hand to indicate that she was fine. She took a sip of water and then cleared her throat.

"I'm fine thank you. As I was describing my shopping to you I remembered that I was out shopping the day that I heard on the TV newscast that Greg had been shot and killed. I...I fainted in the street and had to be taken to a nearby hospital to be checked out. I was fine but the news of Greg's murder was too much for me to grasp. I...I'm sorry if I startled you. I am fine now."

"My dear, I am so sorry. That must have been a great shock to you. I had met Greg Winters several times and he was an outstanding man."

Maddy then thought about Norman sitting at the table.

"Norman, you found Greg's body. I cannot even begin to think how you felt that morning. I'm so sorry for you both."

The three of them sat silent for a moment then Norman raised his glass. All he said was "To Greg!"

The two ladies clicked their glasses with Norman.

Then Maddy said, "I'm sure that Greg would have wanted us to have our meal while it was still warm!"

Elizabeth and Norman smiled and the tension was broken.

Although Elizabeth never really did relax completely that evening, she did feel that Maddy and Norman had come into her life for a purpose. Norman was more reserved while his sister was charming, warm and irresistible. She kept the evening moving along without even really trying. But of course she was trying very hard – it was just that she was good at it!

Elizabeth had not eaten so well since she had moved to Alpine Meadows.

It was well after 9 p.m. when Norman suggested that they retire to the living room for coffee. At first, Elizabeth was reluctant and suggested that she should be heading home. Her hosts would hear nothing of it. To her surprise, and without having being asked, Norman brought out a liqueur while the coffee was brewing.

As Norman handed the liqueur to Elizabeth he said, "Oh, I apologize, I should've asked you if you would have liked a liqueur before your coffee. I'm in the habit of just pouring for Maddy and myself."

Elizabeth accepted her drink – even though she was feeling rather woozy after the wine with dinner.

As the conversation progressed there was more talk of the late Greg Winters. Maddy allowed Elizabeth to speak about Greg. In a way Elizabeth felt more at ease when talking about someone else than herself. Maybe Elizabeth's conversations with Norman had also been a form of healing.

Then almost completely off topic, Elizabeth asked a question – she surprised Maddy and herself!

"You mentioned at the dinner table that you used to operate an art studio, is that correct?"

"Yes - it was my life until the onset of arthritis. Painting and teaching was my passion. Why do you ask?"

'"A long time ago, I thought of taking painting lessons but because of the hectic life that I led at the law offices I worked for, I never took up my interest. I was wondering if you might be available to give me some lessons if you had the time – I would pay you of course."

There was silence in the living room – well, for all of five seconds before Maddy answered.

"Of course, I would! That would be my pleasure! Oh, yes, that would be my pleasure!"

Norman just sat in shock. His sister had not picked up a brush in years and here she was readily accepting to teach Elizabeth how to paint.

"Oh, thank you! ...but I must insist that I pay you for the lessons."

"We can work that out later but for now let's talk about what you would like to do."

After coffee Elizabeth finally succeeded in persuading Maddy to let her go home. The two women had agreed that Elizabeth would telephone in the next few days to discuss a suitable art program schedule. Norman had witnessed a one night bonding experience.

Driving back to the cabin Elizabeth kept thanking Norman and Maddy for having her over for dinner. She repeated herself several times on the quality of the dinner, the great company and the prospect of starting painting lessons. This was very unlike Elizabeth. Maybe it was the wine and liqueur speaking.

At the front door Elizabeth extended her hand to Norman and thanked him again for a wonderful evening. Once she had locked the door and indicated that the alarm system was armed she waved to him and he drove away.

He was hoping that his sister would be in bed when he got home. He was mistaken. She was doing the dishes as he walked in. She had taken her time cleaning up! "Are you pleased that we invited Elizabeth over for dinner?"

Chapter 5

The next day Elizabeth gave great thought to the happenings of the previous evening. After breakfast she sat outside and became engrossed in her thoughts and the splendor of her surroundings.

She often sat outside but she had really not taken in the true beauty of the location. The small dirt track that led off of the tarred road wound first to the right and then to the left. As the gentle left turn was made the small lake came into view. In reality it was no more than two hundred yards long and three hundred yards wide. It seemed to always reflect the sunshine. It looked to be such a happy lake! The sunsets were particularly spectacular. Sharing the sunsets had mostly been a lonely experience for Greg as they were now for Elizabeth.

She looked at the gravestones for Mary and Greg Winters. It was almost ominous seeing them there. She felt as if she were intruding in their private space. It seemed such a lonely place to be after the city life.

The day passed slowly.

All of that week passed without Elizabeth telephoning Maddy. She also did not drive to town but instead did her shopping at another nearby village. She could not bear running into either her or Norman and them asking why she had not as yet telephoned.

Maddy also decided not to telephone Elizabeth that week. She needed to give her time.

On the following Monday, Elizabeth decided that it was time she telephoned Maddy. As much as she believed that she wanted to try painting lessons she believed even more that she should return to San Francisco. She did not know how the conversation would go – except that Maddy would be disappointed.

When the telephone rang Elizabeth thought that it was Maddy calling to finalize the pending arrangements. She could not have been more wrong.

"Hello, how can I help you?"

"Hello, Elizabeth, it's Ken Parker calling. How are you?"

This was not a telephone call that Elizabeth would have expected.

"Oh, hello Ken, I'm fine thank you. And you?"

And she automatically asked, "Is anything the matter?"

"I'm good thank you. Are you enjoying life in the wilderness?"

Elizabeth replied, "Well, it does take some getting used to. Ken, how can I help you?"

"Well, as you know we hired someone after you left us. She seemed okay to start with but it really did not work out for her or the firm. She resigned about two weeks ago."

Ken continued, "We have shortlisted a number of potential candidates and we were wondering if you had the time to come to San Francisco and assist us in the selection process."

Elizabeth hesitated before she answered.

"Well, I have the time. When were you thinking of me coming in?"

"We were hoping to do the selection on Thursday and Friday. We'd put you up at the hotel near the office. We would cover your costs - if you wanted to stay for the weekend that would be fine too."

Elizabeth agreed to drive in for Wednesday evening. On Thursday and Friday she would form part of the panel that would interview the candidates. She readily accepted to stay in the city until the Sunday.

Elizabeth telephoned Maddy.

"Hello Maddy, this is Elizabeth McKenzie, how are you?"

"I am fine thank you, and you. I was hoping that you would telephone soon."

They exchanged pleasantries for a minute before Elizabeth broke the news.

"My old law firm have asked me to come into San Francisco and assist them in selecting someone to fill the position that I held. Things did not work out with the first replacement. So, I will be going into the city this Wednesday and will only be returning on Sunday. We will have to delay our classes."

"Are you still interested in painting lessons?" she asked.

"Yes, but they would have to be delayed."

"Tell you what, why not pop around for a quick cup of tea before you leave and I will provide you with a list of the tools of the trade that you will need for when we start our lessons. There is a great art supply store in The Bay area."

Elizabeth felt a little trapped but she agreed to visit with her that afternoon and pick up the list. She was not sure if she would visit the store or not. They had an enjoyable hour together that afternoon.

Elizabeth drove into San Francisco and checked into the hotel near the law firm.

Elizabeth felt uncomfortable as she parked her car at the law firm the next morning. The anxiety only increased as she walked towards the entrance of the building and then took the elevator to the upper floor of the building.

When the elevator door opened, she saw that Wendy was sitting at the reception desk – just as she had done for the last twenty-five years.

Wendy escorted Elizabeth to the "war room" where the interviews were to take place, but they were stopped several times as the staff saw Elizabeth and came out to greet her. It was a strange feeling as Elizabeth felt both wrong to be back and so right in being home.

The war room held so many memories for Elizabeth. Once Wendy left her to settle in, Elizabeth sat for a few moments and looked around. She needed to go to the ladies restroom to dry a few tears.

Ken was waiting for her on her return.

Two interviews were conducted in the morning and two in the afternoon. The following morning, there were two further interviews to be conducted. On the Friday afternoon Ken and Elizabeth were in the war room – it was decision time.

"So, what do you think? Any front runner?"

Elizabeth thought carefully before she spoke.

"All of the candidates had good legal executive assistant backgrounds. I tried to balance their experience, administrative skills and personalities together, as a match against what I think the law firm expects. Some had great skills but I don't think that they would be a good fit for the firm."

"I agree. I had the same feeling. Some candidates were good but I did not get that feeling of comfort. I think they might lack the passion that we are looking for."

Ken thought for a moment then said,

"The partners and I would like to add another name to the list."

Elizabeth looked at him but did not expect to hear what he said.

"We would like to add the name Elizabeth McKenzie to the list. We would really like you to consider coming back to the firm."

Elizabeth sat in silence. Maybe, when Ken had telephoned her earlier in the week, she had thought that he was calling to offer her job back. After he mentioned the interview process she had completely dispelled the thought from her mind. Now this.

Ken just looked at her and smiled.

She did not know if she should smile back.

Ken sat and waited for her answer.

Finally she answered.

"Ken, I don't know what to say. I really don't know what to say. I hadn't expected this." She was silent again and just sat there. Another endless pause took place. Neither of them spoke.

"Look, I know that this might be a surprise to you. The fact is the firm is not the same without you."

Still Elizabeth just sat. She could not even get an initial thought to pass through her mind.

"Tell you what, I will be in the office tomorrow morning, why not think about it overnight and then pop by and we'll see where you stand."

"Yes, thank you, that will give me some time. What time would suit you for me to come by?'

"Why not call me from the hotel and tell me when you are ready to come over, say about ten in the morning?"

Elizabeth had a terrible night.

She went through a very personal assessment about her life and what her future expectations were. Finally she came to a decision.

The next morning she telephoned Ken right on 10 a.m. When she parked her car, Ken was waiting at the entrance of the building to let her in.

They walked through the deserted offices to the war room.

After they sat down Ken decided to let Elizabeth speak first.

"Ken, I've considered your offer. It stunned me. I was honored. I could not find the words to answer you yesterday and my apology for that."

Ken nodded and said, "Yeah! I suppose that we did blindside you but it is something that we wanted to ask. You are our first choice. The offer that I made yesterday still stands."

Elizabeth hesitated and then answered, "I am absolutely flattered by your offer. My time with the firm was the most rewarding of my life - even with all of the teasing that I had to endure from you and Greg."

Ken had a broad smile on his face. "Yes, it was fun, and maybe we over did the teasing!"

Elizabeth continued without comment.

"I still cannot comprehend why Greg left me so much money in his Will and his cabin. I have never been able to rationalize why he did that."

Ken interrupted, "He did that because he admired you, he often said that without you he would not have been successful as a lawyer – he said that to me many times. He said that you were his confidant, a stabilizing force in his life. He often spoke about his wife and how he missed her – but he had you next to him – I suppose that more than anything else you were his true friend."

"Ken, my life in Alpine Meadows is so different from here in the city. It is not easy to fit into a small town where not much ever happens and there is no burning rush to get things done on time. In many respects next week is better than tomorrow to get things done. It is a strange sensation living where there is little time pressure.

There isn't much for me in Alpine Meadows. I haven't met many people – and to an extent I'm the woman who was left Greg's cabin. And I know what people might think about that.

So, I looked at my life there and my life here. This is where I functioned as an individual, where I felt the pressure, where I feel that I belonged...but it's no longer home."

Elizabeth sat for a moment before she continued,

"It's strange to hear myself say this but I don't feel that I want to come back. It beats me as to why I feel this way – maybe it's like getting off of the carousel – when you're on it life just flashes by, then when you get off you look at it and realize that because it is spinning so fast you cannot get back on.

Ken, I don't know what awaits my life in Alpine Meadows but for once in my life I must go with my gut and not my mind. Alpine Meadows is where I must stay."

I'm sorry but I can't accept your offer to return to the law firm. I hope that you understand."

"Elizabeth, we knew that it was a long shot but we felt that we should give you the opportunity to consider coming back. It's tough to accept but I respect your feelings."

He stood up and opened his arms. Without even thinking about it Elizabeth stood and the former colleagues hugged.

After they sat down again Elizabeth pulled out a sheet of paper.

"Do you still want my opinion for whom you should hire?"

She handed the folded piece of paper to Ken. He took it and placed it on the table. From his attaché case he pulled out the score sheets of all of those who had been involved in the interview process. Ken laid the papers in front of Elizabeth. Her name was on the top of every assessment sheet.

"So, eliminating the top name." he smiled.

In due course Beverly Ann Scott would be offered the position with the law firm. She would accept the position. She would excel – with her own style.

"Before I let you go there's one more thing that I would like to propose.... think about it...can we contract you to assist Beverly on the telephone if she requires any guidance? I was thinking of about 3-4 hours a week when she is settling in and then it might reduce after a few months...we can play it by ear."

Elizabeth agreed to assist Beverly. As Ken walked Elizabeth to her car he doubted if she would ever come back to the firm and visit. They hugged again and Elizabeth drove away. She headed to the Bay area to buy the art supplies that Maddy Wilson had suggested.

Chapter 6

The next few months passed by very quickly. Summer was beginning to give way to fall. It was a spectacular time of the year. The days were still warm but the evenings were beginning to get cool.

The painting lessons were a distraction. Elizabeth had already decided that she did not have the talent to paint!

Maddy had the same thoughts but, for her, it was the company that mattered. In fact Elizabeth felt the same way.

Elizabeth would drive into town two mornings a week and spend time with her in the studio that Norman had set up in one of the rooms in the house. There was no strict start time or scheduled break. By noon, they would stop for the day. More often than not Maddy insisted that she make lunch.

There was no doubt that the bond between them was developing fast. They almost felt as if they had known each other for many years.

Norman was the perfect host. He would be around or leave the two women to talk – he made a judgment call. If Elizabeth visited the Wilson home on a Saturday or a Sunday then Norman would BBQ and Maddy and Elizabeth would prepare the salads. Sometimes he felt as if he had two sisters.

One Saturday afternoon when Norman came to fetch Elizabeth, she was locking up to leave the house when he arrived.

"Hello Norman, how are you?"

"Good, thank you Elizabeth, how are you?"

"I'm fine thank you. If you have a moment before we leave could you take a look at my BBQ? I wanted to invite you and Maddy over for next week but when I looked at the BBQ it appeared to be pretty beaten up."

"Sure, where is it? Have you not used it since you moved in?"

"It is around the side of the house near the rear kitchen door."

Norman followed her around the side of the house.

"And as to your second question...no, I haven't tried to use it since I moved in...I'm not great with things like that." She smiled and Norman returned a smile. He thought, *"I wish that she would smile more often."*

Norman took one look at the BBQ and started to laugh, "I don't think that Greg used it in years. Well there is good and bad news. The bad news is that it is completed rusted through...and the good news is that I know where the dump is!"

"Oh, is it that bad?"

"Yes, it's a rust bucket...may it rest in peace!"

"I did want to invite you and Maddy over next weekend for a BBQ. I suppose now I will have to buy a new one."

"Tell you what, let me swing by one afternoon next week and I'll take you shopping for a new BBQ. How does that sound?"

Dinner that evening was a delight. Neighbors came over and the group played various card games. When Elizabeth looked at her watch it was almost midnight. The evening had just flown by.

As Norman drove Elizabeth home she could hardly keep her eyes open. At the cabin Norman checked that everything was locked up. As he said goodnight Elizabeth did the unexpected. She went up on her toes and kissed Norman on the cheek, "Thank you for a lovely evening!" Then the door was shut and she was setting the alarm system. The alarm bells in Norman's brain was ringing too! He did not expect the kiss and it took him completely by surprise. Elizabeth was in an equal state of shock. "You silly woman what must the man think of you. I hope he doesn't tell Maddy!"

The following Saturday Norman and Maddy arrived at about 3 p.m.

The two women hugged.

"Maddy, I said not to bring anything. What are all of the things that Norman is carrying inside?"

"Oh, just your favorite dessert and a salad or two, hope you don't mind!"

Elizabeth smiled and thanked her friend.

Maddy had never been to the cabin before and Elizabeth gave her a tour.

After the three friends had refreshing lemonade on the porch, Elizabeth suggested that they go for a walk through the surrounding forest. "I have not walked too far since I moved in as I felt nervous by myself but with some company I thought we could explore a little. I found a map that Greg must have drawn that shows a number of different routes that he used to take. I thought that we could take the shortest route and then come back and start the BBQ."

"Sure - that sounds like a great idea – Norman are you up for a walk?"

"Yes, it sounds like a plan." He laughed, "It would increase my appetite!"

"Norman Wilson, you do not need anything to increase your appetite!"

Even the short walk proved to be tough going. The distance could not have been more than two miles. The vistas of the lake through the trees were spectacular.

"Elizabeth, we should set up our painting equipment here one day. This would be a wonderful scene to paint."

"Oh, yes, it would be great – just too bad that I wouldn't do justice to the scenery!"

When they stopped for a breather and sat down on a large dead tree trunk that had fallen over, Maddy joked, "At least I have an excuse of being the oldest one here." She looked at Norman and said, "But in your case as chief of police you have no excuse. How do you expect to pass your physical exam next year if you can't even go for a walk through a forest!"

Norman knew that he could not defend his position. With a degree of rejection all he could muster was, "I know, I know...I need to do something about it I suppose."

"You suppose! You suppose! Is that all that you can say? I think that I will ask Elizabeth to take you for walks every weekend so that you can lose some weight!"

Elizabeth decided to stay out of the conversation.

After they all got their breath back Elizabeth suggested that they walk back to the cabin. No one said much on the way back.

After another round of lemonade Elizabeth asked, "Norman, could you try out the new BBQ for us? I'm sure that you will do a much better job than me!"

Norman readily accepted – it would also keep him away from the wrath of his older sister.

Once the tension was broken the evening went by swiftly as they always seemed to do when they were together. Elizabeth felt very sad when she bade her guest's goodnight and saw them drive off. It was about 11 p.m. She faced another night alone in the cabin.

Chapter 7

Elizabeth faced the prospect of her first Christmas away from San Francisco and in a small town – and alone in her cabin in the woods. She had thought about the upcoming holiday season for some time and had contemplated driving back to California. She dispelled this thought, as in reality she had no one there either.

Her dilemma was solved for her.

While taking their tea break during a painting lesson Maddy said,

"I'm not sure if you have any plans for the holidays but if you like why not spend the Christmas week with us in town. We have plenty of space in the house and a bathroom upstairs that is never used. We would be delighted to have you as our guest for the week."

"That's very kind of you. But a whole week that would be too long to impose on you..."

Maddy interrupted, "Impose! Who would be imposing? We would love to have you. There are lots of things to do in Alpine Meadows over the holidays and you should share in the activities. We really are a great community."

"What does Norman think of the idea of me visiting for a week?"

"Oh, he is totally in favor of the idea – he would love to have you stay with us."

The white lie was carried off with conviction and confidence. She had not as yet even raised the topic with Norman. But she knew he would come around to the idea.

In the weeks leading up to Christmas, Maddy felt very tired and she delegated the decorating of the Christmas tree to Norman and Elizabeth. She sat feet away from them, giving a continuous set of instructions as to where the decorations should be hung. Elizabeth had never decorated a real Christmas tree before and she was happy to follow the instructions – she left most of the bickering to take place between Norman and his sister!

Elizabeth was at a loss as what to buy as gifts for Maddy and Norman. She drove into Reno and explored the stores until she found something suitable. This was a new life for her.

Finally Christmas Eve arrived and the three friends attended church. On Christmas morning they exchanged gifts. The Wilsons gave Elizabeth a beautiful shawl. Elizabeth gave Maddy tickets to an arts exhibit in Reno – Norman received a set of murder mystery novels. They again attended a church service and then returned home to prepare for the major luncheon event. The Wilsons had invited several friends over for the lunch and the home was full - and full of joy.

The week passed by quickly and Elizabeth had had a wonderful time.

The New Year seemed to bring a downturn in Maddy's health and although the painting sessions continued, there were less painting and more just spending time together. Sometimes instead of painting the two close friends would sit and read.

With Maddy not leaving the house much in the winter, Elizabeth spent more and more time with Norman. They would meet at the diner or go to a movie together. They were still stiff in each other's company. Norman had realized a long time ago that Elizabeth McKenzie was a disciplined and intelligent woman. She was widely read on many topics. Still, with all of the time that they were spending together Norman knew very little about Elizabeth. That seemed to be a closed book.

Sitting with Maddy one day Elizabeth asked, "Next week will be one year since Greg was shot dead in his cabin. I just feel very uncomfortable staying there that night, would you mind if I slept here?"

"Of course you can. I would feel creepy too – your room will always be here for you if you need it."

On the night of the first anniversary of the shooting, the three friends had a very quiet dinner. Both Norman and Elizabeth spoke about Greg.

Elizabeth was filled with grief as she had been so close to Greg – never threatened by him – but just bonded by mutual respect.

Elizabeth said, "I have a box at the cabin that is filled with all of the action figure dolls that Greg used to buy for me when he and Ken Parker used to be out during the day and stop for a quick meal." She laughed, "He sure used to tease me – and then had to find a way of making things up to me – either by way of chocolates or with action figures. I think that there must be twenty dolls in the box! The chocolates never lasted very long!"

Chapter 8

Maddy was at her direct best one evening when she asked Norman, "So, are you dating Elizabeth?"

She caught Norman with a mouth full of food and he almost gagged on it. He swallowed the wrong way and went into a deep coughing spasm. Maddy quickly got him a glass of water then sat down and watched the coughing bring tears to his eyes.

Finally, he managed to squeeze out an answer, "Are you crazy! I could have choked to death." He took another breath then continued, "That was a fool thing to do...do you really want to kill me?"

She looked at Norman without any sympathy or emotion. After a short moment she said, "You didn't answer my question, are you dating Elizabeth...and before you answer let me tell you that if you are not then you are a bigger fool than what I think...so...?"

Norman looked at his sister. He wiped more tears away from his eyes and then coughed again.

His sister just sat and watched him.

He had never left a plate of food unfinished, or walked out on his sister. He did both that night! He stood up from the table, thanked her for dinner, said good night and walked up to his bedroom.

Maddy went about washing up. She was not sure if she had over stepped the line. Maybe she had. Norman was a grown man. She made him lunch to take to the police station the next day and left a note for him on the kitchen table. The next morning, Norman left earlier than normal. He did not take his lunch box with him. He had breakfast at the diner.

Not by design but on the evening following his spat with Maddy, Norman was called out to a collision outside of town. He called her to say that he would be very late. He only arrived home after 2 a.m. He again made a point of leaving very early and did not take the new lunch that she had made for him.

Later that afternoon he was at a grocery store outside of town that had been robbed. The key witness – and someone who could identify the vehicle used in the heist and could also recall the license plate of the vehicle – was Chubby, the gas attendant.

After taking down all of the details of the crime and alerting nearby towns to be on a look out for the vehicle used in the getaway, Norman ordered a coffee and sat outside on a bench. The weather was cool, as spring had not yet taken the chill out of the air. It did give him time to think. Had he offended his sister by getting up and leaving the dinner table?

Then the bolt of lightning struck.

Norman's head spun, stopped and then spun again.

He thought, "If not now, then when?"

He was only five minutes away from the cabin.

He tried to control himself as he drove at the speed limit.

He turned off of the road towards the cabin.

Elizabeth was about 50 yards from the cabin. She was trying to paint a winter scene of the lake and the forest. She did not hear the buzzer go off in the house as the police vehicle crossed onto her property. She looked in surprise as she heard the vehicle come around the bend in the road. When she saw that it was a police vehicle coming towards the cabin, her immediate thought was that something had happened to Maddy.

By the time Norman pulled up at the front of the cabin, Elizabeth was next to him.

"Norman! Is it Maddy? oh god, what has happened to Maddy?"

"Elizabeth, Maddy is fine, she's fine!"

"Oh, I'm sorry, I wasn't expecting you and my mind just jumped to Maddy...is something the matter, you look pale?"

"I'm sorry that I startled you. I was nearby and decided to come by."

"I'm glad you did. Are you sure that you're well? Can I get you something to drink?"

Norman accepted the offer and they walked into the cabin.

As Elizabeth walked out of the kitchen with a glass of water Norman spoke, "Actually, there is something that I'd like to ask you."

"Sure, what is it?"

Norman hesitated then said, "Elizabeth, will you marry me?"

Elizabeth stopped dead in her tracks. The words that Norman had just said did not register. She tried to replay the words one at a time and, in doing so, she felt the color drain from her cheeks.

Elizabeth looked down at the glass of water in her hand. Instead of giving it to Norman she drank half the glass. Norman did not know what to say. Had he made a complete fool of himself? Damn Maddy and her crazy ideas.

"What did you just say?" asked Elizabeth.

"I asked you if you would be my wife – would you marry me?"

Elizabeth sat down on the armrest of the one couch. She looked down at the floor. She had to think. Also by looking down Norman could not see her face.

"I'm sorry if I caught you off guard – it was a wild idea that just came to mind while I was at the grocery store – I do have significant feelings for you – but I'd understand if you said no. I do not think that I am the best catch that you could make."

Elizabeth sat for a few more moments then she stood up and walked over and stood in front of Norman.

"You certainly caught me off guard. Whew! I didn't expect this!"

She paused then continued.

There was another long pause.

"Norman, yes, I will marry you!"

This time Norman felt the blood run from his cheeks. Before he fell over Elizabeth gave him a hug and they kissed.

When she pulled away she said, "But there is one condition."

He thought, okay, here it comes…whatever it is here it comes.

"We can be engaged but I will only marry you when you lose some weight and get fitter. How much do you weigh?"

He said "God, it's always my weight!!!"

"255" he lied.

Elizabeth looked at him. It reminded him of the way that Maddy looked at him!

"Closer to 265." He said.

"Right, let's say that when you reach 210 then we can set a date for the wedding. If I marry you I want us to be together for a long time – do you hear me?"

This would be a steep mountain for Norman to climb. Over the next few months Elizabeth would change his diet, he would eat salads at the diner, herbal tea replaced coffee and he would go for long walks through the forest near the cabin on weekends.

"Let's go tell Maddy!" he suggested.

They walked hand in hand to collect Elizabeth's painting equipment, which was still near the lake. Their embrace and kiss on the edge of the lake would be the first of many that they would share at that beautiful spot.

Maddy heard the police SUV pull up in the driveway. It was a little early for Norman to be home. She hoped that they could be civil to each other after the events of the other evening. As she looked out of the window she was surprised to see Elizabeth walking around the side of the vehicle.

She came to the front door to greet them, "Is everything all right? What happened?"

"Hi, no need to worry, I was driving by the cabin and stopped in and invited Elizabeth to come into town with me. You don't mind do you?'

As the two women hugged each other Mandy said, "Of course not, come in, come in!"

They sat down on the porch.

"How did the investigation go at the grocery store? Will you apprehend the thugs?" asked Maddy. Norman seemed distracted when he answered. "Oh, yes, we will get them, young Chubby at the gas station gave us the license plate and make of the vehicle used in the robbery."

Almost without taking another breath he continued, "There is some other news that might interest you." Maddy was looking at Norman. If she had been looking at Elizabeth she would have seen her blush and her eyes begin to swell up with tears of joy.

Norman continued, "I..." He seemed to lose his voice!

"I ..." Still nothing. "Norman, are you alright?" asked Maddy.

She looked at him with some concern. What could be the matter?

Norman cleared his throat and tried again.

"I asked Elizabeth to marry me and she said "*yes*".

It must have been the longest ten seconds in history. Maddy looked at Norman. Her color was white marble - no expression at all, just white frozen marble. "What did you say?"

Elizabeth replied, "Norman stopped by the cabin and asked me to marry him and I said yes!"

Finally the message got through and she burst into tears.

Both Norman and Elizabeth stood up and hugged Maddy as she sobbed.

"I hope that these are tears of joy!" said Norman with a broad smile on his face.

"You big lug – you could've at least told me that you were planning to ask this dear woman to marry you!"

"Well, I in fact only thought about it this afternoon – and I drove straight over to see Elizabeth."

"You did this all by yourself!" She was not going to spill her secret desire that Norman and Elizabeth should get married. Nor would she disclose her discussion with Norman. That would forever be their secret.

"Elizabeth, I can't tell you how happy I am for you both. You're a wonderful woman – and I've loved our time together since we met."

After more hugs and tears, Norman stated the condition to the planned wedding.

"Elizabeth has put a condition on us setting a date for the wedding. She wants me to drop my weight to 210 pounds before we can get married!"

"I knew that Elizabeth was a strong woman – and what a great idea – well done for setting down some ground rules!" Maddy was smiling just as much as Norman seemed to be dreading the weight loss ordeal.

Within a few hours of the engagement the entire town of Alpine Meadows heard the news. They also heard about the condition that Elizabeth had placed on the wedding. Within days lawn signs were posted "Congratulations Sheriff – good luck with the weight loss!"

Elizabeth finally felt accepted in Alpine Meadows.

The day after the engagement Elizabeth telephoned Ken Parker and shared her wonderful news with him. Ken almost fell out of his chair when he heard that Elizabeth was getting married. He ran from office to office telling everyone in the law firm. The reaction ranged from "What!!!" to "No Way!" and to "Awesome - that's great!!!"

Chapter 9

Norman's progress in losing weight was initially slow. He was less than enthusiastic. Between Elizabeth, Maddy and the population of Alpine Meadows, he had a strong support team. He had no choice but to start to participate in the town wide event!

It took two months before any real progress was made, at first it was five pounds and then ten and then fifteen pounds. There was a minor celebration when his police uniform trousers had to be taken in at the waist! Norman was good-natured about the interest in his program – and particularly so in the prize at the end of the rainbow – Elizabeth. Their relationship blossomed. They truly seemed happy.

Maddy gave thanks every day that Norman and Elizabeth were a couple. She wanted to see her young brother happy. Her health was failing and she looked tired most of the time. Painting lessons were now infrequent. She also missed many visits that Norman paid to the cabin.

She felt that Norman and Elizabeth should be alone.

Sometime later a celebration took place at the diner in town. It was Norman's birthday and he looked like a new man. He was thinner and even his skin had more color and texture to it. He looked very different.

The diner was selected as a "Weigh Sheriff Wilson" event. A large crowd gathered. Finally the time came for Norman to stand on the scale (he could not order his meal until he co-operated with the guests!)

He slipped his shoes off and stepped onto the scale. The dial moved and finally stopped. The dial pointed at 225 pounds. Norman had lost 40 pounds. A huge cheer went up around the diner and Elizabeth kissed and hugged Norman. It was becoming easier for her to put her arms around him!

"So, can we set a date now?" he asked.

"No." replied Elizabeth. "Just 15 pounds to go – almost there – you will have to be patient and work a little harder!"

Another cheer went up around the diner. The crowd was certainly into the event!

Norman drove Elizabeth back to the cabin after the weigh-in event. He hated leaving her behind. He had often asked her if she would like to move into town with him and Maddy but she had turned the offer down.

"Let's talk about that when we get married. I don't want anyone in town talking about us before then." She would not budge on the matter and Norman finally gave up.

The telephone hardly ever rang in the cabin. Norman would telephone Elizabeth every evening to check on her before bedtime. Sometimes it took thirty minutes to say goodnight!

When the telephone rang at 4 a.m. the following morning Elizabeth almost fell out of bed with the loud noise in the cabin. It took her a few second to realize that it was the telephone and to turn on the bedside lamp.

"Hello, who is this?"

"Elizabeth it's Norman, sorry to startle you. Maddy has had a heart attack – she's on the way to the hospital."

"Oh my god no, ...how is she?"

"Not good by the looks of things. I'm driving behind the ambulance. Can you come into town?"

"Oh yes, I'll be there as soon as I can. I love you!"

"Drive carefully."

The seven miles into town and the dark roads seemed like an eternity. Elizabeth had to watch the speed of her car as she tried to reach town as quickly as possible.

Elizabeth found Norman in the Intensive Care Unit.

"How is she?' she asked as they hugged.

"I don't know but it doesn't look good. She looked real bad at home when it happened."

They sat holding hands for an hour while they waited for an update from the doctors.

Finally the doctor came through.

"How is she?" asked Norman.

"She suffered a major heart attack. She's lucky to have made it so far ...I am sorry to tell you that she's very weak and she could go any time. I am truly very sorry."

Elizabeth buried her head in Norman's chest and burst into tears. "Maddy is the first woman that I have ever loved – even more than my mother." Norman held her tightly and kissed her on the head.

"Can we see her?" asked Norman.

"Of course – and in fact she asked for you both. Follow me".

The doctor led them through the doors of the Cardiac Intensive Care unit.

They were shocked when they saw her. She looked old and so pale. She had aged dramatically. Elizabeth fought back the tears and she felt Norman holding her hand for his own steadiness.

"Just a few minutes please" said the nurse as she left them alone.

Norman took Maddy by the hand. She opened her eyes and tried to smile but she could not. The three of them just seemed frozen in time and space. Elizabeth walked around to the other side of the bed and took her other hand.

Maddy lifted her hand and motioned for Norman to come closer.

As he leant forward a very weak voice said, "I would like to see you married before I go."

Norman straightened up and looked at Elizabeth.

"Did you hear what Maddy said?"

"Yes...yes, I did."

For what seemed like an eternity Elizabeth and Norman looked at each other. Then Elizabeth said, "Can we do it here, now...can we get someone to marry us now?"

"Are you sure that you want to get married now. Right here in the hospital?"

"Yes, I'm absolutely sure! Please hurry!"

Norman almost took the door off of its hinges as he ran out of the room. Elizabeth was left with Maddy. A nurse walked into the ward and stood just away from the side of the bed.

Maddy had her eyes closed and she seemed so distant. Maybe she was having a foretaste of her next life. Elizabeth could not take her eyes off of her. She was so full of love for her and she was begging for her to hang on. Please, please hang on!

It took almost twenty minutes for Norman to return to the ward, followed by a doctor and the hospital priest. It had taken the priest all of five minutes to be woken, dressed and to reach the hospital.

The wedding service was very brief. It was very simple and touching. Maddy was woken up to a full room of people around her bed. She was told that Norman and Elizabeth were to be married. The faint suggestion of a smile had come to her face. She stared blankly at the bride and groom throughout the brief wedding ceremony.

"I now pronounce you husband and wife."

The bride was dressed in casual pants and zip up sweater and the groom dressed in sweats pants, t-shirt and windbreaker. They kissed.

Madelyn Wilson passed away about thirty minutes after the couple took their vows. They were at her bedside as she silently slipped away.

Chapter 10

The couple had a more public wedding after Maddy's funeral. It was a joyous occasion but fairly somber in the context of the recent events. Ken Parker, his wife and several other members of the law firm drove to Alpine Meadows for the wedding and small reception that took place afterwards.

Several weeks after the funeral, Elizabeth and Norman were sitting on the porch of the house in town. Although married now it did not feel as if they were truly a couple. The planning of the funeral and the emotion of losing Maddy had gripped them and the town. In respect, the fun lawn signs about Sheriff Norman's weight had been taken down.

Norman had struggled to find the right time to ask Elizabeth a question. Now was as good as any.

"Elizabeth, the night at the hospital you said that you loved Maddy more than your own mother. That surprised me. You haven't told me much about your life – but I'd like to know more – and why you made that comment."

Elizabeth sat for a second. Her mind raced as to what she should tell Norman.

"I meant what I said that night." she paused then continued. "My mother suffered from mental illness – there were no fancy words for the illness in those days. The doctors just said that she was mentally ill – whatever that meant."

She paused again.

"Of course that opinion was only made known later in her life. As a small child I remember her as being so loving. As a little girl I remember my mother always smiling and being happy. But she started to change. She began to yell at me and told me that she hated me – I was the cause that she had lost her figure and put on weight. My father tried to calm her down but her moods seemed to blow with the wind."

Elizabeth wiped her eyes. She began to feel very emotional. Norman held her hand.

"The worse she became, the more my father pulled away. He eventually started seeing other women. I didn't know this at the time but I remember hearing them yelling at each other about his affairs. My mother said that I had caused her to lose her beauty and that is why he was seeking out other women. I cried myself to sleep feeling the guilt that I was the cause of my mother's condition.

At an early age I went to stay with an aunt who lived in our town – I think that my parents gave up on me and dropped me off one day. I'm not sure of what happened I just remember that I was now with my loving aunt. I think that I was about eight years old when my mother was put into a home. She had seemed to lose all sense of reality. Before that she would sit and never get anything done – no housework, nothing at all...I suppose that her behavior influenced me in later life that I always wanted to get things done and as professionally as possible."

Elizabeth stopped for a minute as Norman sat with his new bride and waited for her to continue.

"My teenage years were terrible. My mother was in a home and my father drank and womanized. And everyone knew about it. I had no friends. My aunt died just as I was finishing high school.

When I graduated, I told my father that I would like to go away to college. He agreed and set up with his bank that my annual student fees and living expenses would be paid out of an account that I had opened. Three days after graduating from high school I left town. I never returned."

"Did he ever visit you at school?" asked Norman.

"Yes, once. He arrived with some bimbo and they were both drunk. I told him never to come back again."

"Did you ever see him again?'

"No, he crashed his car a few years later and died from his injuries. He was drunk at the time."

"And your mother, what happened to her."

"My mother died several years later. At the end I believe that it was a blessing for her. So, I graduated from university with neither of my parents there to see it. I was alone and knew that I had to make it by myself."

Norman rose from his seat and lifted Elizabeth up to him. He hugged her so dearly and he felt her heart beat almost inside him. He kissed her and said; "Now you have me! I love you and I will make you happy!"

"Thank you. I love you too."

Although Alpine Meadows had its own charm, Elizabeth was bored. Her eager mind required stimulation. Then she had an idea.

One night in bed Elizabeth was tucked up next to Norman with her head on his shoulder. "Are you still awake?" she asked.

"Yes. Just lying here thinking."

"I was growing weary with my painting lessons. It was being with Maddy that really mattered. I think I know what I'm going to do now."

"What?" he asked.

"I am going to write a book based on Greg's life. I'm going to call the book The Solar Murder."

Part 2

Chapter 11

All he remembered before he went to sleep every night was their fighting, his father yelling and his mother's feeble replies. The more she mumbled, the louder he yelled at her. Even putting his small hands over his ears, he could not block out their argument. Neighbors would call out from their homes for them to quiet down – and sometimes the police were called. It was not a happy environment for a young child.

The other thing that he remembered was hunger. On so many nights his mother would forget to cook an evening meal – she just lost track of her day. The child would not have dinner. His dad would come home and there would be no dinner for him either. And then the fighting would start again. The boy was either ordered to his room or went by his own accord – either way he went upstairs hungry.

Sometimes during the day when his mom was in her own special place the child would wander down the road alone. Ruth Kempster would see him sitting on her front lawn. He would never respond to her and it took some time for her to realize that the child was starving. His little body was pale and drawn and he looked so sickly. In those days there were no child-aid programs.

She would make him a big grilled cheese sandwich and a glass of milk. She would place it on the lawn next to him and then walk away. At first he would not touch it but soon, like a trained stray animal he realized that he needed the food.

Mrs. Kempster was in her late seventies and lived alone. She never invited him into her house but she would always make him something to eat if she saw him outside. He would not eat if she tried to sit near him but as soon as she closed the front door he would grab the sandwich and gobble it down.

She would watch him through her front window – sometimes she cried as she watched him. It was not her place to interfere but she wondered what sort of life he was leading.

Without her he would surely have died at a young age.

At that stage in his life the boy did not know what his father did for a living. They never spoke to each other. In reality his father was more like a lodger in the house. He used to entertain his lady friends in the living room or in the back room of the house while his mother was upstairs.

It was some time before he found out that his dad was a fireman in town. Jobs were hard to find. His father most likely got the job because of his fire-fighting services during the war.

His father had been a fireman in the US Navy on a war ship during World War 2. He was just twenty-two years of age when peace was declared in 1945. Maybe the experience of the war, fighting fires and seeing men burn to death had affected him – and now these demons could well influence the actions of his son in the future.

After the war he had tried a number of different jobs but for young men there were not many opportunities. He was in his early thirties when he applied for, and secured, a job at the local fire hall in a small town.

The boy discovered in later years that his dad was a pretty good firefighter and his drinking habits were tolerated – just as long as he did not drink on duty.

As his mother slipped further and further into her state of poor mental health the more the young boy understood that he was alone in life. His father still lived at home but the distance between them seemed wider than the Grand Canyon.

When he started at elementary school there was hope that the more social climate of having other kids around him would improve his silent disposition. It did not.

He was rude to his teachers and despised his classmates – and they despised him. It seemed like every week he was being sent to the principal's office because of his bad behavior in the classroom. If he got something wrong in class or did not complete his homework correctly, then his personality changed and he would ransack the classroom, and drive the fear of god into the teacher and his classmates.

Several times his father was called in and a heated debate took place behind closed doors. The only result was that his dad would give him a whipping when he got home. Maybe in a way, it was to get his father's attention. The whipping was extremely painful but at least he had access to his dad. The mental sickness in the young boy was growing.

Maybe it was one particular afternoon that things were set off. The boy was sitting in his bedroom when he heard the fire engines, with sirens blaring, coming down the road. He ran down the steps and onto the front lawn. He made it just in time to see the red trucks go flying past. He caught a glimpse of his father sitting in the cab with his helmet on. The boy ran after the truck as it sped down the road.

Not a half a mile away the trucks came to a screaming halt. An entire house was up in flames. It took the boy another minute or two to catch up to the trucks, arriving just as the firemen were assembling their equipment to commence fighting the raging fire. He saw his dad – in command, taking charge, yelling out instructions.

All the boy saw from his vantage point was his father – the burning house was only a backdrop to watching his father co-ordinate the firefighting activities.

Not for a moment did he take his eyes off of his father. Even as the crowd was pushed back to a safe distance did he take his eyes off of his dad – "*that's my Dad*!" he thought to himself. As the crowd swelled he was pushed away by the adults and he could no longer see what was happening. He squeezed his way through the back of the crowd. He looked up and saw a large tree – without any further thought he ran towards the tree and climbed it as if he had done this type of thing all of his life. He dragged his way out onto a large branch and from there he had a birds-eye view of the fire scene not thirty yards from where he was perched.

The fire raged high above the house and the smoke was drifting directly towards him but he was not going to move. *"Where is dad? Where is dad?"* he kept asking himself. The firefighters were spraying water on the home but he could not see his father. Then from out of the fire and smoke and water, he saw him, bursting out of the front door of the home. He was carrying a woman over one shoulder and a young child in his arm. He dashed forward and was caught by his colleagues as he dropped to the ground. Those that he had rescued were rushed away for medical care. His dad rose again and headed back to the house. But this time he could not go back in - the flames were too fierce.

Finally the fire was brought under control. The boy had not moved from his place in the tree. He had been there for several hours. He had not moved an inch. He saw everything that had happened. He watched every move that his father had made.

Then a realization hit him. How was he going to get out of the tree?

He looked down – it was at least twenty feet. Going back along the branch seemed impossible. How he had sprinted up the tree and out onto the branch was beyond his comprehension. He yelled and yelled until someone heard him.

A familiar face placed a ladder up against the tree and climbed up and carried him down over his shoulder. His dad said nothing. He just put him on the ground and went back to his crew.

The boy walked back home. Once back in his room he undressed, as his clothing smelled of smoke. He washed himself and threw his soiled clothes into the wash basket. If his mother had been lucid he would have told her all about his adventure. But she was in her own space – in her own world.

A plan hatched in his mind and he sat in his room thinking about it. Not all plans are good ones.

When his father came home the boy ran downstairs to greet him. But instead of a warm welcome and hoping to share the excitement of the afternoon's activities all he got was a reprimand for leaving the house, climbing a tree and having to be rescued. But there was no beating that night – no punishment.

Hungry in bed he thought about his plan again.

The following day the town radio station and newspaper carried full coverage of the fire on Main Street and the heroic service of the boy's father. Everyone thought that he was a true fearless firefighter. There was a whole set of photographs of the fire scene and shots of his father bringing out the survivors from the burning house.

Several weeks later the fire fighter was presented with a medal of bravery by the town mayor and received a citation from the regional fire chief. The only two people that seemed left out of the new media exposure were the man's wife and his young son. The boy in the tree, who was so proud of his father that day, received no warmth or love. If only the town folk knew what he was really like – an unloving father, a drunk and a womanizer. But still the boy needed attention – he had to find a way of attracting his father's attention.

Chapter 12

Nothing much changed over the next year or so. The cycle was the same. His parents argued, his father brought women home; his father drank when off duty and the growing boy was basically fed and kept alive by a kindly elderly woman who lived down the street.

What also did not change was his behavior at school. The teaching staff and administrators disliked him intensely. He was rude, exploded in temper tantrums and taunted them with psychical harm. He was suspended several times, whipped by his father and then went back to school. The cycle seemed never ending.

School Board doctors were brought in and the general diagnosis was known in those days as a "child mental disorder". In later years it would become known as Oppositional Defiant Disorder (ODD) – kids who become easily angered, have temper tantrums, refuse to obey orders and have low self-esteem. Maybe in a way they were crying out for attention – maybe it really was a conduct disorder that could lead to further escalation of bad behavior.

His father did not seem to care. No one seemed to care.

The plan that the boy had begun to formulate at the time of the house fire was still in his mind. Now a year later, nothing had changed. He was still angry inside. He would teach them all a lesson one day. But one step at a time!

The first incident caused the fire trucks to be called out at 2 a.m. one spring morning. A small fire had broken out in the garbage cans at the back of the local school. At the end of each school day the janitors collected all waste papers and put them into bins at the rear of the school. The fire fighters believed that vandals had set the fire – it was easily contained and no damage resulted.

In those days there were no outside cameras at schools so no evidence existed of how or who had started the fire.

The local newspaper reporter was working the late shift and was on hand when the fire crew put out the fire. In the next edition of the town paper there was a story on the fire and a photograph of the boys dad overseeing the dousing of the flames. The young boy took a cutting of the photo and kept it in a small box under his bed. Over the next few years the box would become filled with several articles of small local fires and the crew that had put them out.

Several months later there was another fire. This time it was also late at night behind a local bar. Again it was a Class 1 fire – started by paper and matches – and no real damage was caused. After a third fire near a local church, the newspaper reporter began to suspect the same person as being behind the incidents. They did not expect more than one person to be involved, as the fires were too small to be that of a group activity.

The fires stopped for a while when the boy heard his father talking about the incidents with a neighbor. This would give him more time to plan his next move. He had dreams of his father burning to death.

The boy was now in high school. His personality seemed to be in turmoil. At some points in time he almost seemed to be tolerable and drew close to several kids at school and then at other times he became withdrawn, sullen and almost evil. Even his eyes seemed to change color when he lost control. An inner villain took over his soul. He felt as if he was in control if he visualized them burning. Then he would return to himself and almost forget his deep evil thoughts.

He hardly comprehended it when his mother died. Maybe by taking her own life she was set free. He had loved her and she him. She was all that he had – and only for a short period of time.

He lived in a house without any affection. He believed that he had received her instability.

His father was losing control. The hero figure in town was now known publically for his drinking habits and his flirtations with countless women. His reputation was waning. In truth, the Fire Chief had warned him that his job was on the line. Now in his early 40's he seemed to be on a downward spiral. At his age he might not be a fire fighter for too much longer.

The teen was now independent – he fed himself in the mornings and at night. His standard diet was sandwiches with jam. Mrs. Kempster was now in a retirement home as her arthritis prevented her from looking after herself. He never once visited the woman who had kept him alive with her sandwiches and milk. He felt as if he did not owe anyone anything.

The high school annual concert was a highlight in the events of the town. Both teachers and students participated in the program and it was staged four times over two weekends in early May of each year. Every year all of the concerts were sold out. Students auditioned for the various parts in the play. Competition was always hot to be included in the annual cast of characters.

In his first two years in high school the teen had ignored the annual event and had not even attended any of the performances. He had no interest at all in participating in school events, especially not in school events where other kids brought their parents – like normal families.

This year seemed different – well at first.

The boy sat at the back of the school gymnasium and listened to the kids going up to try out for the singing parts. Some of them were good and others not so much. He sat and listened not really paying any attention. Then a voice said, "Why not try out?" He looked up and saw a redheaded girl from his class. He did not answer. After several more prods from her and no response from him she said, "Tell you what, if I go up will you go up with me? I'm so nervous but I can't go alone". He looked at her and then to his own amazement he said, "Okay" and he found himself following her to take a number.

Standing in line she tried to make small talk with him but he did not respond. He watched her as she went up on stage and was handed a song sheet. She looked down at him and smiled nervously. The teacher coached the girl, played the music for her once or twice and then asked if she was ready to try the song.

Her voice was shallow. The teacher stopped her and tried to coach a little more. This time had more life but it still was lacking depth or conviction. After several tries the teacher thanked her and called up the next student.

Panic hit him, as he was about to walk up on stage. He felt himself glued to the floor and could sense the anger building up inside. Soon it would overtake him and he would either explode or flee. Then he felt a very soft arm on his sleeve. It was the girl. "You'll be okay, just go up and try!" He could not recall ever being touched by a fellow student – let alone by a girl. Yet he seemed not to mind. Before he knew it he was walking up on stage. He looked down and she was smiling up at him.

There was still panic tearing around inside of him and yet he felt calm at the same time.

The teacher went through the same coaching and playing of the music as she had done before. Now it was time to sing.

Twice the music started and nothing came out. Not even a panicked croak. The teacher was very calm and told him to relax and breathe normally.

They tried again. The music introduction – and then he saw her telling him to start singing.

The first line of the lyrics came out slowly and there was stiffness in the new voice. The teacher stopped him said, "Almost there, let's does that again."

The rowdiness in the school gymnasium quickly came to an end. The voice from the stage was sorrowful, deep and tender – and though untrained it possessed soul and raw feeling. After one verse the teacher said, "That was great, let's just try it once more!" This time was even better. A rough stone always requires polishing.

The chatter went through the school like wildfire. "Did you hear the crazy guy sing?" No one could believe it.

After the audition, fellow students spoke to him. This was not natural for him to be the center of attention. He felt himself shaking and pushed himself out of the crowd – he just needed to be outside and control himself.

He felt the fresh air begin to bring him back to normal. "Congratulations!" He swung around. She was standing there.

He hadn't heard her come outside.

He just looked at her. "I'm sure that you'll get the part – you were great!" She was smiling at him. He looked at her then walked away.

Two days passed before the names of the successful students were posted. He had the lead male part. The girl who had encouraged him to sing got a minor part but they were going to do a duet together. He was not sure about this development.

In a way he was very proud of himself and other students liked his voice. He needed to find a way of telling his dad. Maybe he could get some recognition. He was wrong – it was several days before he saw his father. When he told him the news, his father looked at him and said that plays were a waste of time. He then turned and walked out of the room. The boy stood alone in the living room. "God, I hate him so much!"

Chapter 13

The school year passed by in a flash. He was by no means fully accepted by his fellow students or the teaching staff but he was more tolerated. There was still the sarcasm, edged comments, and outbursts of bad temper. By now most of his behavior was well known. Frequently after a cooling off period following one of his tirades, he would return to some level of normality. "Normality" is such a misleading word.

The plan in his mind was now almost complete. He would give his father one more chance.

The rehearsals for the school play were progressing well. The rehearsals were held three afternoons a week and every Friday night. The boy totally kept his own schedule. He hardly ever saw his father. Some of the work shifts at the fire hall were for 72 hours at a time. During this period his dad would sleep and eat at the station. The boy had the small house to himself. It was better that way. There would be money left for him to buy groceries but never so much as a note of affection or encouragement.

A notable absence in the town newspaper was the lack of small set fires, unlike the prominence given when they had occurred in previous few years. In one editorial, the comment was made that maybe the culprit had either left town or grown out of the habit. Neither speculation was true.

On his sixteenth birthday he was congratulated at school as part of their Birthday Club. The school tried so hard to have different celebrations for the students. After school that day he went home to an empty house. Not even a card from his father. A house but not a home!

The school play was scheduled for the third last week of school.

The following week exams would be held and then the wrapping up of the school year.

The rehearsals had begun to be like therapy for the boy but at the same time he knew what was counting down in his head.

He had not bonded with the young girl at school but she was always there to encourage him and keep him involved in the development of the play. He thought that she looked troubled herself. Maybe that is why she was reaching out to him. They never spoke much, but from time to time they sat outside of the school and talk about things. Her dream was to be rich and one-day drive a convertible sports car. He wanted to sing – but he knew that was not likely to happen after the last night of the play.

She did make him promise that, should he ever become famous, he would buy her a red sports car. Such is the idle chatter of young adults. In a way he knew that he liked her but he had no space inside of him for any real affection.

The school concert was a success. The students and teachers enjoyed performing and the audience appreciated the substantial effort that had been put into the entire production. In a way, it was an annual bonding of the entire community. The stars shone brightly on the nights of the school play and none more so than for the gentle, rough but soulful voice of a sixteen-year-old student. His two songs and duet with his female friend were the highlight of the production.

On the final night of the play he had hoped to see his dad in the audience but he had checked his father's schedule and knew that he was on a long shift at the fire station. In a way that was perfect.

The boy walked home after the party, held for the school cast and the production crew and staff. He had not chatted much to the girl that night. Maybe he had nothing to say. He went up to his bedroom and waited. Close to 1 a.m. he dressed in dark clothes. He went down to the basement and very carefully took out several containers from behind a closet. He placed them into his backpack.

He casually walked the few hundred yards to his school. He almost passed the entrance before he quickly doubled back and made his way down the side of the old large school building. He paused at the back, waited and listened to if see if anyone had followed him or maybe heard him making his way along the school building wall. Nothing.

He waited another minute, walked on through the schoolyard and off the property. The school building was not his target. He left his backpack behind a tree at the beginning of the lane, taking the contents of the backpack with him. He would collect it on his way home.

At the end of the schoolyard was a lane that ran almost to the beginning of downtown. He walked very slowly down the lane. Near downtown he turned left off of the lane and walked right into the backyard parking of his target.

Before he walked across the small parking lot, he stopped and listened again.

He saw his father's truck parked in the yard. He looked up at the windows where the firefighters' communal sleeping quarters were situated. The lights were out. The firemen would be semi-dressed in bed and ready to respond to a call. The target was not so much the fire hall as was his father.

He thought that he would have about five seconds from the time that he lit the fire until it broke out in a major gasoline explosion. His plan was to light the firebomb and then run across the parking lot and into the lane and disappear into the night, collecting his backpack and make it home.

He took out the box of matches. He lit one.

Chapter 14

Like most developing towns in the late 1880's there was a great deal of drinking on weekends. Most of it was harmless fun but sometimes fistfights would break out and some cooling off time was required.

This town was no different. It was a copy of so many situated across the USA.

Most times the perpetrators of these minor crimes were tossed in the cellar of the saloon until they sobered up. Then it was realized that when they came to, it was like waking up in heaven with whiskey bottles all around them.

Construction began on the town courthouse and prison in 1882. Completed, it was the most impressive building in town, a two-floor stone building on the outskirts of town. There were cells in the basement and a courtroom and some offices on the ground floor. Upstairs were the judge's chamber rooms and some space for town administration staff. It sure was an impressive building – solid as a rock.

The building served the town well for almost forty years until it became too small and a new building was erected in the mid 1920's, just before the Great Depression took hold of the throat of the nation.

During the Depression the building was used as a soup kitchen and flophouse for the unemployed. It certainly had stories to tell. By the mid 1930's the building stood empty again, a great scarred stone structure. It looked sad as people passed by on their daily commute into town. The boarded up windows seemed to hurt its personality.

In the war years it was opened again and used as a home for badly wounded soldiers; those who had returned from the theatres of war where the American forces fought for world freedom. Many screams of torment would be heard as the mentally scarred soldiers suffered the emotional aftershocks of combat.

After the war it stood empty again.

In 1947 the building was gutted and fitted out as the town fire hall. The one side stonewall was removed and behind two large pull up doors stood the two new fire trucks that had been acquired by the town. The entire inside of the building was revamped. When complete, it had a reception desk and offices downstairs, a glass partition looking onto the fire trucks and a meeting room. Upstairs was a kitchen, recreation room and sleeping quarters for the crew on duty. The basement was used for storage.

During the reconstruction it was found that the stone outer wall at the back of the building was badly worn and chipped away. The decision was made to leave the damaged stone and to build a modern façade around the entire building. The façade was made of wood and gave a more cabin-like look to the building. Though the original stone-faced character of the building was lost, it now looked more appealing to the town folk.

The most popular feature of the fire hall was the firemen's sliding pole.

School trips to the fire hall always included kids taking turns in sliding down the poll. The boy had been on one of these trips and drew a map of the inside of the fire hall when he returned home after school. He had remembered everything that he had seen that day. It was as if the field trip had been ordained for him!

Over the years the fire hall had been updated several times and, for a small town, was a feature of the local landscape. It was situated just off of a small lane at the back of the building near the high school. Staff parked their vehicles at the rear of the building when they were on duty.

Not much had changed for the on duty fire crew over the last twenty years. The crew would still report for long shifts. The beds were all in an open plan room that served as the sleeping quarters.

Chapter 15

The fire crew reported for duty at 6 p.m. on the Thursday evening. Their shift would be over by 6 p.m. on the Sunday.

The town had several teams of fire fighters and depending on how the shift rotation worked out the composition of the four-man team could vary – but not by much as it was a small town.

Each core group of men did the same things whenever they were on duty. They hoped never to be called out to fight a fire but they were always ready. During the day they practiced various fire drills and kept the equipment clean and functional. If ever the fire bells rang the equipment would have to function. Lives could depend on it.

On this particular weekend the team got together to all help in the making of their Saturday night dinner. Firemen are a close brotherhood – even today. They would take their dinner plates through to the recreation room and watch TV while they ate.

They watched the "Lawrence Welk Show" and the "Jimmy Durante Presents the Lennon Sisters" on ABC before switching over to NBC and watching the Saturday Night Movie. If the movie was no good then they used to listen to the radio and follow the countdown of the Hit Parade. In May 1969 the hit music was "Spinning Wheel" by Blood, Sweat and Tears, "Wichita Linesman" by Glen

Campbell and "In the Ghetto" by Elvis. And of course not to forget the fun song, "A Boy named Sue" by Johnny Cash!

Some nights the crew would amble off to bed after they had watched TV. Other nights they would move to the table in the recreation room and commence their poker game.

From outside of the fire hall it was impossible to know what the firemen on duty were doing, but by about 1:30 a.m. they would usually all be in bed.

The boy took out his box of matches. He lit one.

He watched the flame come to life.

Half way down the match he blew it out.

He had thought that he would feel the pent up hate and anger building up inside of him as he prepared to send his father up in flames. But there was nothing.

He heard a sharp crack behind him. He froze. It sounded like a branch breaking. His heart raced as he listened. Nothing! Maybe it was just an animal in the bushes behind the parking lot. He waited another minute but there was no further sound. He turned back to his task at hand – to kill his father.

He thought to himself, *"This is no time to quit!" This is no time to quit!"*

He threw away the burnt out match that he was still holding. Then he quickly bent down and picked it up and put it in his pocket. He sat and tried to gather himself.

"Think about him, just think about him, just think about him!"

He tried to stir up the anger and hate that had taken root inside of his soul since as far back as he could remember.

Then he began to feel it. The hate was coming. The other part of his personality was taking over – he could feel the pressure building up inside. He could visualize his life with his father – the feeling was becoming more and more powerful..."*I hate him! I hate him, I hate him!"*

All of a sudden he was sweating. He could feel it running down his forehead. It was time to act, now before he began to doubt himself.

With control and purpose he took out another match. He held the gas-drenched cloth in his other hand.

He struck the match and as it burst into flame he held it to the cloth.

It caught fire in an instant. He threw it onto his prepared gasoline bomb. He heard a whoosh and then a flame spread quickly towards his gas canisters. He turned and ran. He was across the parking lot and into the lane in just a few seconds! Behind him he heard a gigantic crackle as the fire spread across the dried wooden frame – below the sleeping crew and more particularly his father.

As he ran down the end of the lane he grabbed his back pack and dashed onto the school property. From there he walked home. When he reached the safety of his bedroom he could hear the commotion from the other side of town.

He changed and put the dark clothes items into the washing basket. He sat in his pajamas on his bed. He turned on the transistor radio. The local station would certainly have the emerging story covered almost as it developed. "*I hope that he died in the flames – just tell me that he died in the flames!*"

He did not have to wait long.

"We interrupt our music program to bring you breaking news.

A blaze has broken out at the fire hall downtown. The alarm bells rang at the station itself at approximately 1:45 a.m. We are trying to obtain more information and will bring it to you as soon as we receive an update."

The music had hardly resumed when the night shift DJ interrupted it again.

"We have Todd on the roof of our studio. Todd, what can you see?"

"Mike, the flames have engulfed the rear of the fire hall and I can see that the roof is ablaze. I am trying to look if there is any activity from inside the fire hall but I cannot see that far... I guess that we must be a quarter mile from the blaze but I can't see any more details. I think that I'll have to try getting there on foot."

It took about another ten minutes for the boy to hear a further update from the radio station.

"We have now made contact with Todd...Todd can you hear me?"

"Hello Mike, I am near the fire hall but still about a hundred yards away. The police are holding us back...I really can't see much detail. There are people fighting the fire but I can't make them out at this distance."

"I hope that he burns. I hope that he burns!" The boy sat on his bed. He had not been this excited about anything in his entire life.

It took another two hours to put the fire out.

Through sheer exhaustion the boy had fallen asleep on his bed. It was around 6 a.m. when he awoke with the chill of the early morning air on his body. At first he did not remember the events of the night before. He was physically and mentally exhausted. Then he heard the radio next to him.

"The blaze at the fire hall is under control. We believe that there are injuries. Two fire fighters were taken to the hospital during the night but we have no further details to report at this time. It does appear as if the fire started in the rear of the building but we will have to wait for the press conference that the mayor and fire chief will be hosting later this morning."

The boy drifted back to sleep.

When he awoke again it was almost 10 a.m.

He did not turn on the radio. He just knew that his plan had worked.

After he made himself breakfast he went back upstairs to his room. He thought that he would wash up and then walk down to the fire hall and inspect the damage. Half of the town folk were there and it would look strange if he, the son of a fire fighter were not there. It was while he was washing up that he heard the front door of the house open.

He froze.

He listened carefully without making a noise. He heard someone move. The home had a small downstairs shower and he heard the water running. He looked out of his bedroom window. His heart almost stopped. In the drive way was parked his father's truck.

At first he could not comprehend what he saw. Then he began to shake with both rage and fear - rage that his father had escaped the fire and his fear that his father might uncover that it was him who had tried to kill him. He had to leave the house before his father came out of the shower – he needed to be outside and get fresh air before he fainted.

He tiptoed down the steps and took flight out of the back door of the house. If his father caught up with him in public it was unlikely that he would whip him. That might come later when his father was drunk. Without realizing the distance that he had covered, he was already at the scene of the fire. The back end of the fire hall was badly burnt and the roof was missing – it had collapsed inwardly as the old wooden beams burnt.

"Hey, did you hear that your dad was a hero last night?" He turned and looked at a bunch of students from his school.

"No, I was sleeping what happened?"

"The police think that someone set a fire at the back of the building. It must have spread really quickly and two of the firemen had smoke inhalation – you dad carried both of them out – he saved their lives – I wish that my dad was a hero like yours!"

Kids were patting him on the back as if he were a hero as well.

He could not contain his emotions. He walked to the curb and sat down and started to cry. He cried not from joy but from disappointment, and from the fear of what his father would do to him if he realized who had set the fire. Maybe his father would never know who had set the fire hall alight but he could not be sure. He had rolled the dice and lost.

He did not hear her walk up and sit down next to him. The first he realized that she was there was when she spoke.

"Are you okay?"

He turned sideways and saw her. She was looking at him with his face full of tears. Not the thing that a sixteen-year-old boy wants a girl to see. He bent his head forward so that she could not look at his face.

"Here" she said and pushed a Kleenex into his hand.

"This might help".

He looked up and took the Kleenex from her. She smiled and then stood up and walked away. He had not even said "Thank you".

After he recovered, he milled around the scene of the fire. There was no reason to stay there but he feared going home.

He was sitting under a tree near by to the fire hall when he saw his father drive up in his truck. He was sure that his father did not see him. He walked straight from the truck and up to the Fire Chief who was directing operations. He wondered what they were discussing.

Then the Police Chief arrived in his vehicle. Arrangements were being made for an address to the public. The boy went and stood near the rear of the crowd that was gathering.

"Good morning everyone" said the police chief, "As you can see we had a fire here last night. The fire started at approximately 1:45 a.m. At the time there were four crewmembers on duty. They were all awake at the time and were seated in the recreation room".

There was no mention that they were playing poker.

"The crew heard the combustion fire break out at the rear of the building at the parking lot. The fire spread quickly – we believe that an accelerant – probably cans that contained gasoline – was used to start the fire. The crew reacted quickly – the fire trucks were removed from the building and driven around the back of the fire hall. Two of the crew suffered smoke inhalation – they collapsed inside of the burning building – their lives were saved by their crew lead.

Within a few minutes back up teams arrived and the crews set about containing the blaze. Trucks from nearby towns arrived within an hour.

The fire was brought under control by 4am. An initial assessment of the damage indicated that the roof of the building was destroyed. Apart from the water damage from the hoses the inside of the fire hall is not too badly affected. It's too early to make a full assessment but the stone structure of the building saved the fire hall from major damage. I would now like the Fire Chief to make a statement and then we will take some questions."

"Good morning. As the police chief has mentioned the fire hall has sustained some damage, but not as bad as what it could have been. If it was not for the quick action of the crew on duty the damage could have been much worse."

The chief covered most of the same information that the police chief had mentioned. The first asked question from the press was what everyone expected. "Do you believe that the fire was arson or an accident?"

"We are in no doubt that the fire was arson. We found a number of cans of gasoline and clothes at the rear of the building. And to pre-empt your next question... we have no leads or suspects at this point in time."

Whether he was telling the truth or not was something that the boy had to consider. He looked at his father standing near the Fire Chief but he could not read any emotion in his face. He could not anticipate what may await him when his father came home. Did he know who had set the blaze?

The chief continued, "The building was saved because of the large stone blocks behind the wooden outer façade. The fire could not penetrate the building because of the stone. The old construction of the courthouse certainly saved it from major damage. Whoever set the blaze most likely did not know that just behind the wooden façade was the old stone building."

The boy swore under his breath. He did not have knowledge of the stone blocks of the original building. Anyone born after the late 1940's might not have known this fact. He swore. *"Planning, planning, all this planning and you did not check on the construction of the building!"*

He did not hear the rest of the media briefing. His mind was spinning too fast for anything to register. He felt faint. He had to flee. But fleeing might have been noticed. He slowly worked his way to the very back of the crowd and then walked home. His heart was almost bursting out of his chest when he reached his home. He felt as if a raging fire was consuming him.

He feared for his life. What would happen to him if his father knew that he was the target? If he fled town then everyone would work out that he had set the blaze. If he stayed he might have to face his father's wrath. He waited for his father to come home.

Chapter 16

The boy spent all afternoon in his room, in dread of what might happen.

At dinnertime he made himself a quick sandwich and retreated upstairs again.

Finally at about 11 p.m. he fell asleep. Half asleep was a more accurate description. Monday was a school day and he might feel safer at school than at home.

When he awoke the next morning he peeked into his father's bedroom. The bed had not been slept in. His father had not come home that night.

At school he was again congratulated on the heroism of his father. Everyone reminded him that this was the second time that his father had saved people from a burning building. His mind flashed back to when he had climbed a tree to watch close up as his father saved the young woman and her child. He thought then that his father was a hero – now things were different.

It was awkward to be the center of attention. He did not enjoy it and he knew that within a day or two most of the kids would again be very cool towards him. Nothing would really have changed in his mind.

He also had to face a barrage of compliments about his performance at the school play over the last two weekends. If he felt terrified at home, he felt even more so at school – he could not cope with people being around him.

His father did not come home that night or the night after. The suspense was driving him crazy. Maybe his father did not suspect that he had set the blaze.

School examinations commenced on the Thursday and ran through until the following Wednesday. He had spent the entire week and weekend at home and had not heard from, nor seen his father. The boy saw a copy of the local newspaper and the coverage given to the fire and the heroism of the crew.

On the following Thursday he spent his day sitting outside his house. The Friday would be Report Card day and the close of the school year. He had no plans for the summer. Most kids in town did not have plans either but he would spend it alone, as he had done so many times before. The other kids had each other for company but he was excluded – or just forgotten.

He saw her walking towards him. He was not sure if he should go inside the house or wait for her to walk by. He still felt embarrassed by her giving him the Kleenex to dry his tears.

"Hi, how are you?" she said as she stopped in front of him.

"Hi", he said. He did not know what else to say.

"Can I sit for a while?"

"If you want."

"You okay?" she asked.

"Yes."

"Doing anything this summer?"

"No".

"Me neither." She replied.

He wanted her to leave and he wanted her to stay.

If he spoke to her then he might just let something slip about the fire.

"Remember what you promised me?"

"No, what did I promise?"

"You said that if you became famous that you would buy me a red sports car. Did you forget?"

"Oh that! It was just talk. I will never be famous."

"Well, maybe you should start working on it over the summer!" She smiled at him.

Then she stood up. As she turned to walk away she said, "Maybe we could get a soda over the summer."

Mechanically he answered, "Sure".

She was already walking away when she said, "Strawberry".

He watched her walk on down the street and then turn at the end of the block. He stood up and walked inside the house.

The next day at school the report cards were distributed early and the students were dismissed by about 10 a.m. He did not see her at school – he heard the girls saying that she was sick. He heard them say that she was weird and that she frightened them sometimes. He wondered what they meant. She seemed a little strange but at least she spoke with him.

He walked home from school and thought to himself just how long the summer was going to be. A strawberry soda seemed like a good idea.

Sometimes things never work out the way you expect them to.

He was sitting in his room at about dinnertime when he heard the sound of his father's truck pulling into the driveway. Fear gripped his entire body. He had not seen his father in the almost two weeks since the fire. He froze - froze and sweated at the same time.

He heard the back door of the house open and his father walk inside.

About thirty seconds later his life changed forever.

"You up there" yelled his father.

"Yes sir" he replied.

"Get your ass down here right now!"

He came down the steps and walked into the living room where his father was standing. The town hero figure – not his father!

"Sit down!"

"Yes sir."

He sat on the edge of the couch.

His father paced in front of him but said nothing. The boy could feel the sweat running down his back.

His father turned and looked at him.

"There are a few things that we need to discuss – so listen carefully, I am not going to repeat myself, you hear!"

"Yes sir!"

Again there was a silence. Then his father spoke.

"Kid, you are not my son."

"No, no, you are making this up!!" he yelled.

"Shut up and listen before I whip your ass to the wall, do you hear me!"

He whispered, "Yes sir".

"Your mother was with this guy every month when he came to a nearby town. I only found out when she fell pregnant, then I knew that she was screwing around."

He took a breath and then continued, "I was injured during the war and while I was in hospital recovering, the doctors took a number of tests. They broke the news to me that I had a sperm-count deficiency and that I would not be able to have any children. Pretty shitty thing to have to tell a young man!

After the war I was drifting around. I came to town looking for work and I met your mother. At first we thought that we loved each other. But we both had problems. I enjoyed drinking and had a dysfunctional body while she, well, she was a little crazy sometimes. You know that about her. She got worse over the years. You know that too.

So, when she told me that she was pregnant I knew that it was not my child. Our relationship fell apart. Everyone thought – and maybe still thinks that you are my kid but you are the son of a travelling salesman and a deranged woman."

The boy jumped up from the couch, "No, you are making this up! It is not true!"

His father – this man in front of him - spoke calmly but very precisely, "Sit down and shut up. Do you hear me! Sit down!"

Reluctantly the boy sat down.

"Hear me out, just hear me out!

After you were born we decided to stay together but it didn't work – she slid into that state of personal madness. I knew that she had stopped seeing her lover, but I could not love you – you weren't mine. I turned to other women. I'm no angel. I have never pretended to be one. Maybe one day I'll pay the price for my drinking."

There was a pause. The boy dared not say a word.

"I've known for years that you started fires in town. You were careless right from your first fire. I had some magazines at home that went missing. When we put out the fire I found burnt pages. I had marked some things on the one page and there it was in the ashes of the fire. Some pages remained unburned in the place where the fires were started - the page with my handwriting on it".

The boy put his hand up to speak – almost asking permission. His father nodded his head.

"Why didn't you not turn me in to the police?"

There was another long pause.

"I'm not sure. Maybe I thought that you would outgrow it. I don't know."

Everyone needs to know that they are either loved or that someone cares for them. The boy had known for all of his sixteen years that his father had no feelings for him – he had come to accept the coldness and being ignored. But to hear it spoken out loud to you is like a dagger cutting open your soul.

He just sat there stunned in his shock and swelling hatred for the man that stood before him.

The man just stood in front of him in the room.

After a while the man continued, "I know that you started the fire last week – I know that you were trying to kill me." The statement was cold and matter-of-fact – devoid of all sensitivity.

"How did you know?" He was not just going to sit there in silence.

"I'd been expecting something to happen. You were careless. You went to purchase gasoline from the station in town. You told Bob that my truck had run out and that I needed a gallon to ride back into town. I saw Bob a few days later and he asked if I had made it back. I knew right away that you were stockpiling gasoline. I told Bob that I had made it back all right. People talk when you make plans. You should remember that people talk."

People talk when you make plans.

How that statement would haunt him in the years to come!

"You thought that we were sleeping when you started the fire. We were in the recreation room. Maybe if you had started the fire at 3 or 4 in the morning we would all have been in bed. Then maybe your plan might have worked."

He paused.

"You tried to murder me. There's no point in denying it. I can't let you have a second chance. Maybe next time you'd succeed."

"Why haven't you turned me in?"

"I thought about it but decided that too many questions would be asked. Also right now I'm a bloody hero again – so why shatter their illusion of me by having the town know that my son is a life-long firebug. I thought that I was on my way out of my job because of my behavior but your failed fire attempt has given me another few years before I become a nuisance again."

"So what are you going to do?"

"I am going to get rid of my problem – you!

You're sixteen now and of the right age to quit school and move away. You will go upstairs and pack your gear and get out of my house, out of town, out of state and never come back. I don't want you in my house or in my life...kid, it's time for you to go."

The boy sat in stunned silence.

Eventually he whispered, "I'm not finished school..."

Before he could finish the man interrupted him, "Kid, I don't give a fuck...get out of my house. You have fifteen minutes to pack and get the hell out. There's a bus leaving town in about an hour ...be on it. If not I will turn you in to the police."

He pulled out an envelope from his jacket and threw it on the couch next to the boy. "There's $200 in there – a lot of money. Maybe start a new life somewhere – your time here is up. You had better start packing, the clock is running."

With that last comment he turned and walked out of the house and drove away.

The boy sat for what seemed like an eternity. He was filled with anger, hate, pain, and raw emotions that could have sparked an inward explosion. His hands shook and his eyes filled with tears. In reality he died a little that afternoon – we would anyone in the same position.

He had the thought of burning down the house before he left but then thought, *"What is the point? Just pack and leave town".*

He looked at his watch. He had forty-five minutes to get the bus.

He ran up the steps. He pulled out his backpack and a sling carry bag. He began to throw things into the bags. He realized that he really did not have much stuff. He packed old jeans, t-shirts, sweaters, socks and underwear, his toothbrush, toothpaste and a towel into the larger bag. There was still space in the bags.

He walked out of his room. He stopped. He walked back into his room. He removed a photo of his mother from a frame – he was standing next to her, holding her hand. Once again just as he was about to walk out of the room he stopped. On his dresser was the sheet music from the school play. He picked it up and with the photo placed it in the side compartment of his backpack.

He went into the kitchen. He took all of the apples and bananas. He filled a bottle with water. He grabbed the packet of cheese out of the fridge. He knew everything that was there – as he had bought them himself with the grocery money that was left for him every two weeks. He took some cans of beef and the opener. He packed a knife and fork. Then he ran out of the kitchen and into the workshop. He picked up an old knife from the shelf. He thought that he might need something to protect himself with if he was alone.

The knife that he picked up was a switchblade. On the handle was the US Navy insignia and was engraved with the words "US Navy 1941-45". He took it not for sentimental reasons but for protection.

Inside the house he picked up his total worldly possessions and walked out of the front door. At the gate, he stopped. He dropped the bags and ran back inside the house to the living room. He picked up the $200. He closed the front door as he left the house. It was the closing of a part of his life.

Ten minutes later he walked into the Greyhound station. He purchased a ticket on the last bus to leave town that day. He never looked back as it pulled out of town.

In a truck outside of the bus station a man sat and watched as the bus left town.

Chapter 17

As night came, the rain intensified. At first it was just a regular rainstorm. Then it came down harder and harder. The wind picked up as the storm worsened. No one in a sane state of mind should have been out in this weather. Driving in these conditions was sheer madness.

Trooper James Williams was one of those that had to be out driving that night. He was on duty. Duty comes first – even when the weather is almost beyond description.

Trooper Williams did however have a description. "Holy shit" he said to himself. "I have never seen anything like this – what the hell am I doing out on the roads?" He mumbled far less polite words to himself.

He slowed the police car and looked out the windshield for a safe place to pull over. The visibility was so bad that he was disorientated. After fifteen years driving this stretch of road he thought that he knew every curve and bump. Indeed he did, but tonight he felt lost and confused.

Driving at about 20 miles per hour was about the maximum speed that he could do. Just then the radio crackled. The instruction was for all patrol vehicles to find shelter as the storm was going to get even worse.

He acknowledged his radio instruction and had taken his eye off of the road for a second. When he looked up he saw something lying half across the road in front of him. In a split second he braked and swerved to miss the object. The patrol car skidded and aquaplaned off of the side of the road. In a flash the vehicle tipped and rolled onto its right hand side. It came to a stop against a tree with a massive thump.

The trooper was trapped in his seat. After the crash there was silence, as if nothing had happened. There was just the harsh sound of the lashing rain and the wind.

It took about a minute before the trooper moved.

“Think! Think!” he said to himself. ”Shake your head. James, wake up! Wake up! You’ve got to move.”

It was another full minute before he began to focus and take control back. Then he felt the pain in his leg. “Broken!” is all he said to himself.

He reached for the radio and called in the crash. “I am okay, okay, maybe a busted leg but okay.” He had no idea of where he was on this patrol route. He knew that his colleagues would find him.

He sat back in his seat and tried to breathe. Besides his leg he felt pain in his chest and one arm. “Okay, buddy you must get out of the vehicle – got to lay down some flares.” It took him an eternity to open his door and then try to lift himself out of the vehicle. The pain in his leg and chest was almost unbearable.

Standing up outside of the vehicle, he was in the full force of the storm. He masked his face from the biting rain as he hobbled around to the back of the vehicle. Twice he slipped and fell. The pain from his broken leg shot up through his entire body. He gritted his teeth and tried to endure the stabbing pain.

He opened the trunk and took out the flares. He was not going to chance hobbling back up onto the road with his broken leg. He ignited two flares and threw them back up towards the road. He hoped that they would not be washed away with the rain. He scrambled his way back to the driver's door and threw two more flares towards the road coming from the other direction. He needed to find cover until help arrived. He held up his hands to protect his face from the lashing rain. He looked back down the road and maybe thirty yards away he saw the object that he had swerved to miss. In his panic to get out of the police car he had forgotten about the object in the road.

"Better check that out before other vehicles come along."

Hobbling proved to be impossible – the strength of the wind just blew him over. He crawled on his stomach back up onto the road and towards the object. "Please God protect me from being run over."

Thirty yards could have been three hundred. Crawling with the wind and rain lashing his body was an ordeal that was almost too much for the trooper. Each time that he pulled himself forward, the pain from his broken leg, his ribs and his wrist reached every part of his body.

Finally he reached the object. He opened up his jacket and deployed two more flares, one on either side. Then he turned his attention to what lay in the road. It was not a tree.

Trooper James Williams looked down in horror. Laying face down was the body of a young man. He rolled the body over. Even in the poor light he could see that it was a boy and that his face was covered in blood. The rain was washing the blood off of his face so that the trooper could see the significant injuries. His eyes were bruised and ballooned shut, his lips were torn open and it looked as if his nose was broken.

"Holy shit, holy shit, who would have done this!"

The boy looked no older than in his mid-teens.

As the trooper started checking for vital signs he looked down and saw that the boy was not wearing trousers or shoes. He was naked from the waist down.

There was only a trace of a pulse but nothing more.

James Williams took off his heavy rain jacket and placed it tightly around the boy. He then gently lifted him to try to keep him warm. He sat in the pouring rain with the boy in his arms waiting for help to arrive. He would never forget this experience for the rest of his life.

In situations like this, one loses all sense of time. Trooper Williams sat there, not moving. The rain was driven across the surface of the road with great intensity, powered by the near gale-force wind.

He was not going to let go of the boy in his arms. If a vehicle came down the road in the storm, they could both be killed. He just sat in the lashing rain trying to protect both himself and the boy. He whispered. *"Oh God, keep him alive – oh God keep us both alive."*

The oncoming lights seemed to play tricks on his water filled eyes. The lights flickered, moved and then seemed to stop near him. He could not look up, as the lights were too bright.

"Trooper! Trooper! Are you all right?"

Williams looked up and tried to protect his eyes from the flashlights shining in his face.

"Thank God, thank God you're here. Someone left this kid in the middle of the road to be run over. He's alive but only just."

Hands took his bundle away from him. As he moved he gripped his leg, "I think it is broken!" Then he passed out.

Williams did not remember being loaded into an ambulance and driven away. He could not feel the hands of paramedics working on him or even hear their voices. He had passed into a deep state of unconsciousness – his body had shut down to protect him from further harm.

He woke up the following afternoon. Consciousness and reality came back slowly. Gum seemed to keep his eyes shut. The more he struggled to open his eyes the more they seemed determined to remain shut.

Then he heard a voice. "Good, you are awake – just lie still."

The gum finally released his eyelids and he squinted from the light that poured into his eyes. The hospital ward was dark but the lights still hurt his eyes.

"Where am I?" he asked.

"In a warm and safe hospital ward!" The nurse was standing just to the left side of the bed.

"You have a broken leg, two broken ribs and a fractured wrist.

Your body took a beating out in the storm last night but you will be fine! You wait right there while I call the doctor."

"Yeah! As if I am going somewhere", he thought to himself.

"Trooper Williams, I am Doctor Perez. You took a hammering last night but you'll be fine. Be off work for a while."

"The boy, what happened to the boy? Did he make it?"

"Yes, he made it – but only just. He is in ICU. We'll update you on his condition once the police department gives us the go ahead. You did a very brave thing last night. You saved his life." The doctor smiled at her patient and then turned and left the room.

Unbeknown to Trooper Williams the story was all over the local TV stations and newspapers. He was being hailed as a hero. The young boy would certainly have died –

either by being hit by a vehicle on the road or from exposure and his inflicted injuries.

It took three days before the boy was slowly brought out of an induced coma. He had received a severe facial beating. That was evident immediately when he had been discovered on the road and taken into hospital. What only became evident later, when he was fully examined, was that he had been raped.

Beaten, raped and then dumped on the road to die. Who could have done something like this? The boy was lucky that he had survived and been discovered by Trooper Williams.

Chapter 18

"Hello can you hear me?" He could not open his eyes. He felt as if he was drifting. Drifting between the conscious and the unconscious.

"Try to open your eyes. Very slow – try to open your eyes."

The boy struggled to open his eyes but finally after more encouragement from the voice that he kept hearing, he finally managed to flicker them open. He could hardly see – his eyes were badly swollen.

"Where am I?" It is difficult to talk through a heavily bandaged face.

"You are safe in a hospital bed. Welcome back - you've been sleeping for several days."

The boy turned his head towards the sound of the voice. In the darkened hospital ward he saw a woman in a white coat.

"I am Doctor Perez. You took a beating – try not to move."

The boy looked around the room and saw a number of other people standing just away from the bed.

"Why am I here?" he whispered.

"You were found on the road outside of town by a police trooper. He almost ran over you in the storm. He saved your life."

The doctor paused then spoke again.

"Do you remember what happened to you?" The doctor did not mention that he had been raped – that piece of information would come later.

"No." he could not keep his eyes open

The doctor stood next to the bed for another minute or two and then turned to the police officer that was standing at the end of the hospital ward. "He should rest now. He will be more lucid in a few hours. Now he must rest." The room cleared. The boy lay very still – he looked almost dead – or close to it.

Each time he partially regained consciousness, he remembered how sweet sounding the voice was next to him. The nurse was talking in such a gentle manner. She checked all of the machines that he was connected to and even gave him a sponge bath once or twice. He could not remember. His world was blurred and his memory blocked.

When he asked what had happened to him all the nurse would say was, "The doctors will be back soon. They will tell you what happened. You just try to rest."

The next day the doctor and her party entered the ward again. With them was a high-ranking police officer.

"I hope that you are feeling better. The IV has given you a little more strength."

"Why am I here – what happened to me?"

"Do you remember anything at all about your ordeal?"

"No. Nothing."

"I am going to let the police officer speak with you. Try to answer his questions. I know that it might be difficult to remember – and it might be painful to speak as your face is bandaged up – but try to remember if you can."

The police officer stepped into the line of sight.

"I am Officer Gellis. You were found on the road outside of town three nights ago. I would like to ask you some questions."

Swollen eyes looked out through the bandages.

"You had no identification on you. What's your name?"

The boy thought and then replied, "I can't remember."

"Where do you come from?"

Another pause.

"I can't remember."

"Where were you headed?"

"I can't remember."

"Why did you not have any identification on you?"

"I don't know."

The police officer asked a few more questions before the doctor stepped forward again. "I think that we should let him rest." The officer nodded and stepped away from the bed.

"You get some rest – we'll come and see you later."

The entourage walked out of the hospital ward.

Outside of the ward Officer Gellis asked, "Do you believe him when he says that he cannot remember anything?"

"I don't know – too early to say. Let's try a few more sessions before we bring in the hospital psychiatrist."

Over the next two days the doctors and the police officer visited the boy several times.

The questions were the same - always the same. The answers were the same - always the same.

On the third day a round-faced man with a very gentle voice came to see the boy. This time there was no one else in the hospital ward. Not even the police officer detachment that had stood inside his ward on eight hour shifts since he had been admitted.

"Hello, I am Dr. John Michaels. How are you feeling today? Do you need anything?"

To his surprise the boy answered almost immediately. "I'd like a Coke."

"Sure thing, let me arrange that for you – be right back."

The doctor left the ward briefly. When he came back to the side of the bed he said, "One Coke coming right up." True to his word not a minute later there was a tap on the door and a police officer walked in with two cans of Coke. He handed one to the boy. "I needed one myself". He said, "You don't mind if I join you?" The doctor smiled at the young man.

The doctor opened the cans and placed a straw in the one for the boy.

The doctor took a sip from his can and said, "Ah, I needed that!"

The boy just looked back at him.

"The staff here have called you Joe – nice enough name but I'm not sure if you look like a Joe to me – can you remember your name?"

The kid did not answer. The doctor sat next to bed and waited.

"Why am I being held here? – I want to leave."

"I'm sure that you would like to leave but we need to get you healthy first – and besides everyone here likes you a whole lot – so you'll have to stay a while longer." The doctor smiled at "Joe".

Another pause. The doctor just waited.

They both took awkward sips of their Cokes.

Then the breakthrough came. It just needed some time.

"You asked me my name. Still interested?"

"Yes. If you remember your name I would like to address you properly."

"I remembered who I am and where I came from."

The boy whispered his name. The doctor took no notes. All he said was, "That's a nice name – better than "Joe!" Again he had that gentle smile on his face. He knew that the boy was telling the truth.

"How old are you?"

The boy looked at him. He seemed deep in thought. "I'm 16 – just turned 16 on April 4."

"A belated happy birthday – that is a great age!"

The doctor gently steered the conversation along – there was no rush.

"Where are you from?" The boy answered him without hesitation.

"Do your parents know that you are away from home? Maybe they are worried about you?" This time the answer took a while to come out.

"My mother is dead", then a pause, "I left home – my father and I agreed that it was time for me to find my own feet. He knows that I left home."

"That's tough – to be off on your own so young – it's a tough world out there!" The doctor thought to himself "*As you have found out!*"

There was no change in his facial expression as he processed the information that he was receiving.

"Would you like me to contact your father? Where did you live?"

Again there was a pause. Each time the boy took his time responding the doctor notched up a red flag that the boy was holding something back.

"If you want. I don't really care. I am sure that he doesn't care either."

"Ok, let me take down the details."

Once the doctor had taken down the details on his note pad he read the information back to the boy.

"Your name is Anthony McKinzie, of Vale, Oregon…that's only a few hours from here – at least you are still in your home State!"

Anthony nodded in acknowledgement.

"Ok, got it! And your address is, 7 Third Street. What is your dad's telephone number?"

"My dad! He is not my dad!" He thought to himself. He gave the doctor the telephone number of the house where he used to live – never a home - only a lonely house.

Dr. Michaels provided the information to Officer Gellis.

Firstly Gellis made a telephone call to the police department in Vale. It is always useful to have some background information before approaching a father about a potential run away child.

He briefed the Chief of Police on the case and they agreed that the following day they would meet in Vale and make joint contact with the father.

At 5 a.m. the following morning, Officer Gellis set off on the 330-mile drive to Vale. He could have discussed matters over the telephone with the Vale police department but he preferred the personal contact. He was very pleased when his counterpart in Vale suggested that he drive there.

He arrived in Vale just after noon and was met with a warm handshake, a mug of coffee and a sandwich – homemade by the Chief's wife.

Gellis briefed his counterpart and one of his senior officers. He described the severe beating and the rape of the young man. The teen was known to the police department – not for any misdemeanors but because he was the son of a local firefighter hero. Gellis sat and listened to the heroic acts of the kid's dad.

"So the boy has no criminal record of any sort?"

"No, none at all. We are aware that the dad has a drinking problem and sometimes has come close to losing his job because of it but he is one hell of a firefighter – so the town puts up with him. But no, the boy has no record."

"Any whispers of child abuse?"

"Well, most kids get a whipping every so often around here – common practice you know – but nothing that required us to intervene. The old man and his wife used to fight like crazy years ago but she died some time back. What goes on behind closed doors today we will never know."

After about an hour together, the three police officers drove out to the dad's residence.

The dad answered the door and seemed surprised to see three police officers standing outside.

"Hello Bill, sorry to worry you but we have some news regarding Anthony... could we come in?"

"What crap is he up to now?"

"We'll explain once we are inside." There was no choice but to allow them into the home.

Once in the living room he said, "What is this all about?

Anthony doesn't live here anymore – he moved out after the school year ended."

All three police officers could smell the stale odor of liquor in the house. Since coming off of another 72-hour shift, Bill had hardly been sober. They also noticed a woman's high heel shoes laying on the floor in the living room.

"So, what's this all about?"

"Let me introduce Officer Gellis of the Hood River police department – I will ask him to provide the details to you."

"Sir, several nights ago your son was found on a road near Hood River. An on duty police trooper almost ran over his body on the road during a violent storm. Your son was lucky to be found. He had been heavily beaten - and he had been raped. He was lucky to survive the ordeal."

The police officers looked for any signs of shock or remorse from the dad – they noticed none.

All he said was, "What happened?"

"He can't remember what happened that night. Our doctors believe that his mind is shutting out the events that took place. We believe that he was either hitchhiking or was with someone in a vehicle – most likely before the storm broke. If our trooper had not found him he would most likely have died before dawn."

Bill did not know what to say. He hated the boy and he always had. He was shocked at what had happened but he felt no parental emotion – he was completely detached from Anthony.

"Anthony could remember his name and address here in Vale. He also said that he had agreed with you that he had left home. Is that correct?" asked Gellis.

"Yes. He left home. We discussed it and we thought it time that he headed off on his own."

"That is pretty young to head out?" said the local chief.

"Look, there is no hiding the fact – we didn't get on. We both felt that it would be in his best interests if he headed out and started a new life. There was no more than that."

"When did he leave home and where was he headed?" asked Officer Gellis.

"He left home on the evening bus – I think that it was Friday a week ago. He got the last bus out of town but I have no idea where he was headed."

"How do you know this?"

"Because I was in my truck and I saw him get onto the bus and then watched as the bus pulled out of town."

"So, he just took off never to be seen again? Or was he expected back after the summer?"

Bill answered in a very clinical manner. There almost seemed to be ice in his voice, "He took off to start a new life – I don't think that he was thinking of ever coming back."

Silence filled the room and no one really knew how to proceed. The police officers felt very uneasy about the type of response that they were receiving from the dad.

"Bill, what did Anthony take with him when he left?"

"I'm not sure. I suppose that he took clothes. I haven't been to his room since he left."

"Did you did see him pack – did he leave in a hurry?" asked Officer Gellis.

"Look, I have told you that we decided that it was time for him to move on. We agreed to that. He packed and took the bus out. What are you implying?" Bill was beginning to lose his temper.

The officers down played the situation. They would make more inquiries later in the day. They had confirmed that Anthony purchased a single bus ticket to Ontario.

"Would you mind if we checked his room?" asked the local Police Chief.

"Sure." Bill stood up and walked towards the staircase. Two of the police officers followed him up the steps. The third one remained downstairs – that would give him an opportunity to look around.

In Anthony's bedroom they found that the drawers were empty and that there were a few odd garments still on the bed. Anthony must have decided not to take them with him. It looked as if he had packed in a hurry. There was no sign of any struggle. His father had not even bothered to move the clothing off of the bed after Anthony left. On the way out of the bedroom Officer Gellis noticed an empty picture frame on the dresser. "Do you know what was in the frame?" he asked.

"I'm not sure. It could have been a photo of his mother."

Back downstairs the officers were preparing to leave when they popped some difficult questions.

"Did Anthony leave home with any money?"

"Yes. I gave him $200 in small bills. It was all that I could afford."

"That is a great deal of money for a young man to carry on him."

Bill did not answer.

Gellis thought to himself, *"You planned the whole thing – drew the cash in small notes – and then kicked the kid out at short notice. You then sat in your truck and made sure that he left town. What are you hiding?"*

In the doorway Gellis turned around and said, "Anthony had no identification or cash on him when he was found. Whoever assaulted him must have taken it. Before we can release him from the hospital we will require that he have new identification documents. I am sure that you would not mind going to the town offices and requesting a new set for him."

Bill looked at the police officer. Going to do anything for Anthony would be too much to ask. But he believed that he had no choice.

"Sure. I could do that." he replied.

The local chief indicated that he would assist in expediting the new documents for Bill.

"When the documents are ready would you like to drive them to Hood River – then you can see your son in the hospital."

He was being trapped by the police officer. He did not like being trapped.

"No. I will mail them to you. Please give me the contact details."

"He doesn't even want to see his own son. The bastard!"

Then there was another surprise for Bill.

"There is also the matter of the hospital expenses. It will come to a good amount – the kid has no money. We cannot release him without his new identity documents or without settling a portion of the bill. Will you be paying the amount so that he can be released in the next week or two?"

The three policemen knew the answer even before the dad could get it out.

"No. I gave him what I had. There is no more – he wanted to leave and make it on his own. He must find a way of settling the bill. It's no longer my business what he does."

The officers thanked him for his time and drove back to the station house.

"Something is fishy there but we have no grounds for any investigation", said the chief.

It was too late to drive back to Hood River that evening, so Officer Gellis checked into a local motel for the night.

He ate at a small diner that evening. The food was excellent but he hardly tasted the steak in front of him. His mind was thinking about what had happened between the kid and his father. How could any dad hate his kid so much? One could almost feel the distaste oozing out.

Gellis did not sleep well that night.

The next morning he took an early breakfast and then drove home. Although this was his case, he had no jurisdiction over matters in Vale. He felt uneasy about the events leading up to Anthony leaving home. But there was no case – there was no evidence linking the father with the assault. The dad had been working the night that the events took place near Hood River. He felt sorry for the boy.

When he walked into the police station in the early afternoon he decided not to go to the hospital that day. He telephoned Doctor Michaels and set up an appointment for the next morning.

After dinner that night he sat with his family to watch Bonanza. He could not focus on his favorite program. When he stood up from the couch and said that he was going to bed, he kissed his wife and his two teenage daughters. The thought, *"Thank god I have a normal and happy family!"*

Chapter 19

"How is he doing?" he asked Doctor Michaels. "Are there any improvements in his condition and in his memory?"

"His injuries are healing – the bandages came off of his face and the swelling is down. Whoever beat him up really did him over. As for his memory of the events of that evening – well, I think that is a much more difficult issue."

He paused then continued.

"I do believe him when he says that he cannot remember what happened to him on the road that night. He recalls getting the bus from Vale and then getting a late bus to Pendleton. He said that the bus got in at about midnight. He said that he spent the night in the lounge at the Greyhound station – we checked with the manager of the station and he confirms that a young man meeting the description of the boy was there overnight.

Anthony told me that he spent the morning in town. By mid-afternoon he decided to hitchhike and reach Portland. He said that he got a ride with a couple – a John and Maureen Houghton – they dropped him off at the intersection of highway 84 and regional road 97 – they were headed to Madras. He said that they offered for him to spend the night with them – but that meant that he would have to double back down the 97 the next day. He said that they warned him that the weather was closing in but he insisted that he would make it to Portland.

We spoke with the police department in Madras and they gave us the telephone number of John and Maureen. One of your Troopers telephoned them and they confirmed what the boy had told us. They were very upset that something had happened to Anthony – we of course did not go into details – but the Press has had a field day with the story – and Trooper Williams is now a local hero as you know."

Officer Gellis listened as the doctor gave his update. He thought to himself, *"Kid, why did you not go home with the good folk from these parts – they would have accommodated and fed you – and you would not have been assaulted!"*

"So, I think that he genuinely can't remember what happened after he started walking down the 84. I believe that his mind has shut down the memories of the beating...for now, I think that we've hit a dead end on his story."

"What did you pick up on your visit to Vale?" asked the doctor.

The doctor sat in silence while Gellis gave a detailed account of his visit with Anthony's father. Every so often he would purse his lips or nod as a sign of understanding. He could tell that Officer Gellis had suspicions about the circumstances under which Anthony had left home.

"We could not establish any motive for the boy leaving home so suddenly – seems very odd but we have nothing. Maybe after all it is just a dad and son not getting along. Tough to believe that but there is no proof of anything else going on.

So doctor, where does that leave us? We seem to have no reason to hold him once his new identity documents arrive. And of course the paying of the hospital bill."

"Unfortunately I agree. We would have no legal reason to hold him – a compassionate one but no medical or legal case."

Gellis decided to see Anthony after his meeting with Doctor Michaels.

He was surprised at seeing Anthony without the bandages on his face. He was rather pale skinned but good looking for a young kid. The bruises were very evident on his face and the lump under his right eye still looked very puffy and purple. *Who could have hit the kid so hard and often? Why would he do it? Even if provoked why continue to hit him?*

"Good morning Anthony, good to see you looking better. How are you?"

"Hello" that was the only answer that the officer got in reply.

"I visited Vale and spoke with your father. He knows about what happened to you."

The boy just looked back at him. The officer detected a change in color in the boy's face. He was turning red with deep anger – then he seemed to take control of himself again. Gellis did not comment on the reaction. He merely waited for the boy to calm down.

Gellis gave a very scant report of his visit to Vale. There was no need to give the boy the bad news that his father was not interested in him – after all the boy seemed to know that already.

"When can I leave the hospital?"

"We expect your new identification documents to arrive within the week. By then you should be fit enough to leave – the only thing to sort out will be your portion of the hospital bill." Officer Gellis hesitated then he said, "Your dad said that it was your responsibility to pay the bill."

Anthony did not react at first. What was there for him to say?

The news was a shock but not unexpected.

"I have no money."

"I know. Let me try to work on that one – you just rest and get better!"

Gellis turned and walked out of the hospital ward. He wiped away a tear from his eye.

Chapter 20

Trooper James Williams had been slated as a hero for keeping alive the young man that he had found on the road the night of the violent storm. That was two weeks ago now. His recovery had also been slow. This however, did not stop the media from covering the story over and over again. The boy's identity had been kept private (due to the fact that the boy could not remember who he was at first) – but also because the police and hospital had put an embargo on the information.

Trooper Williams had his photo in the local newspaper and he had been featured in newscasts across Oregon. The Mayor's Office had issued a statement that, once fit the Trooper would receive a decoration for his heroism. To James Williams, he had just done his job but he knew that he had to accept the laurels being accorded him. Personally he did not like the attention. He was a proud police officer and not a poster boy.

He had been to see Anthony in the hospital. It was an awkward meeting, because it seemed as if the boy would have preferred to die on the road that night. Still, they shook hands. The boy thanked him for saving his life. He was with Anthony for all of two minutes.

On the day that the trooper was being discharged from the hospital Gellis came to see him. He had just been to see the boy. After enquiring how the trooper was doing he mentioned that the boy would be discharged after receiving his new documents but that the dad had refused to pay a portion of the hospital fee.

"Officer Gellis, why don't we start a fund for the kid. He has nothing. He lost the money that his father gave him. Even if we covered the cost of the hospital he can't just walk out – he has no clothes – nothing. Sir, could we do something for the kid?"

The proposal was made to the Chief of Police in Hood River and was then referred to the hospital and the Mayor's Office. Buy-in was swift. The boy was informed of what they had in mind and he seemed very pleased – not thankful, just pleased. All he really wanted was to get the hell out of the hospital. He was getting very heated deep down inside and he needed to run before he lost control again.

The local radio station helped launch the fundraiser. It was an instant success. The response was overwhelming. They even received a check from the Houghton's.

Money was very tight in 1969 but what was raised was just about seven hundred dollars.

While the campaign was going on, a parcel arrived from Vale for Gellis. It was from the boy's father. Inside the parcel were the new documents. Also enclosed was a sealed envelope marked for Anthony. Gellis wondered what was inside.

"This came for you today." Gellis said, handing him the parcel.

Anthony opened it and pulled out the new set of documents. Then he took the envelope. He sat in the chair next to his hospital bed and looked blankly at the envelope.

He looked up at Officer Gellis. "Do you know what's inside?" he asked.

"No, I don't." He then turned and walked out of the ward. He felt that Anthony needed and wanted to be alone.

Anthony tore open the envelope and took out a number of items. He had lost the photograph of him and his mom on the night that he had been assaulted. Now he held another photograph of the two of them. He swelled up and started to cry. *"Mom, how I miss you. You loved me! You were the only one who ever loved me!"*

There was another photograph in the envelope.

The photograph was of a man and a woman.

There was a date and some information written on the back of the photograph. He paid little attention to it.

There was another folded piece of paper. It was a certificate from his high school congratulating him on his achievement in the school musical.

Anthony rose from his chair and placed the envelope and its contents in the drawer of the dresser next to his bed.

Outside the ward a police officer had heard him cry.

But there was nothing that he could do about it.

Chapter 21

Anthony had agreed to go out with Trooper James Williams and his wife to pick out new clothes. He would have preferred to go alone but he really had little choice in the matter. He picked jeans, t-shirts, shirts, socks, shoes, underwear, a towel, and a light and heavier jacket and other personal items. Mrs. Williams insisted that he purchased more than what he thought he would need. They had the foresight to stop at the camping store first to buy a good quality backpack. The backpack was a limiting factor in what he could buy – or what Mrs. Williams wanted to buy for him.

Before setting aside money for the portion of the hospital bill, there was still several hundred dollars left over. Very reluctantly, Anthony accepted the funds. He would have preferred to start out with an amount of two hundred dollars – as he had been given a few weeks back.

A few hundred dollars to start a new life with was not very much.

There had been offers of jobs in Hood River or to complete his high school diploma in town but he wanted to move on. He wanted to prove to that man he had lived with, that he could start a new life. He was determined not to fail. He would succeed at something and then stick it under the man' s nose!

"So kid, is there anything else that you need before we let you fly away?" asked Gellis.

Anthony thought for a while and then he answered, "I would like to buy a guitar. Where could I get one in town?"

"Do you play?"

"Not much but I would like one." Then almost as an afterthought he said, "I sang in my school musical a few weeks back."

A few weeks back he thought. Seems like a lifetime ago. Kicked out of home, left school, beaten up and raped...a few weeks...life changing.

"I didn't know that you could sing!"

"I only know a few songs, the ones that I sang at the musical."

"Well, I'll be!" replied the officer.

"Tell you what, I know just the place to get you a guitar, but only on the condition that you sing to us before you are discharged from the hospital."

"My face kinda hurts still." He was interrupted "No way out kid, your choice." The police offer had a broad smile on his face.

"Well, ok, but I'll need to practice and I'll need the lyrics to the songs that I know. I can't play the guitar so I will need some background music."

Not only did Anthony obtain the lyrics of the songs that he required but he was also given the guitar by the storeowner.

Anthony had two more days in the hospital before he was to be discharged. He closed the door to his ward and tried to sing the songs that he knew. He was lent a tape deck with the music. He struggled to get the songs right.

On the morning of his discharge, he stood in front of a large gathering of hospital and police staff. Williams and his wife, Gellis and the doctors who had cared for him sat in the front row. Doctor Michaels looked very proud and winked at Anthony as he walked forward to sing.

When the music started to play, a rough but solemn voice came out.

The audience loved Elvis Presley and this voice could not compare to the King but the singing of "Love Me Tender" and "Are You lonesome tonight?" left them all in tears.

The school play was "A Tribute to Elvis" and the boy had discovered that he could sing.

After the two songs and the round of applause and back patting were over it was time to collect his gear from the hospital ward and to check out of the place that had been his home for more than two weeks. Without the care and love given to him in the hospital he would surely have died.

He was packing his final things when Gellis walked into the ward with Doctor Michaels.

"Almost ready?"

"Yes."

"Kid, before you go there is something we need to tell you. Take a seat."

Anthony looked at them and after a few seconds he sat on the end of the bed. "What's up now? Am I still leaving?"

"Yes, you're still leaving but I have some news for you." Gellis paused then continued; "I had a telephone call from the police department in Vale this morning...your father died last night. I'm sorry kid."

Anthony looked at him in stunned silence. He didn't seem to comprehend the message at first. His first reaction when he had heard that the Vale police department had telephoned was that he might have been found out – that he had set the fire that night...but now his mind was racing...he man was dead...he was dead.

"Kid, did you hear what I said? Your father died last night."

It took another long period before the boy answered.

"How did he die?'

"He burnt to death in his home."

"What? What did you say?"

"I'm sorry kid. From what we understand your father was on a binge-drinking spree for the few days before he died. He was at home and the house burnt down. He was found dead on the floor in the kitchen."

"He died in a fire!" "He died in a fire!"

"Yes. I'm sorry."

"Why! Why! Why could it not have been MY fire?"

"Kid, I am very sorry. Are you ok?"

"Yes, yes, I'm ok" He felt shock, joy and disappointment all at the same time. Then the tears came. Tears of hate and joy!

After a minute, the police officer continued, "There's more... the police chief in Vale told me that the fire had been set. It was deliberate. The house was torched while your dad was drunk. Most likely he woke up but could not get out of the house in time. Someone wanted your father to die. The police chief now thinks that there is a link between the fires at the station a few weeks back and this fire. Your father was the target in both. Whoever failed the first time around, struck again."

Anthony did not know what to think. He had set the first fire. He had wanted to kill the man that he hated so much. Who had set this fire and why?

"Do they suspect anyone of staring the fire?"

"Not as yet but it could be a husband of one of the women that your father was seeing. Maybe it was a crime of revenge. We don't know anything further. I'm sorry to have to give you this news. I really am."

Doctor Michaels watched the heart-breaking scene.

"See you at the reception desk after you have said good bye to the staff." That is all he heard as they walked out of the ward.

Anthony sat on his bed. He grabbed onto the bed railing to steady himself. He could not believe that the man was dead. There was no heart-felt emotion or grief. There was nothing really. Maybe disappointment that he had failed in his quest – and that someone else had succeeded. He had been deprived of his prize!

He tried to control his breathing. His heart seemed to be beating outside of his chest. He could hear it pounding. His mind struggled to comprehend the fact that maybe now he was truly alone and that he had to make it on his own. He could not go home – there was no home and no one to go home to. Finally he realized that his disappointment of not having been the one who had set the blaze that killed the man was in fact an advantage. He was not a suspect in the fire of a few weeks earlier. He was free of the man, the town and now free of suspicion.

"Anthony, the staff is waiting; are you ready?" It was the nurse who had been at his bedside when he first woke up. In her stiff white uniform she looked like an angel.

"Yes, I'm ready." He walked out of the ward with his entire worldly possessions.

The goodbyes were difficult. He was thankful for the love and care but he did not know how to respond to people. This was, and would be, a life-long issue for him. Most people had been mean to him – but in truth his behavior and temper tantrums had not endeared him to anyone. Kids at school had mostly avoided him. Except for a young girl in his class who tried to talk with him from time to time.

As he stepped into the police vehicle the last one to shake his hand was Trooper Williams. "Good luck kid!" "Thank you for saving my life!" said Anthony.

"Make sure that you have a life!" was the reply.

Gellis parked the vehicle outside of the Greyhound station.

"I don't think that I should go in. Might look as if I am making sure that you are leaving town!" he smiled. The kid replied with a weak grin.

"Where are you headed?"

"I'm not sure. I think that I will go to Portland for a while. Maybe head on to California by the winter. Wherever I can get a job I suppose."

"Thank you for what you have done for me."

"You take care of yourself. I'm here if you need me."

They shook hands. Anthony waited until the police car drove away and then he walked into the Greyhound station. He purchased a one-way ticket to Portland.

Chapter 22

There is always a degree of suspicion when a young boy travels alone. Will he pay for his meal or his accommodation or would he run? Anthony was aware of this.

In Portland he located a Rooming House and paid for one week of accommodation up-front. He thought that he would give himself a week to try to find some work. If not then he would move on. He slept with his moneybag around his neck – he could not afford to lose his money again.

On his fifth day in town he saw a sign in a restaurant window for a dishwasher. The job paid minimum wage and provided one meal per day. He took the job.

For the next month, he worked 40 hours per week. The restaurant owner was fair to him but, other than that, he met no one. He would get a bus to and from work – always with his money with him. He knew that he was taking a risk carrying so much on him but he did not know or trust anyone.

When he was not working, he walked around the city or sat in his room trying to play his guitar. Several times he was yelled at to stop playing as it kept people awake at night. He took refuge in a nearby park when he wanted to play after work.

Nothing special happened in that month. He liked Portland but he did not when it was overcast and rainy.

It was a pointless job and he felt that it was time to move on. He had covered his daily living expenses with his job and his moneybag was still fully intact.

He gave notice at the Rooming House and quit.

He decided to head south. The next stop was Sacramento.

Before he purchased his Greyhound ticket from Portland to Sacramento he stood looking at the map on the wall in the bus station.

He changed his plan. He decided that he would first stop in Salem and then Eugene on the way down south. When you have no agenda or time frame then stops along the road of life – in particular a new life – seem justified.

Although he had grown up in Oregon he knew very little of the State. He justified his decision in the name of furthering his education.

He enjoyed both cities but in Eugene in particular. He ended up spending a few days there before he thought that he had better move on and look for work.

It was now late June and the scenery was stunning as he headed south along highway 5 by bus. His next destination was Sacramento.

The bus pulled into a rest stop. The complex consisted of a gas station, a diner and bar and a large truck stop area. In front of the stop and across the street was a valley. Behind the stop were forests and hills. One could not miss the beautiful view while walking to the restaurant.

The lunch stop would be for thirty minutes.

He walked into the diner with his backpack slung over one shoulder.

It was a large building. To the left was the diner and to the right was the bar. He purchased a sandwich and finished it in double quick time. He decided to walk through to the bar area and kill time until his bus was due to depart.

The atmosphere was much darker inside. Even during the daytime with few people inside, it looked murky. It was a very large room and must have accommodated at least two hundred people.

On the one side of the room was a long bar. On the opposite side was a stage with band equipment on it.

He stood taking in the scene when his eyes saw a large sign on the wall just next to where he was standing.

HELP WANTED
DISHWASHER/BUS BOY
TO START IMMEDIATELY
SPEAK TO GUS.

He stood and looked at the sign then thought "Why not!"

He walked over to the bar.

"Is Gus here?'

"Yeah. I'll call him"

A very large man walked out from the kitchen area near the bar. He towered above the barman. He looked elderly but was still well muscled and looked pretty tough.

"You wanted me?"

Anthony had taken the sign off of the wall and he handed it to the man.

"I would like to apply for the job."

Gus looked at him. "How old are you?"

"Sixteen. I have experience. I worked as a dishwasher and bus boy in Portland for a month."

"I think that you're too young to work in a place like this. It gets pretty rough here some nights."

"I can look after myself." he lied. "Why not give me a chance."

Gus looked at him for a long time.

"You got a place to stay tonight?"

"No Sir, I just came in by bus – the bus that leaves in about five minutes."

"Tell you what kid, you work here tonight and I'll give you a place to sleep. I need the help – then we can talk tomorrow."

"You got a name?"

"Anthony...Anthony McKinzie."

Anthony made double quick time running back to the bus and telling the driver that he would not be driving on with him. Back inside the bar Gus was waiting for him.

"You are too young to work in the bar so you stay put in the kitchen. If we need you to clear up I'll call you. Understand?'

"Yes Sir!"

"Ok, let me show you where you can sleep tonight."

Through the back door of the kitchen, there stood an old camper. It had seen better days. Gus opened the door and stepped up. Anthony followed him.

"This should do for the night. There's a washroom and shower just off from the storeroom – use it."

"Rest up and come and see me at 5:30 p.m. and I will show you what to do. Your shift will end around 2 a.m."

Gus walked out of the camper.

Anthony was excited and weary. He did not know what lay ahead for him that night. He did not unpack his backpack but pulled out a shirt that would be good to work in. He found the shower and washed up. The camper needed some cleaning but he made it suitable for a one-night stay. He then lay down and rested. He almost missed his shift.

Anthony worked like he had never worked before. He washed more dishes that night than all of his stay in Portland. He felt as if his arms were going to fall off. He worked for almost four hours straight before he was given a dinner break. He could not believe that it was still only 9:30 p.m. – and he still had another four hours to go after his break was over.

"How are you doing – holding up?" asked Gus as he walked in with a plate of dinner and a Coke for the kid.

"Good – I'm good." he lied again.

"Good to hear! We have another rush that comes in now when the band starts to play so enjoy the break!" Gus smiled and walked out of the kitchen.

It was almost 3 a.m. before Anthony got to bed. He feared that he had lost all feeling in his shoulders, back and arms. As painful as his body was, he still managed to fall instantly into a deep sleep.

"You awake in there? – It's time to raise your butt." Gus was knocking on the door of the camper.

There was no reply.

Anthony was still out cold.

"Hey kid, move your butt, time to get moving."

It took another round of knocking and tempting the kid with breakfast before Anthony rose and came to the door.

"What time is it?"

"Almost 10:30. Wash up and come through. Do you like hot cakes?"

The smell of hot cakes energized the kid and he washed and dressed in five minutes flat.

He charged into the kitchen.

"You washed your hands?'

"Yes Sir!"

"Your face – you washed your face – it still looks dirty!"

Anthony stopped dead in his tracks. His face was not dirty. It was still the remnants of the injuries to his face that made his face look darker in places. How should he answer the big man sitting opposite him at a table in the kitchen? Maybe the truth! Maybe he should tell the truth.

He looked at Gus and said, "I got beaten up a few weeks ago. My face is still bruised in some places."

Gus looked at him for a long time. It was as if he was taking a head to toe x-ray of the kid. He said nothing.

"Eat your cakes before they get cold." He stood up and walked out of the kitchen.

The plate of hot cakes was staked five-high and had all of the fixings with it. Anthony devoured the meal and the tea that Gus had made for him.

He sat back and felt like a king. Fat on cakes and hot tea.

His state of euphoria did not last long.

"You done?"

"Yes Sir, thank you!"

"I suppose that you want to be on your way now?"

Reality struck the kid like a sledgehammer. His night of work was over and it was time to move on.

"Where are you headed?"

"I was thinking of heading down to California. Nowhere special. I just need a job somewhere. No rush to go anywhere."

Gus looked at him.

"Kid, I'll tell you what, you tell me something about yourself and then maybe I could keep you for a few more days."

Anthony was silent. He did not want to relate his life story to a complete stranger – and just to get a job. That was unfair!

He sat and looked at his hands. He did not answer.

After a silent pause Gus said, "How about I tell you about myself and then you tell me about yourself – then we will both know something about each other." The big man smiled at him.

"Ok, if you want."

"Right. My name is Gustav Pedersen. I was born in 1903, that makes me 66 this September. My family came to the States in the mid-1800s from Sweden. I was raised in the mountains near here and know the woods like the back of my hand. Lived outdoors most summers growing up. Me and my dad used to sleep under the stars most nights..."

Anthony felt a deep pain in his belly. "...me and my dad used to sleep under the stars most nights..." He had never had that experience. He never had a dad – just a monster. That deep down anger wanted to rise up again inside of him.

"Kid, you still with me?"

Anthony took a deep breath – the anger subsided.

"Yes Sir!"

"I was a trapper and huntsman before the war. Pretty good with a knife and axe. I was brought up real tough – and I loved it.

When the US entered the war in 1941 I was too old for fighting but I volunteered and became an instructor for hand-to-hand combat. I trained many young guys to survive outdoors, use a knife, or even worse – to kill silently."

Gus paused.

"Many a young kid that I trained went off to fight and never came back. But hopefully I trained some that did survive.

After the war, there wasn't much going on – no jobs and no prospects. I went back to trapping and hunting. I married, but it didn't last too long. She preferred living in town and I loved the mountains.

Then trapping became unpopular and I moved here. Started as a barman right through those doors." Gus pointed towards the bar.

"Then a few years later I bought the place - the gas station, truck layover and the bar. That was about twenty years ago.

I live in a cabin about fifty yards up in the woods behind the bar. I spend about eighteen hours a day here every day."

Gus then looked at the kid. "Your turn!"

Anthony did not know what to say or where to start.

"I left home in May –I wanted to make it on my own. I got beaten up and was in hospital in Hood River for a few weeks. Then I moved to Portland. I washed dishes in a diner for about a month. Now I'm here."

"That's it? That is all you've got?"

"Yes Sir!"

While Anthony was in the hospital his story was all over the newspapers. Gus knew exactly who he was from the minute that he had walked into the bar the day before. He also knew folk from Hood River and he had made some telephone calls earlier that morning. He wanted to see if the boy would tell the truth – if he did not, he would have been on his way.

"OK, kid, tell you what, I'll hire you for a few weeks over the summer. I need the help. If you want we can tidy up the camper and you can move in. I will pay you minimum wage and you'll get two meals a day. You will work six days a week – it'll be tough but maybe you need some experience."

"He's offering me a job here!"

He seemed to forget the pain in his back, shoulders and arms from the night before.

"What do you say?"

"Thank you - I will work hard."

"You do that – if not I'll whip your hide you hear!" Gus smiled at him. The man that he lived with for all those years did whip his hide but he doubted if Gus would do that to him. He did not want to find out!

"Yes Sir!" Anthony smiled back at him.

"Right then, no time to waste, your day shift is from noon to 3, then you are back on from 6 until close. You had better unpack and let's try to make the camper livable."

"What do I call you?"

"Most people call me Big Gus. You can call me what you like.

Chapter 23

Just three days after taking up employment with Big Gus there was a special project to be undertaken.

"Kid, every 4th of July we do a special BBQ outside and have fireworks as soon as it gets dark. We get really busy so you'll be sweating blood the whole day – and night. You up to it?"

"Yes Sir!" Anthony returned the smile that Gus had given him.

"Good. We need the BBQ"s brought out and cleaned. I will show you where they are. Ray will help you get them out and set them up." Ray was the handyman and fixed everything from fridges, to gas stoves, broken tables (from wear and tear and the occasional bar fights) to cutting the grass or painting the signs outside of the truck stop and bar.

Besides his regular work shifts, Anthony put in two mornings getting the BBQs loaded up from the storeroom and taken to the side of the bar where the party would be staged. One morning was spent carrying the BBQs and the second was for cleaning them. In the two days leading up to the July 4 celebrations Anthony got less than eight hours of sleep.

On July 4 the celebrations started early. The band was set up outside of the diner and by early afternoon the local townsfolk started arriving. The parking lot was completely full by midafternoon. Anthony was hauled in to cook hotdogs. Paper plates were being used – so there was little washing up to do.

He lost count of how many hotdogs he prepared that day. He could not believe that the population of a small town could eat so much.

"Kid, I need help here!"

"Kid, we need more hotdogs from the fridge!"

"Kid, we need more napkins!"

It never stopped and he loved every minute of it.

The feeding frenzy eased off around 9 p.m. as everyone tried to find vantage points for the fireworks display. Each year since Big Gus had introduced the July 4 celebrations at his truck stop and diner the event had got bigger and better.

"You excited about the fireworks?" asked a young woman.

Anthony turned and looked at her. He felt embarrassed with his answer, "This is my first one – never seen fireworks before."

He hated the reply, "Mother, this boy has never seen fireworks before – where does he come from, outer space!"

He just walked away.

He found a spot on the grass and sat and waited for the sun to set and for the show to start.

"Hey, kid, come sit with us!" It was Big Gus. He waved his arms at Anthony, who walked over and sat with the group that was with him.

"Grab some lemonade." Gus pointed at a large vat standing on the ground near the group.

Just on 10 p.m. Gus gave the signal for the show to start.

Anthony looked up in amazement as the rockets burst in the black night sky. Each set of explosions was better than the last. As the crowd roared with excitement a new feeling started to come over the boy from Vale.

He could picture himself setting off the fireworks. He could see himself becoming the one who brought forth fire.

His emotions were on edge. In the last few weeks he had forgotten about the impact that fire had on his life. He had tried to kill someone by using fire. He had failed – but someone else had succeeded in destroying his target. He had felt cheated when he heard the news about the death of the man that he hated.

By the time the fireworks display had ended, he felt totally confused. His plot had been to kill someone by fire. Although he had failed and there was no one else that he hated, he still seemed to have an attraction to fire. The thought of fire gripped him inside. He wanted to be in control of it. Maybe hate sparked his feelings.

His deep thoughts were interrupted.

"Come on kid. The show is over. We've got cleaning up to do."

It was well after 1 a.m. before everything was cleaned up outside and the remaining dishes washed. Anthony was exhausted when Gus called it a night.

"OK folks that's enough. We can do the rest in the morning – thank you all – now let's get some sleep."

Anthony was about to walk to his camper when Gus called him over.

"Hey Kid!" Anthony stopped and turned around.

"You did great! We could not have done this without you! I have a surprise for you. I am giving you double pay for today – and tomorrow only come in for the night shift...take the day off...and I will also pay you for the shift that you'll miss." Big Gus smiled at him.

"Thank you Sir!"

That night he slept the sleep of the dead.

The next few weeks sped by. Twice Anthony accompanied Big Gus into town to buy supplies for the restaurant and bar. Beer trucks and food vendors delivered directly to the bar but there were always other things to buy. They would drive back from town with the long wheel base truck fully loaded with packs of napkins, toilet paper, boxes of condiments and whatever else needed replenishing.

On one of these trips into town Anthony took his envelope of money into a local bank and opened an account. The bank manager queried why a sixteen-year-old boy would open an account without his parents' consent. It took some time before they permitted the boy to have an account. He still had his $300 intact and had added a small sum to the total.

Whilst in town he purchased more clothes and things that he needed.

He felt independent. Free of deep pain and more relaxed. Maybe he was outgrowing his inner demons.

On the way back from town Big Gus asked, "Are you excited about the Apollo 11 launch on Wednesday?"

"Yes Sir! I haven't watched any of the other launches before."

"Are you kidding – you've never seen any of those giant Saturn rockets blast off?"

"No. I didn't follow the space program until I came here. Then everyone has been talking about it the last week or so. I don't understand how something that big can leave earth and fly to the moon and back."

"Well, the whole thing doesn't fly to and from the moon. The rockets have several parts to them and as they go along the ship gets smaller as the burnt out pieces get jettisoned. Then they have two sections to the final piece. The one goes down to the surface of the moon while the other stays in orbit waiting for the astronauts to return."

"It stays by itself? How do they know that it will still be there when they come back from the surface?"

"No, the one astronaut remains with the mother ship while the other two go down to land on the moon. Then the two ships are linked together after the mission is over."

"That is crazy. How do they know that the guys on the moon will come back?"

"There are sure big risks but NASA has been preparing for this for years – using up our tax dollars as if it was water – so they'd better be ready. Our scientists need to beat the Russians to landing on the moon."

"Will it be on TV?'

Big Gus laughed, "You bet – and the people around the world will be watching!"

"Can we watch it?'

"Hell yes, I think that there will be a hundred people around our small TV."

"I can't wait!"

"He's just a normal kid – I hope that his life turns out ok. It's good to have him around!" Gus thought to himself.

On the morning of the launch Gus offered a special lunch to his guests in the bar. As he had suspected, the diner and bar area of the truck stop were completely full almost two hours before the launch time. As the official count down preceded the excitement became electric. ABC had teams at the launch site, along the coastline of Florida and around the world.

From NASA the countdown continued.

"This is Apollo Saturn Launch Control. We've passed the 6 minute mark in our countdown for Apollo 11...still GO at this time."

Gus walked through the bar, "Last call for bar service closes in one minute – there will be no service until after the launch." There was a frantic calling of orders for drinks. During the final moments prior to the launch no one touched his or her drinks.

Anthony was about ten feet from the small TV. He wished that everyone would shut up as he was trying to hear every word that was being said by the ABC commentators.

"T minus 1 minute, 35 seconds and counting...we continue to build up pressure in all three stages here at the last minute to prepare it for takeoff."

The noise in the bar was deafening as the excitement grew.

Almost by divine intervention the room became very still as the last minute ticked by.

As the fuel was ignited the yellow flames burst out from beneath the bottom of the 363 feet tall Saturn V rocket. Even on the TV the earth seemed to shake as the 6.5 million ton beast roared into life.

"T- 20 seconds and counting, 15 seconds, 12, 11, 10, 9, ignition sequence started, 6, 5,4,3,2,1, zero, all engines running... LIFT –OFF!...We have a lift-off, 32 minutes past the hour. Lift-off of Apollo 11... Tower cleared..."

The commentary continued as the 7,648,000 pounds of thrust lifted the Apollo 11 craft into the blue sky. The silence in the bar gave way to a barrage of whistles, yells, hooting and hollering. This scene was the same across the US and in most parts of the world.

"Eight miles down range, 12 miles high, velocity 4000 feet per second."

"At 3 minutes, downrange 70 miles, 43 miles high, velocity 9300 feet per second."

"Down range 270 miles, altitude 82 miles, velocity 12, 472 feet per second."

As the commentators reported on the launch and NASA provided updates on the staging process, the focus on those in the bar drifted to celebrations. It almost seemed as if "out of sight out of mind" saying was proven true that day.

"Hey Kid, did you enjoy that?" yelled Gus.

"Sure did! Will they show it again?"

"Oh yeah! I would think that it will be shown a million times over the next few days!"

Anthony could hardly pull himself away from the TV over the next few days. As the mission progressed, he became more and more excited.

Gus loaned him a portable radio so that he could listen to mission updates while he was working in the kitchen or while he lay in bed at night.

July 20 could not come fast enough. That would be the big day.

On the Sunday morning Anthony was washed, dressed and sitting in the closed bar well before Big Gus arrived. He had position 1 in front of the small TV.

Over a billion people around the world were watching TV that morning.

As the EAGLE slowly approached the surface of the moon, one could almost hear the heartbeat of the person you were sitting next to. Anthony thought that Big Gus could hear every beat in his chest!

When the "1202" Program Alarm sounded Anthony thought that he was having a heart attack. "You cannot fail now! You cannot fail now!" he said to himself. He gripped the side of the bar stool that he was sitting on. He was white knuckled like Gus and Ray next to him.

Mission Control and Eagle communications were all business, and all professional. The thousands of hours of training and the sheer skills of Neil Armstrong kept the moon landing on track.

Another Program Alarm! More panic. Anthony thought that he was going to pee in his pants.

"400 feet.

300 feet.

120 feet.

60 seconds of fuel.

30 feet.

2 ½ down,

Faint shadow.

4 forward, drifting to the right a little.

Okay, down a half.

30 seconds of fuel.

Contact light. OK, engine stop.

Houston, Tranquility Base here. The Eagle has landed."

"Tranquility, we copy you on the ground. You got a bunch of guys about to turn blue. We're breathing again. Thanks a lot!"

Gus, Ray and Anthony patted each other on the back. It was as if they had landed on the moon themselves. They were not alone in this global mankind moment. They clapped and cheered and danced up and down.

Several hours later the bar was clogged with people. The first potential steps on a foreign heavenly body were about to take place. Service in the bar took longer as the focus of attention was on the TV screen.

"I am on the foot of the ladder… I am going to step off of the LEM now.

THAT'S ONE SMALL STEP FOR (A) MAN, ONE GIANT LEAP FOR MANKIND".

Again the roar went up in the bar.

Everyone listened while President Nixon spoke to Neil and Buzz on the moon. It was the longest distance telephone call ever made.

"Here Man from the Planet Earth first set foot upon the Moon, July 1969 A.D. We came in peace for all mankind."

The re-entry and splashdown down on July 24 1969 brought to end a space journey that billions of people watched and shared. It did not stop wars or conflicts but it proved the ability of mankind to embrace an event that they all felt part of.

After the July 4 fireworks display and the Apollo 11 mission Anthony felt as if his life was full of adventure. There were so many things to learn about and enjoy. Some were good – others not so good.

Chapter 24

Thanksgiving and Christmas were two of the new experiences that Anthony enjoyed. Even at the tender age of sixteen he was maturing fast. He was well liked by the regulars at the bar. He seemed like a kid brother to the other members of staff. Big Gus treated him well. He worked hard and sweated for the money that he earned, but he was content.

Gus invited a few people up to his cabin for Thanksgiving dinner.

The restaurant could not afford to close so the small group had their meal at a midafternoon time slot. Anthony sat at the table and glowed with joy. He sat with his new family – his first family. He also did not have to do the dishes after the meal.

"Hey kid, you've got enough food on your plate to feed an army!" Ray did not speak much but he was a kind man. "Enjoy it kid." Said Gus, "Don't let him tease you!"

Anthony looked at the mountain of food on his plate and felt embarrassed. He was about to try to mumble some sort of apology when he looked up and saw Gus and Ray smiling at him.

"Just make sure you leave some space for pie!"

There was not much talking during the meal. Everyone was totally focused on the meal in front of him or her. For the adults, it was a special event each year but for a sixteen-year-old boy who had never sat down to a Thanksgiving meal, it was super special.

After the meal they all went and sat outside on the small porch in front of the cabin. No one could move!

"Ok you lazy bunch, before you get coffee and pie we have to walk off the turkey – so let's go…up the hill…the last ones up get no pie!"

"You walk up by yourself and enjoy the view!"

"Have a good time! See you when you get back!"

Some of the other comments were less choice.

Anthony turned to Ray, "Is no one going to walk up the hill with Big Gus?"

"Kid, we have the same discussion every year...he forces us up the hill and back...he'll threaten us with no pie if we don't join him but we straggle along. Besides he couldn't let all that pie go to waste."

As Ray stood up he offered his hand to the kid and hauled him up off of the step on the porch. "We had better follow him up the hill!"

At first the dirt road up the hill was a gentle climb but then it turned upwards and the journey became harder. The laughter amongst the guys in the group stopped as they began to pant their way up the hill.

Just as the moaning started Gus brought a halt to the "Everest Explorers".

"Ok that is far enough". Everyone felt out of breath – even the youngest of the group. Being sixteen is no guarantee of being in the best shape.

Earlier in the day Gus had driven his truck up the dirt road and placed an icebox filled with beer and lemonade under a tree. This was now the resting spot.

Sitting on the ground and drinking something cold together was another experience that Anthony would not forget.

"Kid, come over here. I want to show you something."

Anthony stood up and walked behind Big Gus. They walked over some flat rocks and just beyond the line of trees.

"What do you think?"

The view looking down on the valley was the most beautiful thing that Anthony had ever seen. He stood in complete awe looking at the vista in front of him.

"It is so beautiful. I have never seen anything like this before."

He turned and looked at Gus. All he said was, "Thank you." He was learning to say "thank you."

"Sure kid, no problem. Enjoy nature. Always try to find a place with trees – if you listen carefully they talk to you – and they calm your soul." How true this saying would become.

The others had joined them and they all stood overlooking the valley.

Chapter 25

It was after Thanksgiving when he was winterizing his camper that he pulled out his guitar from under the bunk bed. He had not played it since arriving at the bar and taken up employment.

"Hello, sorry that I've ignored you – but Big Gus does not allow me much time off!" He held the guitar as best he could but it felt uncomfortable in his hands.

He took it outside and sat on the benches on the one side of the diner.

He strummed away but it sounded like a cat being murdered.

"You play?"

Anthony looked up. He had not noticed the van with the band members pull up. It was their afternoon to practice before the weekend sessions in the bar.

"Oh no! – I'd like to but I haven't had any lessons."

"Do you want to watch us practice – maybe you could pick up a few things?"

"Sure! I only start work at 6."

Anthony followed the band into the bar. Gus was working the bar shift himself and did not notice the group that walked in – at least he did not see Anthony walk in with them.

The bar was fairly empty so he took up a seat right in front of the small raised stage. He was still too young to be in the bar but sometimes he would watch TV from the set at the bar counter.

The band tuned up and then started playing. Although Anthony had heard them play many times from the kitchen or from when he was clearing plates from the tables, he had never really paid much attention to them at all.

He sat there listening to songs that he did not know like "Hey Jude", "Sitting on the Dock of the Bay" and "Crimson and Clover." Then the band changed tempo and played "Suspicious Mind" by Elvis. Anthony sat up and paid more attention. When the band stopped playing he said, "Do you guys know "Love me tender"?

"Yes. Do you know it?"

"Kinda. I sang it at my school musical in May."

Then he thought, *"May, only six months ago. Six months – so much has happened to me in six months!"*

"You wanna sing it for us?"

"Oh no! I've forgotten it." He lied. He remembered singing it to the hospital staff in June.

"Come on kid – give it a try!"

Anthony thought about it. "Hey, why not!"

"Ok, but I need the words – I might have forgotten them."

"Yeah, sure, we've got them."

Anthony took the sheet music and tried to sing the song in his mind first. Although he had sung the song just a few months ago, it was tricky to try to get it right. Not having had any singing training, he still struggled with his voice and pitch. Then the band played the song and he sang it to himself.

"Ready when you are!"

Anthony took a deep breath and then began singing. He still required a great deal of training but what came out was still as soulful as what it did when he tried out at his high school musical.

Just after he began the bandleader signaled for the band to stop playing and to let the kid sing by himself.

Big Gus looked up as he heard a different male lead sing. He almost dropped the full beer that he had just poured when he saw that it was Anthony who was singing. Gus had never heard a better rendition of the song besides Elvis himself.

When he finished the song, the bandleader indicated that he should sing it again. Although the band played a few Elvis numbers in their sets, the venue was not one for slow romantic numbers. The dozen or so people in the bar stopped talking and turned and looked at Anthony on stage.

"Hey, kid, where did you get the voice from? Wow man, that was cool!" The band members gathered around him and were slapping him on the back.

"Kid, you got to sing more often."

"Where'd you learn to sing like that?"

Anthony still felt extremely nervous about being the center of attention – just like when the kids at school congratulated him when his "father" was a hero for saving people from fires.

"Oh, I just like that song, that's all."

"You should sing more often – maybe we could teach you to play the guitar and sing other numbers!" The bandleader was smiling, "Yeah, you should sing with us sometime!"

Anthony walked straight towards the kitchen. He wanted to put his guitar away before he dropped it. His knees felt weak as he walked by Gus who was standing at the side of the bar. He almost made it but then a voice said, "Stop! Where do you think that you are going?"

He turned and looked at Big Gus.

"Why didn't you tell me that you could sing?"

"Dunno"! He did not know what else to say.

All he got as an answer was a huff and, "You start work at 6. Don't be late!"

He expected some comment from Gus over the next day or two but nothing was said. When next he saw the band members, they asked him about singing and he just shrugged his shoulders and did not answer.

Chapter 26

Christmas had never been anything special for Anthony. He had spent most of the last ten years by himself on Christmas Day. Since his mother had died he had no one around him – it was just another day. No family, no going to church or hearing choirs' sing and no presents under a tree – there was not even a tree. He spent the holidays indoors so that no one could see him or see that he was alone.

Would this year be any different?

His answer came early.

"Do you have anything to wear to church on Christmas Eve?"

Anthony looked at Big Gus in total amazement. *"What did he just say?"*

"Kid, did you hear me? Have you got anything to wear to church?"

"How do I answer him?"

"Tell the truth!"

"Sir, I have never been to church."

"What! You have never been to church? Never?"

"No Sir. Never."

"Right then young man tomorrow we are driving into town and getting you some clothes. Then I will give you the "Big Gus" crash course on Christmas and going to church!"

The next morning after their normal mid-morning breakfast they set off to town.

"You really never been to church on a Sunday?"

"No. There was never anyone around at home. My Mom died and...and my father... well, he was never at home either. I did everything myself. But I never went to church". He hated using the word father.

"I can't believe it! I only go a few times a year but Christmas Eve is special. You will like it."

With long pants, shoes and a smart shirt on, Anthony looked at himself in the mirror in the store. Not too bad he thought.

"You look like a young gent – all dressed up!"

Anthony smiled back at Big Gus.

"So how much is this going to cost me?" asked Anthony.

"Well, let's see those price tags?"

"Tell you what. We'll split the price...I'll pay for it and you can give me half when I pay you next week."

"You didn't tell me the price?"

Gus looked at him. "You are a determined one." He said.

"It comes to about $20 bucks, so you owe me ten. Do we have a deal kid?"

Ten dollars was a great deal of money. He looked at himself in the mirror again. "OK, you got a deal. I will pay you ten bucks next week. Thank you Sir!"

Driving back to the bar the kid was beaming from ear to ear. He could not wait for Christmas Eve.

The magic of Christmas was completely new to him. Everything flashed by as if it was a dream.

Gus closed the bar at 5 p.m. and only kept the gas station open.

Gus, Ray and Anthony drove into town and lined up to get into the church. The Big Gus 101 course on Christmas had been very useful. Still, everything was new and frightening to a degree. "So this is what regular people do on Christmas Eve." he said.

Ray nodded, "Yup, it's very special."

The choir was amazing and Anthony enjoyed the Christmas music. After the service they drank hot chocolate in the large room attached to the main church building. In bed that night he hoped that the small gifts that he had purchased for Gus and Ray would be acceptable. He fell asleep easily but was awake well before dawn.

He had been told to be up at the cabin by 9 a.m. on Christmas morning. It was a short distance to walk and it was chilly out. He covered the distance in record time!

"Hey, come on in kid. Merry Christmas! Breakfast will be up shortly."

Ray and a few other people arrived soon after and the small cabin was full again.

After breakfast they gathered around the decorated tree.

Ray took on the role as Santa's Helper. Anthony had placed the gifts for Ray and Big Gus under the tree.

"Well, what do we have here?" said Ray as he picked up a gift with his name on it. Anthony had given him a new work-overall. The old one was almost falling off and had holes in it. "Thank you kid!"

Finally the gift for Big Gus came out.

Anthony did not know how Gus would react to the gift that he had selected. Gus unwrapped a Swiss Army knife.

"Hey kid, this must have cost a fortune! Thank you, this is great!"

There were just three gifts remaining under the tree.

"How strange, all of these are for Anthony! I wonder what they are."

The gift from Ray was a winter sweater. "I hope that it comes in handy kid. It gets cold here in the winter!"

"Thank you Sir!" Anthony pulled it over his head to try it on.

The remaining two gifts were from Big Gus.

Both were envelopes.

Anthony opened the first one. Inside was a certificate for driving lessons. He looked at it in surprise.

"Kid, it is about time that you learned to drive!"

"So starting in the New Year you will be taking driving lessons in town once a week." Gus smiled, "Then you can start taking the truck into town and buying supplies for us!"

"I thought that I could only get a license when I turned 18? How can I start driving now?"

"Well, you can start lessons now but only get your full license when you turn 18."

This was more than a gift to learn how to drive. It was an indication that Gus wanted him around. He wanted the kid to start taking on more responsibility in the bar and diner. Maybe they both needed each other.

"Thank you Sir!" Without thinking he was giving the man a hug.

"Why not open your other gift?"

"Sure!"

Anthony opened the second envelope.

"To Anthony,
Three months of guitar and singing lessons at The Music Shop".

"Big Gus, is this for real?"

"Kid, you have a great voice but you need training. And the guitar will help you – maybe you'll become famous one day...then you can provide for old Ray and me!" He laughed.

Deep down inside his almost forgotten part of his soul he remembered that someone else had said that to him. Not even eight months ago. How his life had changed.

And it was about to change again soon.

Chapter 27

Anthony did not know what to expect from the guitar and singing lessons. He had never been a good student. He did not relate to taking instructions. His history of bad behavior was still a vivid memory for him. He knew that Gus wanted him to become trained but he really did not know if he could go through with it. Anxiety built up inside of him and he tried to keep to himself after the holiday season. Lessons would start by the middle of January.

Driving lessons were, however, another matter. He could not wait to learn how to drive.

He had just come on shift when he heard Big Gus calling him, "Hey kid, hey kid, come to my office."

Anthony dried his hands and walked through to the office.

"What took you so long? I have a telephone call for you."

"For me?" He thought, "Who knows that I am here?"

Big Gus handed him the telephone and walked out of the office. He shut the door behind him as he walked out.

"Hello."

"Is that Anthony McKinzie?"

"Yes it is. Whom am I speaking with?"

"Anthony, my name is Fred Monk from Ontario, Oregon. I'm a lawyer with Monk and partners. You might have heard of us."

"No. How did you know where to find me?"

"We were able to trace you through the assistance of Officer Gellis in Hood River. He sends his regards by the way."

"And how did Officer Gellis know that I was here? Only Gus could have told him!"

"What do you want with me?"

"Anthony, we represented the estate of your late father, William McKinzie. When he passed away he died intestate – he died without a will. We were appointed to settle his affairs. Once everything was done, there was a small surplus in the estate account. The State of Oregon intervened because there was no will. As you are the only living relative the net proceeds of the estate are yours."

Anthony did not really follow what was being said but the mere mention of the name of Bill McKinzie made him begin to shake. *"Why can't I move on from this man?"*

"Anthony are you still there?"

"Yes. I am still here."

"Well, the State has decided that, although you are the only surviving relative of your father and that you are only sixteen-years-of-age, they are withholding a portion of the sum due to you until you turn 21. The net value of the estate was just on $3000 – they will make $1000 available to you now.

"In order to receive these funds you would need to come to our offices in Ontario to sign for the check. Can you do that?"

Again there was no answer.

"Anthony, did you hear what I said, I have $1000 that you should come and collect."

It took the boy another few seconds before he answered, then he said, "Sir, can I have your telephone number and I can call you back?"

"Sure." He gave the number to Anthony and he hung up.

Anthony sat down in the chair reserved for Gus behind the large desk.

"Why can't I get rid of the monster? I wish that I had killed him!"

He was still fighting the demons inside him when there was a knock on the door. "You done in there? Can I come in?"

"You ok kid?"

Before Anthony could think properly he blurted out.

"You ratted on me that I was here. I thought that I could trust you!"

"Now kid, wait a minute, what's going on?"

"That was a lawyer about my father's estate. He said that Officer Gellis in Hood River helped him track me down. How did he know that I was here unless you told him!"

Gus took in a deep breath.

"Kid, you were all over the media when you were attacked – I knew who you were the minute that you walked into the bar and asked for a job. Everyone here knew it too – but everyone here took you for who you were – a young kid who wanted to start a new life. No one tricked you. You made things happen yourself – you have done good things since you have been here. No one betrayed you."

"Then why did Officer Gellis know that I was here? You must have told him."

"As I said, I knew who you were when you walked in here that day. I wanted to get information on what happened – and I then wanted to see if you would lie to me when I asked you to tell me something about yourself. If you had lied, I would not have given you the job. You told the truth and I appreciated that."

Gus paused and looked at the kid.

"And we've been honest with each other since then," he added.

Anthony's heart pounded and his cheeks were flushed. He was in turmoil.

"I love you like my own kid. I started off thinking that you needed a chance, but I soon came to love you. You might not have recognized it as love but I have treated you like my own. Do you understand what I am saying? I didn't mean to mislead you but I just needed to check you out when you arrived here. That's why I contacted Officer Gellis."

The rage in Anthony's body began to subside. He felt the fires deep down beginning to burn out - those fires that flared up whenever he hated someone. The fires that one-day might still destroy him.

"You telling me the truth?"

"Yes kid, that is the truth – now what's going on here. Let me help you."

Anthony was calm again. He could feel himself breathing normally.

"The call was from a lawyer in Ontario Oregon. My father's estate has been settled. There is $3000 for me from the proceeds of the estate. $2000 will be held until I turn 21 but there's $1000 for me to collect from them.

I don't know if I want his money. I want nothing from him. He never cared for me so why should I take his money now?"

"Did he leave you the money in his will?"

"No. He died without a will. The State says that I'm his only living relative." He was about to say that it was not true but he decided wouldn't. "So the money left over comes to me. I don't know if I should take it."

"Kid listen, look at it this way – maybe he didn't realize that he was leaving it to you. Maybe he didn't want to – no one will ever know. But here's a chance to improve your life – the State determined that the money is yours – you should take it."

Anthony telephoned the lawyer. Three days later they collected the check at a branch office of the law firm in Eugene. The following day he deposited the $1000 into his bank account.

He had promised to keep the law firm informed of his address so that when he turned 21 they could forward the remaining $2000 to him.

He would decide then if he should keep the additional money. This time he had agreed with Big Gus and taken the $1000.

For a sixteen-year-old, he was now beginning to build a good financial base. He left home in May 1969 with $200 and now in January 1970 with his savings and the

$1000 he had almost $1400 – a great deal of money in 1970.

Chapter 28

The music lessons were short-lived. Anthony did not get on with the teacher and the teacher did not like him. The teacher was set on teaching the theory of music and singing whereas Anthony wanted to just "play" the guitar (as if it was going to play itself!) and learn pop songs. After just a few lessons the arrangement was stopped by mutual agreement.

"Hey kid, I heard that you dropped out of your music classes?"

"Yeah! It didn't work out." He replied to the bandleader as the group walked up the steps into the bar. Although it was January, the kid enjoyed sitting outside on the front porch of the bar on his breaks. The air was fresh and crisp.

"What you gonna do now?"

"I'm not sure. Maybe just give up on the idea."

He was still sitting outside when Big Gus and the bandleader came outside.

"Kid we got a plan if you're interested – Bob here says that he will teach you to play. He will not charge you for lessons if you agree to sing a few songs every Friday and Saturday nights."

"I could spare you for say two ten minute gigs during the night – so what do you say?"

"Sure! That would be great! Thank you!"

"Ok, starting from next week you will be a 90% Washer and a 10% singer!

The next week he practiced with Bob until his fingers hurt.

"I think that this week we'll just get you to sing and we will back you up." Bob realized that Anthony was struggling with the concepts of playing the guitar.

On Friday night he left the kitchen at 10 p.m. and went and changed. At around 10:30 he was standing near the bar waiting for the set to commence. Singing in a school musical was tough, singing in the front of hospital staff and police officers was worse but this was knee knocking, sweat-dripping and hand-shaking different.

"Folks, we have a special guest singer this evening. Here to sing two songs for us is ANTHONY!"

There was some clapping but not much of a response. Not even when he walked up on stage did anyone really recognize him. They were too interested in their beers, steaks and burgers.

The band started up and he began to sing. It took about a minute for silence to overtake the noise of the large room. He did not sing an Elvis number that would not have worked with this audience. Instead he sang "Hey Jude" and then "Wichita Linesman."

There was still a long way to go with his voice but he captured the audience that night. Both sets went off well.

"I think that I might need another dish washer and bus boy if you keep doing that!" Big Gus gave him a big smile. "You might even draw some more customers in too!"

The band did not share their gig money with Anthony but a hat was passed around and at the end of the evening he was handed $5. On the Saturday night he was given $7. This was his first payment for singing in public.

Chapter 29

On the Monday he still felt euphoria. He could not stop smiling all day.

That changed on his evening shift.

"Hey kid! Tables need clearing."

"Be right there," he yelled back.

He dried his hands and picked up a big tray to carry the dirty dishes back into the kitchen. He did the first few tables and then as he turned, he knocked an empty beer bottle off one of the tables onto the floor. He put the tray down on the floor and grabbed for the bottle that had rolled under the next table. He stretched to pick it up and, as he lifted his head to table height again, he looked into the face of two giant snakes!

He gasped at the sight and then realized that he was not looking at real snakes but at the fists of a man sitting at the table. As Anthony lifted his head higher he saw that the man had the most enormous arms that he had ever seen. Looking higher he saw that the arms were attached to gigantic shoulders. The cut-away denim shirt left nothing hidden. The man was a giant. Down both arms were tattoos of snakes. The bodies of the snakes twisted under his arms and got bigger as they emerged over his elbows. The bodies grew even bigger as they came down the forearms. The heads of the snakes were tattooed over the hands. When the man opened his fists it looked as if the mouth of the snakes were wide open.

He tried not to stare at the human mountain sitting at the table. It was difficult not to look. He picked up the bottle and placed it onto the tray and stood up.

"Sorry!" he said as he stood.

Then he looked at the man's face for the first time. It was like a delayed explosion going off inside of him. At first there was nothing – not even a simmer – and then he could feel the tremor starting. He felt his arms going numb, like he was going to faint.

When he looked down at the table again his eyes almost popped out of his head. Stuck, point down into the table, was a switchblade knife. On the handle was the US Navy insignia. From a distance of only about two feet from the table, Anthony could see the engraving "US Navy 1941-45".

He held on to tables as he walked, or rather, staggered, back to the kitchen. He was frozen in a deadly sweat. He was both hot and cold. He needed air. He put the tray down in the kitchen and walked to the back door. The cool January air hit him hard. He was struggling to breathe. Then he threw up.

"Hey kid! You ok?"

It was Big Gus.

Anthony was still throwing up.

"You ok, what's up?"

Anthony blew his cheeks out to get some air into his body.

"I'll be fine – just got really woozy all of a sudden. I'll be ok in a few minutes." He lied.

"Take your time." Gus walked back inside of the kitchen.

Besides trying to get his breathing back to normal he was also in an intense mental state of confusion. What had set him off? Did he stand up too quickly? Was he overworked?

He sat outside for another few minutes. When he walked back into the kitchen Gus took one look at him and said, "Shit, you like crap – we don't need to get what you've got – go to bed. I'll check on you later – go on outta here!"

Anthony stumbled the few feet to the camper. He could hardly keep his balance. He opened the door, stepped up and fell forward. His head was spinning again. He stood up and lurched forward to his bed. By pure instinct he pulled the covers over himself.

He closed his eyes. He tried to concentrate. Nothing. He opened and closed his eyes several more times. Nothing. Then as he began to relax, an image began to form. As it became clearer he saw what it was – he screamed but no one heard him. The noise from the kitchen blocked out his pain.

He remembered what happened that night on the road near Hood River.

"You sure that you don't want to come and sleep at our place tonight? There is a storm coming. You need to be warm indoors. Maureen here has soup ready for us with her homemade bread. What do you say?"

"No really, I'll be fine. I'll make it to Portland ok. Thank you!"

"Son, listen to John, please come with us – he will drive you back to the main road in the morning. Please!"

"John and Maureen, thanks for the offer but I need to press on. I will be fine."

"Well, we can't force you. You need to do what you need to do!"

He waved at them as the car turned off on their country road.

He pulled up his gear on his back and lifted the half-filled carry bag. All of the food that he had taken from home when he walked out had now gone. "I need to get to the next town and pick up something to eat and then hit the road before it's dark."

Lying on the bed in his camper, Anthony could see everything unfold as if it were happening right now. He was hovering above the scene.

He could see himself walking down the road. Heading west. It was late afternoon. John had told him that there was not much by way of traffic on this road after dark. The wind was picking up and he could see clouds rolling in. Better move faster he thought to himself.

He stopped on a rise to rest. The backpack was getting heavy. He had bought it with money earned by washing cars near where he lived in Vale. The backpack was black with a yellow strip down each side. He thought that it looked cool. He knew that it was cheap but it was all that he could get with the money that he had.

He heard a loud noise behind him coming up the hill. It was a large black rig. The rig was laboring up the hill. He watched it approach.

"Must be a sixty-footer!" he thought to himself.

Then he heard the hissing of the air brakes as the huge rig began to change gears and slow as it approached him. It came to a stop almost opposite where he was standing. His head was about level with the door handle. He looked up and saw a bright green snake painted on the door.

He was still looking at the beast when the door opened.

"Where you headed?"

"Portland."

"The weather is getting bad. You want a ride – I'm going through Portland."

"Thank you."

He saw himself step up into the cabin of the rig.

"There is space for your gear behind your seat."

As he was settling in, he looked at the man. He was a mountain sitting behind the steering wheel. Both arms were heavily tattooed with ugly looking snakes. Their heads came right down to his massive fists.

The rig came back to life as it began to roll forward.

"You got a name?"

"Anthony. Anthony McKinzie."

"Where you from?"

"Vale."

"Why you up here on the road alone?'

Anthony hesitated. He did not know really what to say.

"I left home. I'm on my way to see family in California." he lied.

"That is a far way for a young kid to travel. Your pa knows where you're headed?"

"Oh yes Sir, I will telephone when I reach my family."

"Anyone expecting you in Portland?"

"No –just when I get to California."

"Well kid, sit back. We'll have you in Portland in no time."

He could see himself sitting in the cabin of the rig with the man. He was edgy but the big man seemed friendly. Now he realized that in just a few questions the man had obtained information that he had left home, was not expected to make contact with anyone soon and that he had no one waiting for him in Portland.

For the next ten miles or so they chatted about a few things. Nothing too meaningful! Then the rig started to slow down and begin to pull off of the road.

"Why are we stopping?"

"Restroom up ahead – see that building near the trees. I need to pee."

The rig pulled off of the road and drew up in front of a small wooden building. There were a few tables near the one side of the restrooms.

"You should pee too. It will take us a while to get to Portland."

He could see himself opening the door of the rig and jumping down onto the ground. He looked like a midget next to the black monster with the snake on the door. It was only when the man walked around the front of the rig that he saw just how big he really was. His chest must have been 55 inches at least and his shoulders and biceps were gigantic. He stood over 6 feet 3 inches tall and weighed close to 280 pounds. There was no fat to be seen on this mountain man.

They walked into the restroom. The man held the door for Anthony to walk through. He opened the front of his pants and relieved himself. At first he did not realize that the man had not come and stood next to him. As he was about to finish his pee he turned sideways.

The man was standing there smiling. The look on his face was like the devil. Like a devil snake that was about to strike! Then Anthony looked down. The man had opened his pants and his long hard penis was sticking out in front of him.

He was frozen in fright. It took him a few seconds to realize what was about to happen.

He stood there in sheer fear.

"Suck it before I ram it into your young sweet ass!"

Anthony saw himself come to life. He screamed and tried to run around the man. It was pointless – the man had blocked the door.

"You take it now before I give you a whipping like you have never had before!"

"Now kid, take it now!"

"No, no, get away from me. Please let me go – please, no, no, let me go."

The monster looked at him and then he raised his arms out on his sides. His arms were like tree trunks.

Then he slowly lowered his arms and took his penis in his hands, "Here, kid, I will hold it for you!" The two snakes tattooed on his arms came down and almost seemed to open their mouths as the man took hold of himself.

He stepped forward towards Anthony. He saw himself crying.

As the man moved sideways, Anthony saw a small space open and he burst into a run. He was quick and pushed himself out of the restroom before the man could get his arms on him. He ran. He did not care in which direction he ran – he just had to get away. His decision to run towards the forest was a mistake. No one driving by would see anything that happened between the trees.

He thought that he had gotten away. Then a vice-grip took him by one shoulder and threw him to the ground. When he rolled over onto his back he saw that man standing over him. His penis was still erect and sticking out of his trousers.

He did not see the first punch come. It hit him like a sledgehammer and his neck snapped backwards. Two seconds later another punch hit him square on the nose and he could hear the bone break. Blood was already dripping into his mouth.

"Last chance kid before I ram it into you anyways!"

He screamed but there was no one to hear him.

The punches rained down on his face like cannon balls fired at point blank range. He never saw them coming. He lost count after about four or five, but deep inside, his body seemed to tear apart with the dull impact of the terror that was being unleashed on him. The man kept punching him until his huge arms hurt. The boy's face was a bloody mess.

Lying on his bed in his camper, Anthony was sweating. He could not cry out. He was hooked into the returning nightmare that he could not get away from.

He could not remember his shoes and blue jeans being removed but he could picture it as he lay in his bed. He could not remember the monster raping him – but now he could feel it. He could feel everything. His body seemed to be filled – he could not break loose.

The evening of the attack, the trucker had left him without his pants. Once done with him, he carried the boy about thirty yards back down the road before the rest stop and dumped him half naked on the road. As he turned to walk away, he stopped and kicked Anthony in the head several times. Then he walked back to his rig and drove away. Behind the passenger seat in the rig he packed the boy's shoes, his jeans and his backpack. It was his prize to be added to the other trophies. Trophies accumulated as far away as Alaska, Florida and Texas. Only about one a year – and the cops could never trace him. He moved around too much.

In the boy's jeans pocket he found a switchblade.

Later that night when the storm was at the height of its fury, Trooper Williams swerved to miss the object lying half on the road. It was a beaten-up body of a young boy who had been raped and savagely beaten. Left to die on the road.

Anthony fell into an exhausted sleep. He had remembered what had happened to him. He could feel the blows hitting him. He passed out as he had done on the night of the attack.

Later that night Big Gus tapped on the door of the camper. "Kid, you ok – you awake?" There was no answer. Gus let him sleep.

The following morning Anthony awoke with hammering on the door of the camper.

"Are you gonna work today? It is almost lunchtime! You ok in there?"

Waking up from a bad dream was not easy. He opened his eyes. Things were real – he must have been dreaming – then suddenly he realized that it had not been a dream. It was rather a recall from deep down inside of his mind. Something had unlocked the key – and he knew what it was. It was a monster.

"You hear me kid?"

"Yeah, I'll be right out!"

He was still fully dressed from the night before. He changed and walked into the shower room near the kitchen to wash up. He walked into the kitchen. Gus looked at him, "You ok?"

"Yeah, just felt ill last night. I was dizzy all of a sudden. But I'll be ok."

"Like hell you are ok –you look like death. What's up?"

"I'll be fine after I've eaten something."

"You sure?"

"Yes Sir."

"You want some hot cakes?"

"Yes please!"

Big Gus made the best hot cakes that he had ever eaten and with tea inside him he felt a lot better – the food seemed to suppress the memories that he had relived. Reliving it was more painful than actually having experienced being raped. He seemed to feel it this time.

The afternoon shift passed by quickly and he had several hours off before the night shift. He went to sleep almost as soon as he lay on his bed. Then the torment started again. This time he thought if the monster would be back in the bar that evening – and had he recognized Anthony. If the man had recognized him then his life was in danger.

When he was called out to clear tables that night he dreaded who he might see in the bar. The man was not there. He breathed with relief.

Late into the shift Anthony was cleaning behind the bar. He asked the barman, "Do you remember that big guy who was in here last night. He had tattoos all down his arms?"

"You know him?"

"No. I've just not seen anyone that big before."

"Well, you stay away from him. He's bad news. He's tough and a mean bastard. He hangs out with a few guys – but no one likes him.

He is an independent trucker. Goes wherever the work is. He drives long hauls across the country. He used to come in here when he worked in Oregon and nearby – fill up the rig with gas, eat here and sometimes overnighted too. He's a bad piece of shit.

Not seen him in a few months. He must have been driving somewhere else for a while."

"He got a name?" asked the kid.

"He goes by the name of SNAKE. He must think that it's a pretty name! But there is nothing pretty about him. He used to be a pro wrestler with the WWF but they kicked him out. He could break someone's face open with one punch. Crazy bastard!"

"I know that he can!" thought Anthony. *"I know it only too well!"*

"Who are you guys talking about?" asked Gus as he walked through from the kitchen.

"The kid was asking who Snake was. I told him to stay away from him."

"He's an animal. I don't like him coming in here but I can't stop him unless he starts trouble – and if he does he'll take most of us with him. Yeah! You stay away from him."

The kid had decided not to ask Gus about the man. There was no way for Gus to know that Snake was the guy who had attacked him.

When the kid crawled into bed that night he was physically tired but mentally alert.

He thought about the small fires that he had started. The fires had not satisfied him. Then he had a bigger target. He had not done his planning right and he had failed – failed to burn to death the man that he hated – and failed in that he made some mistakes. That would not happen again. Not because he had given up on his fire quest but because now he had a new target – and this time he would not fail. He would see Snake burn.

The inner "Anthony" had returned.

He would succeed. He had to succeed. He had to set the fire free.

Chapter 30

Big Gus could tell something was wrong with the kid. He thought of asking him but refrained. The kid looked different – even his eyes looked darker. He even thought of telephoning Officer Gellis in Hood River – what would he say, *"the kid is acting strange!"*

Maybe he should have.

Anthony kept a detailed mental record of when Snake came into the bar, which nights, what time, where he parked his rig. Once he saw him in the bar then he would take his break and check things outside. Snake parked the rig at the end of the parking lot of the sleepover yard. He would arrive at about 9 p.m. and return to the rig at about 11 p.m. The small light in the sleeping unit above the cab would go out shortly thereafter. The big man only had one or two beers with his meal so he would still be alert when he walked back to the rig. The plan was to pour gasoline over the cap of the fuel tank and then light it. No mistakes this time! He had to kill him.

The routine was the same – Snake would come into the bar every Monday and Thursday evening.

Anthony kept no notes of the routine. There would be nothing to implicate him should the police search his camper. There would be no evidence this time. No mistakes.

It was early March and he was building himself up for the big event.

It was the Monday night when things accelerated. Anthony was bringing out clean glasses to the bar when he looked up. The beast was standing at the bar. Their eyes met. Anthony looked away as quickly as he could. He was not sure if the beast had recognized him. As he unpacked the glasses he looked in the mirror behind the bar.

The beast was talking to the barman but he kept looking in Anthony's direction. Back in the kitchen he could feel the sweat running down his back.

The beast had never walked up to the bar before. What was he asking the barman?

Anthony peaked through the door and as he saw Snake walk away, he walked back inside the bar and offloaded a few more items on the shelves.

"Hey kid!" Anthony froze. It was the barman.

"Thought that you'd like to know that the big fellow will not be around for a while. He came up to buy some potato chips and he told me that he is heading south to drive in New Mexico for a few months. Glad that he is going – he gives me the creeps. Said that he was having a beer before he heads to his rig."

"Oh, that is good news!" and Anthony walked away. He had to act tonight or miss his opportunity.

Big Gus was yelling, "Tables need clearing!" It broke his concentration. "Not now, I need to think" he said to himself. He looked at the clock in the kitchen it was 10:40

p.m. – if Snake kept his routine then he would leave for his rig in twenty minutes.

To his disbelief, Gus pointed out which tables needed clearing. It was the two tables next to where the beast was seated. *"Look down, don't look at him!"*

Just as Anthony approached the table the beast stood up – Anthony stopped dead in his tracks. Was there going to be a confrontation right here in the bar? There was nowhere to go – the beast walked right past him and headed off towards the restroom. Anthony thought that the entire bar could hear him exhale.

As Anthony walked past the table where the beast was sitting with his friends, he saw the switchblade stuck into the table. That had become a hallmark of the beast's visit to the bar. Big Gus and the barmen were aware of the intimidating action and kept a very close watch on him while he was seated. They did not believe that he would start anything in the bar but one could never be sure. Big Gus kept a handgun under the bar counter – and had done so for years.

Someone else was also clearing tables behind Anthony.

Then he heard the booming voice from behind him, "Who took my knife? Who took my fucking knife?"

Anthony swung around and looked down at the table. The knife was gone.

The beast was yelling his head off and had knocked some chairs over.

In a flash Big Gus was standing in front of the beast. Big Gus was small compared to the monster.

"OK, what's going on? Settle things down here – what happened?"

"Someone stole my fucking knife while I took a piss!"

"Are you sure it was there?"

"You calling me a liar?'

"No, I am not calling you a liar – let's just calm down and sort things out – no tension let's just keep it calm."

The bar went silent. Everyone stared at the scene but no one said a word.

Snake was breathing like a mad bull ready to run wild.

"Hey Snake, you took your fucking knife with you when you went for a piss – check your pocket." said a friend at his table. He checked his pocket. There was no knife.

"You being funny?"

"No, I thought I saw you put it in your pocket when you went for a pee."

Big Gus tried to smooth things over. "We'll look for your knife – maybe it is in the restroom – we'll check it for you. Let's just calm things down ok?"

Snake looked at him. "It's my knife and I want it back!"

"We'll check for you when we clean up after closing. If we find it we'll leave it for you on the step of your rig. If it is here we'll find it."

Snake nodded.

"OK, folks the excitement is over." Big Gus walked away.

Snake sat down. He yelled for his bill.

It was now 10:50 p.m.

Anthony took his break just before 11. He only had a few minutes to get ready. He would wait for the light in the rig to go out before he acted.

He hurried back to the kitchen with the tray of dirty plates.

He took off the white apron and put on a dark jacket. He walked outside and stood in the shadows near the kitchen. If anyone saw him there, it would be no surprise. That is where he stood to take in some cool fresh air whenever he was on break. He had a clear view of the side of the black rig – he would see the beast walk around the side corner of the building and then walk to his rig.

He would wait for the light to go out on the rig. Then he would wait a few more minutes. He had a small can of gasoline just behind where he stood and waited.

At most, he would have about a minute to wait before he would hear the side exit door of the bar open. Then it would take about another ten seconds before he would see the beast. He had watched him many times over the last few weeks. He knew the routine. He had it all planned out.

Within ten minutes the beast would be burning! And he would be back in the kitchen washing dishes.

He waited. Every second seemed like a lifetime. He could feel the raw anger taking over his body. That feeling of wanting to see someone burn was so strong. He needed to control himself. No mistakes! No mistakes!

Then he heard the side door opening.

He thought that he heard something. Not sure. Sounded like something falling and hitting the ground. Wait. Wait. He will emerge any second. He waited. Nothing. Then he heard a noise. It sounded like a broken faucet running. He strained to hear the noise. It sounded like water gurgling. It sounded like an animal – like an animal choking on itself.

Anthony eased himself out from the shadows. He edged towards the corner of the building. The noise was louder - it was terrifying. He peaked around the corner. There it lay.

Anthony looked down. He saw two massive snakes curled upwards - their closed heads were holding onto something. They were not holding a penis like he had seen before. They were holding onto a knife totally imbedded into the throat of the beast.

Snake was lying on his back and gurgling for air. A knife was struck deep into the middle of his throat. Only the handle was protruding.

As gruesome as the scene was Anthony only had one thought, *"No, No! I wanted to kill him! I wanted to see him burn up in flames! No, I wanted to kill him!"*

Then he heard a voice.

"What's going on here?" Big Gus had come out of the side door of the building. He looked down. "Shit, what happened here? What happened here?" He went down on one knee and looked at the knife imbedded in Snakes throat. Then the gurgling stopped and the two massive arms and their beloved snake tattoos let go of the knife that he was holding. He was dead.

"Kid, what happened here? Did you see anything?"

"No. I saw nothing. I was taking my break when I heard something gurgling – I came around the corner and saw him lying there – and then you came out."

"I didn't do it!" he said almost automatically.

"No, I'm sure you did not. If you had come at him with a knife he would have ripped your arms off of your shoulders before you got near him!"

Anthony did not know why he asked the question but he did, "Did you do it?" Big Gus looked at him. He answered, "Kid, I told once you that I taught to kill silently with a knife. If I had killed him he would have died instantly ...no noise...No, I did not kill him."

Gus looked down at the dead man. He looked closely at the knife. On the handle was the US Navy insignia and the engraved words "US Navy 1941-45."

"He was killed with his own knife."

Anthony looked down at the body. That was his knife but he could not say anything then because Gus would know that Snake was the man that had attacked and raped him.

"OK, I've got to call the cops. You get back into the kitchen. You heard nothing. When the cops come you heard nothing. You understand – you heard nothing! Get going!"

Anthony ran inside of the kitchen and was back washing dishes before he knew exactly what he was doing. His mind was still full of disappointment. Again his fire-prize had been taken away from him. He felt cheated. The beast was dead but he felt cheated.

The police arrived about ten minutes after Big Gus had made the call. The entire area – the diner, bar, sleepover area – was all locked down. All guests and staff were interviewed – including Anthony and Gus.

It was just getting light before the lock down was lifted. Gus had provided coffee to his guests once the police had closed the bar.

Anthony watched the police as they opened the big black rig and began to bring various items out to check out for evidence. Each item was placed on the ground, tagged and photographed. There were a number of backpacks. One was black with two yellow stripes down the sides. Anthony recognized it immediately. He could not believe what he saw. The beast had kept his backpack! Why?

As casually as he could he walked closer to where the items had been laid out. They had been placed in a line near one side of the rig. The police were still taking photographs. As they moved away, Anthony edged even closer. Then as soon as the police officers were out of sight, he darted to the bag – he pulled open the one side pocket.

Inside of was a photograph of a boy holding the hand of his mother. There was also another photograph and a page of sheet music. He quickly placed the items in the front of his apron and walked away. No one saw him. He made his way back to his camper. He placed his treasure with his other personal possessions.

He had successfully removed any evidence that could link him to Snake and with the attack. He hoped that the switchblade would never be linked back to Bill McKinzie.

The police finally cleared the site just after lunch. They had located the keys in the big black rig and had driven it away to be searched further.

The atmosphere in the bar was very tense. Who killed Snake?

Who was strong enough to get near to him? Why did they want him dead? Not many members of the public from the nearby town came into the bar that evening. It was mostly just a few truck drivers getting their meal before either driving on or sleeping over.

About mid evening Big Gus asked Anthony to come through to his office.

"What's up?" asked the boy.

"You knew Snake? He was the guy who beat you?"

Anthony looked at Gus.

"Yes, how did you know?'

"The last month or so you haven't been the same. I saw the way that you watched him – I just put things together."

"Why didn't you say anything?"

"Not really my business is it? I just watched you and hoped that you did nothing stupid. I thought that you might try something but I didn't know what. I didn't want you to get hurt that's all."

“Why do you care about me? I’m just a kid.”

“That, kid, is the exact reason why I care for you. I just want to give you a chance at life – a chance at life and not at hate.”

”What do you know about my life? What do you know about me? Nothing! You know nothing about me!” There was pent up anger in his voice. He had never spoken to Gus like this before.

“I know very little about you – just from the last few months that you’ve been with us. I know that there is anger deep down that I can’t touch – that I have not tried to touch. But I also know that there is a great kid in there too – one that I care for – one that we all here care for.”

The kid looked back at him. He did not answer. He could not find the words. He wanted to be blunt and rude – he wanted to be away from another adult – he wanted to get away from his demons. But he could not say anything. He just sat in a mixed silence of pain and anger – of pain and feeling for the man sitting in front of him.

“Tell you what, tomorrow you and Ray head off into town and buy us some supplies – you take the cash with you and pay everyone that you stop in on and get things from. Then when you are done Ray can drive you to the store and you pick out something for your birthday.”

“My birthday is still weeks away – April 4 – why go now?”

"No reason! Just a thought!" Gus was sitting smiling at him.

Sometimes a smile is worth a thousand words.

"And kid, pack it in for tonight – catch up on your sleep. Good night!"

Then Gus added, "Another thing...that camper could be too cold to sleep in. There's a room in my cabin if you are interested." Gus walked out of his office leaving Anthony just sitting there.

In his camper that night he thought about what had happened in the last 24 hours. He had heard what Big Gus had said to him. Maybe he could not comprehend what Gus had said.

Deep down, he knew that he could not control the fire in his belly. Being loved could be the answer – hating might set it off. He had to stand on his own two feet and sort things out.

He picked up his guitar and sang softly to himself.

He knew what he wanted to do.

The next morning he walked up to the cabin. He knocked on the door. Big Gus opened the door stepped aside to let the kid come out of the cold air.

"You're up early! Something wrong – or did you just come for breakfast?" He was such a gentle man.

Anthony looked at him.

"You're leaving aren't you?"

"Yes Sir!"

"Why?"

"Every time that I walk out of the kitchen I'll see him lying there. I will never be able to get rid of him. He will be there every day. I will see him and remember what he did to me…I can't stay. He will end up killing me inside."

"You sure about this?'

"Yes. I'm sure."

"When do you want to leave?"

"As soon as you find someone else."

Big Gus thought for a while and then he said, "OK, but let me suggest something to you. You might want to think about this. Snake was murdered last night and the police will be all over this thing for a while. They don't need to become suspicious of anything – but if you take off now they might just start linking you and him together. I think that you should stay for a few weeks and then you can quit and leave. By then things would have calmed down. What do you say?"

"Ok, but I am not going to change my mind."

Anthony stayed until his birthday – several weeks longer than what he had planned for. Big Gus and the staff started talking about a birthday party – Gus was smart and played the kid into a corner! Gus wanted him to be there as long as possible and to give him a darn good birthday – most likely his first ever party. Turning seventeen was not a party with balloons and clowns – but there was music for him, games inside and out and a ton of laughing and having fun. Maybe love was the remedy for soothing a fiery soul.

His birthday was on a Saturday. Sunday was his last shift.

He had drawn some money out of his bank account and he had advised the bank that he would contact them with his new address – first he had to decide where he wanted to go. With his pay, his singing money from the weekend gigs and $1000 and the $300 from the folk in Hook River he now had close to $1700 dollars to his name.

The drive to the Greyhound station with Big Gus was very difficult. He had promised to write. He knew that he was breaking the man's heart but he had to move on.

"You make sure that you write. You look after yourself you hear!"

They hugged. Anthony had never experienced that feeling of a tender embrace before. Those from his mother were too far distant in his memory. Big Gus watched as the bus drove down Main Street. Then he drove to his lawyer's office.

Chapter 31

"Are you ready for the interview?"

Mike was his manager and personal friend. They had been together for just a few years but it was already more than a pure business relationship – they were good buddies. They had traveled extensively across the States and done many things together. Some good, others childish, but they had been fun at the time. When Mike had found him he was an unknown and now things were very different.

"Yeah! But do we have to do this?"

"Yes! We have to do this. It has taken me months to set this up. We've discussed it – and you know most of the questions – just remember what to answer – just like we have rehearsed it."

Fame came at a price!

"When will she be here?"

"In about twenty minutes. Her guys are just setting up the equipment in the living room. Half of the interview will be there and then you will switch to the pool area."

The rehearsals had been difficult. He did not like talking about himself. There was too much to think about. Not even Mike knew of what was buried deep in his soul. Mike kept him balanced and focused on work – and at making money – lots of it!

"After you are introduced, then you will go through with her to the living room – once you are both wired then it would just be the two of you. It will be great – no need to worry – just relax!"

The home was large but old. It was situated on a hill overlooking the mountains with trees all around. It was his personal retreat. That is one reason why he did not want strangers coming to visit – let alone journalists – and definitely not a taping for TV stations.

Susan Clayburn was a force in the industry. She was polished, did her homework on everyone that she interviewed. She was gentle one moment and then tough the next. Mike had struggled to get her to do the interview but it was only after the award ceremony that she had agreed.

They had watched some of her previous interviews and made notes. They had also noted that she was single, and in her late thirties, and drop dead gorgeous.

"Don't try to be cute with her! She will slice you to pieces if you do. Strictly business!"

When Susan arrived and they were introduced he felt as if he was meeting a goddess!

"Should we get started?" she asked. It was not so much of a question as a statement.

"Good evening Ladies and Gentlemen. Welcome to our show. Today we have the pleasure of meeting with a very special guest – a guest who has permitted our interview to be conducted in his mountain retreat in Utah. It gives me great pleasure to introduce you to Tony Macey – number 1 singer on the Country and Western Charts and in mainstream music, Grammy award winner and recently the voice behind the soundtrack of the successful Hollywood movie, "A Song for Mary" which starred Anne Grant and Neville Waterson. The single from the movie has recently gone Platinum in the States. The second Platinum record released by Tony Macey…ladies and gentlemen…Tony Macey."

"Good evening Susan, thank you for having me on your program – this is a great honor!"

"You've had some run in the last few years but 1978 has been a knockout for you! Congratulations!"

"Thank you – it's been incredible – and my thanks to my fans! Without them there is no one to really sing to." All rehearsed questions and answers sounded so plastic.

"But let's start at the beginning… where did you start singing?"

"I started off singing in bars and at clubs".

"How old were you at the time?"

"I was in my teens. I kicked off with rock 'n roll – Elvis – just like everyone else was doing – and then I moved onto John Denver, Neil Diamond, and other softer ballads."

"How long ago was that? Were you still at school?"

"No, I only really started in my teens – I moved around and found small gigs."

The interview proceeded through the planned course. Tony kept thinking how good Susan would be in bed. It was difficult to concentrate on the questions and answers.

"When did your big break come?"

"I was singing mostly Elvis songs in the clubs." He smiled, "Earning enough to pay the rent!"

"I then had a long term gig on "Elvis Rock Legend – a salute to the King."

"When was that?"

"That was in 1972 – before that was mostly smaller gigs – nothing really special. I call those my journeyman years!" He laughed. In fact it was true – he had so much to learn – about his own voice and where he wanted to fit into the music industry.

"Is that when you met Mike – your manager?"

"Yes. The Elvis show toured for about six months and I was getting tired of the travel and the songs. I didn't know at the time that Mike had seen the show in several cities – he was traveling with another tour and our dates crossed several times. After one of my shows he waited for me outside the theatre. He asked me if I sang anything else besides Elvis. We had dinner that evening and we spoke about what I wanted to do. The next morning we met and I sang a few of my own songs for him."

"Is that when you signed with him?"

"No, we both had contracts. It was a few months later that we were both able to quit what we were doing. By then I had more material and we decided to collaborate – he would manage my career. Greatest decision that I ever made!"

"And that was about five years ago? Just five years!"

"Yeah! It is insane. It took us about a year to get going. We tried to find a record label but no one was interested. Then Decca agreed to a one record deal. They had nothing to lose, I suppose. The album was good and sold well – the single reached the Top 10 – but we were not happy with the arrangement."

"You quit and started your own label?"

"Yes."

"Where did you find the money?"

This was not a question that he wanted to answer. It was too personal and his private affairs. But he could not avoid the question.

"I was left some money and that helped us get started."

Susan moved on to another set of questions.

Tony remembered receiving two letters. The one was from lawyers when he turned 21 confirming that he was due some money from the estate of William McKinzie – and they asked what to do with the funds.

The second letter was one that he would never forget.

A man that he had respected had written to him say that he was dying of cancer. He asked if Anthony could come and visit him. He remembered taking the long drive at the time – many hours to think about his life.

When he arrived to visit Big Gus, he was shocked to see what was left of the man that he worked for in 1969. They had just nine months together before he moved on. He had written to Gus many times over the last few years. The replies were always short. They always included a money order for $50. And he always received cards for his birthday and at Christmas. He had visited once but he could not bring himself to walk anywhere near the back door to the kitchen. That visit was the only time that he had slept in the cabin.

Anthony hugged Big Gus as he sat in a large armchair. Once he had fitted nicely into the chair but now he was half the size.

Anthony Mckinzie had adopted the stage name Tony Macey in 1974 at the age of 21. That was the time that he had received the letter from the law firm in Ontario.

"You're looking good!"

"Thank you Sir! How are you?"

"As you see – in my early 70s and a ship-wreck!" He tried to smile. His skin was so pale. In just a few months since being diagnosed with cancer he had wasted away dramatically.

They made some small talk and then Gus said, "There's something I need to tell you. Remember the night that Snake died? Well, I lied to you that night. I wanted to protect you. I knew who killed him and I wanted to keep it from you."

Anthony had not expected this topic to be ever discussed again.

"Why?"

"Because I wanted you to have a life."

"You know who killed him?"

"Yes! The person who stole his knife from his table that evening – that's who killed him."

"That's not news. We assumed that."

"Yes we did. But you see I was the one who took his knife."

"You! You took his knife? Why?"

"I saw him looking at you that night. I was sure that he knew who you were. I knew that he would find a way to hurt you again – or most likely kill you. He didn't need a survivor from one of his attacks to talk to the police."

"You killed him?"

"Yes."

"You told me that you taught people to kill silently. If you had done it you would have cut his throat and he would have died instantly. He was stabbed in the throat. That's not the way that you would have done it."

"Twenty-five years before that night it would have been clean and silent. That is how I trained my men. And I was much stronger then too.

I walked out of the exit door on the other side of the building. I knew that he always left the building from the door on the other side – nearer to his rig. I moved around and waited in the dark."

Anthony recalled that he only heard the side door open once – when Snake had walked outside – then he heard something. It was the attack on the beast – the assailant must therefore have been outside already, and waiting for him.

"I thought that he might try to find you in the kitchen by coming through the back door and grabbing you – or that you might even be outside. The barman mentioned to me that Snake had asked him some odd sounding questions about you that night – even when you took your breaks. When you went to clear the tables I picked up a tray behind you and found an opportunity to take the knife."

"Something went wrong?"

"I waited for him. Maybe I was too far away. As he came out of the side door I stepped forward and tried to grab, turn him and expose his throat. I only half grabbed him – and I totally under estimated his strength – he was even stronger than what he looked.

He grabbed my arm and started to swing me around. I had one chance before he would have broken my arm and taken the knife away. I went for his throat. I plunged the blade as hard as I could. He released my arm and grabbed his throat.

As he fell, I turned and headed back around to the exit door. I then walked through back to the door that he had used to leave the building and that is when you and I saw each other."

Big Gus sat in silence. There was no more to tell.

Anthony thought hard about what he had just heard. It made perfect sense to him. Only someone as large as Big Gus, could have attacked the monster. None of the truckers were that big.

"What about any finger prints on the knife?"

"That was a problem. I had no time to clean the handle after I stabbed him. I had to move away fast so that you did not see me. When I came out of the door you were already standing there. If you remember I sent you inside and I was going to call the police. When you left, I cleaned the handle with a cloth that was on the ground. I hid the cloth so that no one would find it. I put it inside one of my own shoes."

"Why are you telling me this now?"

"You need to know that people care for you – you need to trust people.

I love you kid – I wanted to tell you the truth before I died."

They ate a small dinner that night. Not much was said. They shared a few beers after dinner and they went to bed.

Anthony was there for another two days. He sang in the bar the one night. Big Gus sat and listened to him. On the third morning he said goodbye to Big Gus. He sobbed openly in the weak grasp of a dying man. Then he drove away.

He received a letter two weeks later. Ray advised him that Big Gus had passed away.

It was several months later that he was contacted and advised that Gustav Pederson had left him $50 000 in his will and half-ownership in a diner, bar and trucker sleepover business in Oregon. Gus had changed his will the day that Anthony had left – from the bus terminal he had driven to see his lawyer.

Anthony used the money to start his own record label.

He was brought back to the present when Susan said, "Tony did you hear my question?"

"Oh, sorry Susan, could you repeat the question".

"Yes, you recently stated that you would no longer sing Elvis Presley songs. Why is that?"

"I started off singing Elvis songs when I was sixteen. I was told that my voice was good but I was nowhere near The King. But I enjoyed his gentle love songs. They expressed the soul of the man. I had never seen him live. Last year we had the opportunity to see him in concert – June 26, 1977 – it was his last concert before he died. He was completely out of it on stage – as we now know he was very ill, drugged most of the time and overweight. I hated seeing him look like that. My images of him were of course from the 1960s – not like when I saw him. I decided then that I would not sing his songs again – it would be too painful for me."

"You are now 25 years old and some say a very wealthy young man. You have not only owned your own record label for a few years but you now have been made offers to sell it to the big named labels. Some reports are saying that you have been offered several million dollars. Is that true?"

Tony laughed, "Well we have signed a number of up-and-coming artists that are shaking up the charts and yes, there is interest in our label – but at this point we are not contemplating selling." He lied. There was an offer on the table that would make both him and Mike very wealthy. A condition of the sale was that he stayed with the label for five years. If the deal went through then he would be a multi-millionaire by aged 26. That was not something that he was going to discuss.

The interview wound to a close. As Susan rose to leave, she handed Tony her business card. She held it up to him – and for him alone to see. She had written, "Call me!" next to her private number. She smiled and thanked him for the interview.

Later that night a car pulled up outside of his home. He was alone. He opened the door himself. Susan was more than ten years older than him but they spent several enjoyable hours together.

When the TV interview was screened there were many other females who were interested in Tony Macey – he was young and rich. In particular for one person the interest was renewed.

Chapter 32

It was about a year after the interview with Susan. Tony had taken on a three-month gig in Las Vegas. Ten shows a week. The money was great but the stress was getting to him. The weekends were the worst. There were five performances on Saturday and Sundays. Meal times were out of sync and there were always people around him. Sometimes he needed something to take the edge off and put him to sleep. If asked, he would, of course, deny that he was becoming addicted to alcohol and sleeping pills.

One Sunday night he had just completed the late show when there was a knock on his dressing room door.

"Tony, there's a woman who would like to see you." This was not new.

"Tell her to take a number!" He laughed. The security guard smiled. This was not the first time that he had delivered such a message.

"She said that I should give you this note." He handed a folded piece of paper to Tony. He took it and walked over to the sofa and sat down to read it – most likely another offer of marriage or other perks!

He unfolded the note. There were just a few words written on the note.

"You never did buy me a soda, strawberry."

He looked at the note and could not understand what it meant.

"You never did buy me a soda, strawberry."

He was about to discard the note when he remembered.

It was back in Vale – that kid that I sang with – what was her name? What was her name? – Kathleen, yes, it was Kathleen. She was the one who persuaded me to go up on stage and try out for the school musical.

She said that we should go for a soda sometime during the summer. A strawberry soda – I remember it!

He looked up at the security guard. "Where is she?"

"Outside the back stage door. Should I send her away?'

"No – Let me think."

"Where can I get a soda in a small diner in town – anywhere nearby?"

"Excuse me Sir?"

"Is there a suburban soda shop open at this time of night?"

"Yes. There's one near where I live."

"Please call my driver."

While Tony waited, he wrote out a reply to the note that he had received, "One long-overdue soda (strawberry)– coming up. My driver will take you to a place and I'll join you shortly."

She read the reply and smiled.

It had been ten years since Anthony had left without saying goodbye.

The driver dropped her off at a small diner. He then returned to collect Tony.

Tony never carried any money and he was embarrassed to have to ask to borrow $50 from his bodyguard for his soda date.

When he reached the diner, Tony sent the driver home. He would act like a regular guy that night and get a cab back to the hotel.

She was sitting in a booth facing him as he walked in. When she stood up to greet him, he remembered her. Older now, fuller of course, but her face had hardly changed. Neither of them knew what to do so they shook hands and sat down.

"It has been a while!" he said.

"Yes. A long time to wait for a soda!" she smiled. He remembered that look. It was friendly yet vacant, innocent yet strange.

"What brings you to town?"

"I am travelling around and I saw that you were in town so I took in the show." She lied

"How did you know that it was me – Vale was a long time ago?"

"Yes – if I recall you left without saying goodbye – you just disappeared – then I saw your TV Interview last year with Susan Clayburn and I realized that it was you – Anthony from our school.

I was travelling and looked out for your shows – then I saw that you were on in Vegas so I came to see you sing."

"Did you enjoy the show?"

"Yes you were great."

Just then the waitress came over. "What can I get you folk?"

"What would you like?" he asked her.

"A strawberry soda of course!" He ordered two.

The waitress looked at him.

"Sir, are you Tony Macey?"

"No, everyone thinks that I just look like him."

She walked away but she knew that it was he. He was too well dressed and looked too rich for this part of town. Maybe he just had a secret date.

"So what have you been up to?"

"Nothing much really. I graduated from high school in Vale. There are no jobs there so I moved around for a while after school doing whatever was going – not like you."

"Hey! I did the same. I have washed more dishes than what you can count." He laughed. "I did whatever I could to earn money."

She continued.

"I then started dating Daniel – his dad owned the hardware store. Do you remember him from school?"

"Not really – I never knew too many of the kids. But I do remember the store – just off of Main Street?"

"Yes. They had a fancy house just out of town. We got married a few years back." She stopped. "But he died just under a year ago – we were only married for less than two years."

"Oh, I am sorry to hear that. What happened?"

"We were camping and he fell and died."

The two strawberry sodas arrived just in time to break the sad moment that was beginning to build up.

They sat and spoke for another thirty minutes or so and then Tony said, "Well, I am pretty bushed – these shows take it out of me. Let me call two cabs – where are you staying?"

"I'm at a motel just down the road. So only call one cab – drop me off then he can take you home too."

Tony asked the waitress to call them a cab. He settled the bill and slipped her a $10. "Thank you for not blabbing who I was!" She nodded. The ten dollars doubled her tips for the night.

"How long are you in town for?" he asked.

"No plans. I am just moving around seeing different parts of the country."

"How about a late lunch tomorrow? I have Mondays and Tuesdays off I usually sleep late but if you are free we could go for lunch."

"Thank you. That will be great."

The cab dropped her off at her motel and then took Tony back to his hotel.

He could not sleep that night. Memories of his life in Vale filled his head.

They met for lunch the next day. Conversation was difficult – not only because they did not really know each other well but also because it reminded him of his early life. Still it was a link back to where he came from – warts and all.

They linked up several times during the next week.

"I must be moving on." She said.

"Oh, where are you headed?"

"Nowhere really. I am just taking things as they come – but the accommodation here is expensive so I need to find another place to visit and something less pricy."

Tony thought for a moment then said.

"Why not stay for a while? I am sure that I could arrange something with my hotel – how about it?"

"I can't afford my place so how could afford your hotel!"

"You leave that to me!"

The next day Kathleen moved into the hotel. Tony had not asked for a free room he just arranged to pay for it himself. She would never know.

"So, boss what's up with you and the babe?" Mike was fully aware of the time that they were spending together. "She looks a weird one to me!"

"I know her from way back and besides it is none of your business! Do you understand?"

This was the first time that Tony had spoken to Mike like this. It was direct and sarcastic. "Sorry Tony, I was just asking!"

"Well don't ask – it is none of your business who I see. It never has been and it never will be!"

Mike walked out of the room without saying another word.

Tony took things very slow with Kathleen - she had said to him that people called her "Kathy" – but he did not seem ready for that yet.

During his days off they would have his driver take them around Las Vegas. They drove through neighborhoods and saw parts of town that were not too desirable to live in. One area that they both thought to be peaceful and pretty was Summerlin. Kathleen said that it is a place where she could settle down one day.

"The show is coming to an end soon and after a short break we will be heading to South Africa, Australia and then to Japan for four weeks. We are doing three concerts in each country and some R&R in each in between. I was wondering if you would like to come with me."

"What! No way! I couldn't just tag along – I mean it would be great but I could not just come with you. What would people say?"

"I don't care a hoot what people say. Screw them. The question is do you want to come with me?"

"As your friend?" She looked at him with an innocent yet penetrating smile.

"What would suit you? Friend or partner?" It was the first time that he had hinted at anything suggestive to her.

She paused for a long time and then replied.

"Maybe I should check out your hotel suite and then we could decide."

They spent the afternoon together in the suite.

Later that afternoon he telephoned Mike. Ten minutes later there was a knock on the door of the suite.

"Mike, you know Kathy." She was sitting on the sofa in the living room of the suite. Mike nodded at her.

"What's up boss?" asked Mike.

"Mike, Kathy and I are going to get married." Tony carried on speaking but Mike was still trying to comprehend what had just been said.

"Mike, you with me?"

"Yes, congratulations!" He did not mean it.

"Mike, please contact my lawyer to arrange a marriage agreement, then arrange for a small wedding to take place in the hotel before our run at the hotel closes next week – and one more thing – Kathy will of course be coming on our concert tour to Africa and the other places – we'll need visas and other arrangements made!"

"Sure boss!" Mike hugged Tony and gave Kathy a kiss on the cheek.

"What should I tell the media?"

"Oh right, let's get the pre-nuptial in place first then we can make an announcement to the media."

Mike left the suite and Tony walked over and kissed his bride-to-be.

She was smiling – things were going well.

For a wedding present he bought her a red Audi A4 Convertible. She had reminded him those years before sitting outside on a hot afternoon he had promised her a red convertible if ever he became famous.

Chapter 33

Their tour to South Africa took them to venues in Durban, Johannesburg and to Cape Town. Between the Johannesburg and Cape Town concerts they spent three days at a private game park near the world famous Kruger National Park. Seeing lion, elephant, buffalo, leopard and hippopotamus close up were a real treat for them.

In Cape Town they stayed at the Mount Nelson Hotel. They had three days free after the concert at the Good Hope Centre. They had a private tour guide take them – and their large tour party - around the city and into the wine route and to Stellenbosch. They visited the Delheim winery and spent a wonderful afternoon in the company of the owners of the famous wine farm. Michael (Spatz) and Vera Sperling were wonderful hosts. They had been on the wine estate since the early 1950s. They were both originally from Europe but this estate in South Africa was their home and their passion.

Tony was so impressed with his hosts and the quality of the wines that they drank that afternoon; he asked Spatz if he could purchase twenty cases of wine and have the order shipped to his home in California. Unfortunately the order could not be fulfilled because of the United Nations sanctions against South Africa.

The view from the top of Table Mountain was breath-taking. Across the bay they could see Robben Island where Nelson Mandela was imprisoned.

In Australia they played in Sydney, Melbourne and Brisbane. Again they made time to be alone and do some sightseeing – including two nights in the Blue Mountains west of Sydney. But there were always too many people around them.

In Japan it was no different – actually it was worse – they were mobbed wherever they went. There was no private time. But the consoling fact was that outside of the States, Japan was Tony's biggest market. They added two more shows onto their Japan leg of the tour – they could easily have sold more but everyone needed a break and just wanted to get back to the US.

Back in LA the touring party split up for a while.

Tony and Kat – he was the only one to use this name for her - headed up to his cabin in the mountains.

They needed to be alone.

Chapter 34

The next five years were taken up with tours and playing at special gigs in the States and around the world. The pace was brutal.

Tony was beginning to fall apart.

Tony and Mike also produced singles for other recording artists. They worked nonstop.

Kathy had become part of the team – Tony had her appointed as Vice President of his fan club – much to the dismay of Mike. However the fan club more than doubled in size and the merchandising of *Tony Macey* t-shirts, caps and other items quadrupled.

The relationship between Mike and Kathy had never been good – and the relationship between him and Tony seemed to be deteriorating. She was always in the way.

Record sales were down and the latest single hardly made the charts.

The five-year lock-in period that he had to remain with the record label was due to expire. At one time they had expected that it would be extended but now there was no talk from the company.

Tony was still struggling to sleep at night and his pill taking had increased substantially. Kathy knew that he took "stuff" but she did not seem to mind at first. Now it was becoming more of an issue. She would wait for him in bed at night but he seldom joined her. He said that he was concerned about the softening in his sales and in his career. Once on a spiral downwards, it is difficult to stop. Tony was drinking excessively and was taking pills to help him sleep.

He was booked for a six-concert tour in the northeast but it was only half sold out. Music tastes seemed to be changing.

When the record company released him at the start of the last year of the five-year contract period he was paid a bonus of $2 million dollars – of this $750,000 was due to Mike. Kathy and Mike had a scene about it.

"What have you done to deserve the money?" she blurted out at him.

"What business is it of yours? I found Tony and put him on the map – I made him!"

"You made nothing. He gave you everything that you have!"

"Who do you think arranged his gigs – his $25, 000 a show in Vegas, his international tours...you? Who do think you are?"

"I'm his wife!"

"More like his sponge. I know that you are drawing large sums out of his accounts. Our accountant keeps me in the picture!"

Kathy slapped him.

"Get out!" she yelled at him.

The next day Mike terminated his relationship – professionally and personally – with Tony Macey. They never spoke again. In over ten years together they had both become multimillionaires.

Tony's decline accelerated after Mike left him. He had no one to plan his life for him. And no one to put up with his behavior!

In the next year he struggled to find gigs. He struggled with his addiction to *Estazolum.* He needed something to help him fall asleep. A cocktail of one tablet and a shot of whiskey helped – but it could prove fatal.

Kathy had led a good life with Tony. Her plan to link up with a rich man to provide for her had worked. Initially he felt comfortable with her. Maybe they were just two misfits who could understand the problems that they both had. Kathy had worked hard to help Tony build his brand name. As a Vice President of his business she drew her own good salary but she wanted more.

They had only been married for a few years but things were unraveling. His moods became deeper and he often spoke about hell and wanting to burn things. .

She had found another man for comfort but she had to be careful.

They needed a plan.

Each week she went to have her hair washed and styled.

"Hello Kathy, good to see you!"

"Hello Mary, how are you?"

As Kathy sat down in the chair she removed her dark glasses. Mary stared at her face.

"What happened to your eye?"

"Oh, it was a silly thing. I slipped in the kitchen and whacked my face on the side of the counter top – gave myself a black eye."

"It looks terrible!"

"I know. I have tried not to go out since it happened but I did not want to miss our appointment!"

Several weeks later Kathy walked into her bank and she had her left arm bandaged from the wrist to the elbow.

"Good morning Mrs. Macey. What happened to your arm?"

"You would not believe what happened. I got up during the night and went downstairs to the kitchen. I didn't put on the light and I missed a step and fell down. I bruised my arm and seemed to twist the shoulder. It was a silly thing to do but I will be fine."

"Where have you been?" Tony asked her as she came home well after midnight one night.

"I told you that I was going out with some girlfriends. We went for dinner and a few drinks afterwards. Why so suspicious?"

He just looked at her and sat back on the couch.

"*God you have let yourself go*!" she though. "*You must have put on forty pounds in the last two years and you looked glazed most of the time!*"

"I'm going to bed." And she walked out of the room.

The next morning Tony telephoned one of Kathy's friends. He knew her well. "Was Kathy with you last night? She has lost a broach and I thought that you might have seen it."

"Yes, we went out for dinner. No sorry I did not see a brooch at the table maybe she had lost it before getting to the restaurant."

"Yeah maybe. Did you go for drinks after dinner?"

"No, we were done by about 9:30 p.m. and we all went home."

"Thank you."

"I hope that she finds her broach!"

"Oh yes, thank you!"

He hung up. He now knew that she was seeing someone else.

Deep down he could feel that evil part of his soul re-emerging. It had been still for many years now. As long as he had been successful, had buddies around him and even felt the love of a woman, he had been calm. But now he knew that it was re-emerging.

Should the feeling continue to grow, then he knew it would break out in his desire to either set fires or to kill by fire. He remembered how he became a slave to the feeling of wanting to burn things – and people.

It seemed that every time they were out somewhere, it would end up in an argument. Kat seemed to set him off – and he reacted badly. He was losing control but instead of Kat loving him she tormented him – and his demons got worse.

Standing outside of their home one day, the argument started. All of the neighbors standing outside heard him yell at Kat, "I will burn you to death! Do you hear me! I will torch you!"

"You are a disgrace! You are a disgrace!" and she ran inside the home.

Almost no one on the exclusive block of homes now talked with Tony.

The next argument was when Kat wanted to go out one evening.

"Where are you going tonight?" he asked.

"None of your business!" Kat replied.

"Are you seeing someone?" he bolted back at her.

She hesitated then said, "Yes! And what's it to you. You are not a husband anymore!"

"Without me you would have been nothing! I gave you everything that you have!" he yelled back.

She knew that this was not true. She had made some money before they were married but she had never mentioned it to him.

Kat just looked at him.

Then surprisingly he said, "I am also seeing someone!"

The statement shocked her at first. It was a sincere statement and his tone was more even than it had been just a moment before.

"You seeing someone! In your state which woman would see you?"

His answer was even more of a shock.

"It is not a *her,* it is a *him."*

Kat looked at him – "You disgust me!" and she walked out of the house. He thought about what he had just told her – *too late now!*

Chapter 35

Both parties to the broken marriage needed a plan.

Kathy tried hard to think of something but could not. In a divorce she would not get much – essentially leaving her with the funds that she had set aside for herself.

Tony began to realize that he only knew one way out. His two previous attempts had failed. Both times someone else had stepped in. First was the person who took revenge on Bill McKinzie after the fire- hall failure. The second was with Big Gus stepping in to save his life by killing Snake. This time he was determined to complete the unfinished business – if ever he was going to rest in peace then he knew what he had to do. Kathleen had to die in flames.

Tony was at home one day when he bit into an apple and chipped his tooth. "Shit! That hurts!" He was half way through a bottle of scotch when it happened.

"Hello, this is Doctor Webster's office can I help you?"

"Yes lady that is why I am calling you! It is Tony Macey here. I need to see Dick. I have chipped a tooth and it hurts like hell."

The receptionist ignored his rudeness.

"Mr. Macey could you come over in about 30 minutes – the doctor has a free slot then?"

"Yes, I will be there!" He hung up without saying "Thank you."

About twenty minutes later he walked into the dentistry.

"I'm here. Is he ready?"

The receptionist looked at him and said, "I will go and check."

In the back office she saw the doctor washing his hands. "Tony Macey is here – I think that he has had a great deal to drink. Do you still want to see him?"

Doctor Dick Webster had known Tony for many years.

"Yes, take him through, I will be there in a moment."

As Doctor Webster walked into the cubicle Tony said, "What took you so long? I'm in pain here!"

"Hi Tony, what is the problem?"

"I think that I chipped a tooth – hurts like hell!"

The smell of booze filled the room.

"Ok let's take a look shall we."

"Yup, there is a small chip – not a problem to fix. Get it done in no time at all. Just one question, I will need to give you an injection so tell me how much you have had to drink."

"None of your business!"

"Tony, I need to know otherwise I cannot give you a shot."

"A couple of doubles!"

"Right then, let me prepare the injection for you. When he stepped out of the room Doctor Webster only took a quarter of the normal injection quantity. Tony would never know the difference.

"Ok, let's give it a minute to take effect and then I can start working on you. How are you?"

"You mean besides the pain!"

Dick smiled, "Yes, besides the pain."

"Well Dick old pal I'll tell you just how good I am – but only after you've done my tooth!"

It took Doctor Webster about 20 minutes to replace the small piece of the tooth that had been chipped.

"I would like you to sit for a few minutes while it sets. Then you'll be fine".

"You were going to tell me how you were! What's up?"

"Dick old pal, I got a plan. I got a real good plan. I want to murder my wife." In his state of mind this was not a subject that he should have spoken about to anyone. He would not remember that he spoke about his plan to the doctor.

Doctor Dick Webster was told what the "plan" was. He really did not want to hear of it but Tony just blurted it out.

After Tony left the dentistry Dick Webster went to his office and closed the door. He made a telephone call.

Chapter 36

Kathy was struggling to put her plan together. She had worked out some aspects of the plan – she had been working on these for a long while. For other aspects, she was at a loss as to how to make it happen. What she knew was that she wanted a new life.

Sometimes opportunities present themselves without any real planning at all.

Kathy answered her private line at home. "Hello, Kathy Macey speaking." She listened. "Oh, when?" She listened again. "Tomorrow! You sure?" She listened to the voice on the phone. "Yes, ok." She hung up the telephone. She was sure that no one in or around her home office had heard the call.

The next afternoon she went out, filled her car with gas and found things to do to keep busy. There were things to do in the garage that kept her occupied.

Later in the afternoon she was in the kitchen when she saw Tony walk out of the garage. That was strange because he hardly ever spent time there.

As he walked into the kitchen she said, "Not like you to be in the garage."

He stopped dead in his tracks. He did not expect to see her standing there.

"Just looking for some old boxes of music." He walked out of the kitchen. Without saying another word.

Kathy thought, *"Has he forgotten that he keeps his old music in the room next to his studio! He does not know what day it is sometimes!*
Shit you have wasted your life!"

As per usual, they hardly spoke over dinner. The cook prepared the evening meal and then left after it was served. After dinner Tony went through to the TV room with his glass and bottle of scotch.

It was about 10 p.m. when Kathy came downstairs.

"I am going out."

"Whatever!" he mumbled.

He would never forget the date. It was burned into his memory *September 24, 1987.*

Kathy backed her car out of the garage and headed off down the street. From there she turned on to the small country road that was a short cut to town. At this time of the night there would be little or no traffic on the road.

It was only a few minutes later that there was an explosion. Kathy's car was engulfed in flames. There was no time for her to scream.

By the time the Emergency vehicles arrived, the car was still an inferno. Whoever had been in the car had long died. It took the crews another 30 minutes to put out the fireball. By the time they got near to the car, all they saw was the completely burnt remains of the driver. It was a very gruesome sight. To call it a human body would have been a complete mistake. It looked more like a prop from a Hollywood horror movie. The rear license plate of the car was still intact.

Tony was still watching TV when the front door bell rang. "Crap, who can that be? Kathy left her keys somewhere now I have to let her in?"

When he opened the door he saw two police officers.

"Are you Tony Macey?"

"Who do you think?"

"Sir, can we come in?"

"What's up?"

As the officers moved forward he had little choice but to move aside and let them into the house. Once he closed the door he pointed towards the front sitting room.

"So, what's up? Pretty late to come around for a donation!"

"Sir, where is your wife?"

"She went out – maybe an hour ago, not sure. Is she in trouble with the law!"

"What type of vehicle does your wife drive?"

"A red Audi A4 convertible. What the hell is going on?"

"Sir, there has been an accident. We were called to a car fire on Malcolm's Lane – the car was completely engulfed in flames. The driver had no chance. I am sorry."

"What the hell are you saying? Kat is dead?"

"We will have to undertake a post mortem on the remains to formally confirm that the driver of the vehicle was your wife. You do not know where she was headed tonight?"

"No. I did not ask."

The police officers left Tony. They would return in the morning with further news of the fire.

Tony had showed real remorse when he had received the news. He was pale and shaking when he sat in front of the officers in the living room.

Trained police officers look out for the reaction from people when they break bad news to them. Their first impression was that Tony had been visibly shaken.

And Tony was shaken. He thought that he had been cheated again by disposing of someone with fire. The question was could he remember his actions of that afternoon.

He did not sleep well that night.

The following morning the inspection team had removed the human remains from the car and taken it away for the autopsy. The fire had been intense and the human remains were in very poor shape. On a finger on the left hand was a wedding ring. Around the neck was a melted necklace.

"Hey, come look at this!" the police officer called out to his colleagues.

"I think I know what started the fire."

"Mechanical?"

"No."

The trunk lid of the car had been blown off. In the trunk were the remains of what looked like a five-gallon container and a blown-out propane gas cylinder.

"Looks like someone might have poured gasoline all over the trunk of the car. With the gas cylinder it must have gone off like a bomb. The car was booby trapped to catch on fire."

When the inside of the car was checked there was also the remains of a small can of gasoline under the driver's seat. As the gasoline poured out in the trunk and the propane ignited it would have exploded in an instant. Whoever booby-trapped the car wanted the driver dead.

The media was already all over the case. There was still speculation if Kathleen Macey had driven the vehicle at the time of the fire.

The police made no further statement except that the human remains were to be examined and that the burnt-out car would be inspected in order to determine the cause of the fire.

Tony Macey did not take calls at home. His assistant blocked all telephone calls with the statement that Mrs. Macey was unaccounted for at this time and that no further comment would be made until the police confirmed their findings.

Later in the morning, the police pushed their way through the throng of people gathered outside of the Macey residence.

"Mr. Macey we recovered these items from the body in the vehicle."

They showed him the melted wedding ring and the necklace.

Tony sat and nodded. He could not speak.

"Can you confirm that these belonged to your wife."

He rose and walked out of the room. He returned a few minutes later with an envelope. Inside was the insurance certificate, which contained the date of purchase, value and a set of photographs of the ring.

"Sir, we still need to confirm the identity of the remains – that might take a few days. But we do believe that the car was set to catch fire. We believe that the fire was no accident."

The policemen watched as the color drained from Tony's face.

"What do you mean?"

"At this stage we believe that the car was booby trapped to explode."

Tony stayed indoors for the next twenty-four hours. The media was almost camped on his front lawn and TV trucks blocked the road outside. Although Kathleen Macey was assumed dead nothing formal could be announced until the body had been identified.

The break-through came when Doctor Webster received a visit from the police department. He was requested to identify the remains of Kathleen Macey from her dental records. Her remains were too badly burnt for any other official form of identification.

In the background, the police had been conducting interviews all over town. They were interested in finding out as much about Kathleen as possible. They focused on where she went and whom she saw. The information that they received from the hairdresser and from the bank manager proved to be very interesting.

The housekeeper let the police detectives into the home. "I will tell Mr. Macey that you are here." They had been into the home several times over the last few days.

"Gentlemen, I did not expect you so early!" It was almost noon.

"How can I help you?"

"Sir, we have a warrant to search your home." The one detective handed the order from the District Attorney's office to Tony.

"What is the meaning of this? I don't understand? Do you think that I was involved in Kathy's death?"

"Sir, your wife died under mysterious circumstances – we need to check everything that we can. If you like you can telephone your lawyer but he can do nothing as this document is from the DA."

Within minutes another dozen police officers were in the home. The residence was broken down into segments and the search commenced. They were not sure what they were looking for but every room would be covered.

Three key pieces of evidence were discovered.

The first was found in the garage. It was two small cans filled with gasoline. The cans were the same as the one found under the driver's seat in Kathy's burnt-out car. There was also an empty five-gallon can. Tests would later confirm that it was the same make as the one found in the trunk of the car.

When asked about the cans Tony said that he had purchased the gasoline the previous week as the gardener had asked for gas for the lawn mower. "Sir, is it the norm that you buy gasoline for the lawnmower yourself?"

"No, not normally but I was headed out and he was outside and mentioned that we were out of gas."

The gardener confirmed the story but he had not as yet cut the grass. He suspected that the five-gallon can of gasoline should still be full. It was not.

Tony could not account for the missing gasoline.

The second discovery was that the gas bottle from the propane BBQ was missing. Tony could not account for the gas cylinder.

The third piece of evidence was just as damning.

"Sir, I think that you should see this." The officer whispered to the detective. They walked through to Kathy's office.

Another officer was holding what looked like a small journal.

The police officer drew the attention of the detective to three entries all made in Kathy's handwriting.

The first one read, "We fought again today. He was out of his mind with the booze. He punched me so hard that I fell over. My eye looks a mess."

"Sir, we checked the date and her Day Planner. The notation corresponds to her appointment at the hairdresser. If you recall the hairdresser told us that Mrs. Macey came in the one day with a black eye."

The second entry read, "He chased me out of the bedroom. I ran but he pushed me down the steps. I twisted my shoulder. So much pain that I can hardly move my body."

This date was just the day before her visit to the bank when her arm was in a sling.

The third entry read, "He keeps threatening to set me alight. He is crazy. I am so afraid of him." Subsequent interviews with the neighbors confirmed that Tony Macey had threatened his wife in public. He had said that he wanted to burn her alive.

The lead detective on the case telephoned the police chief and the DA's office. After the two telephone calls Tony Macey was arrested on suspicion in the death of his wife.

When formal charges of First Degree Murder and Assault were brought against Anthony McKinzie (also known as Tony Macey) he denied that he had ever hit his wife. He also denied that he had booby-trapped her car the night that she died a terrible death in her car.

Maybe he just could not remember.

Chapter 37

The news of any celebrity falling from grace makes world headlines.

From a rising star at the age of twenty, he became a superstar at twenty-five. After several golden years and earning millions of dollars each year, he had begun to crash. The media covered it all - from winning Grammys to touring the world - from gold and platinum records to appearing on every TV special with such artists as John Denver, Frank Sinatra, Dean Martin, guest appearances on the Carol Burnett Show and even singing with Barry Gibb. He had done it all. But the pressure was too much.

In the court of public opinion he was first thought of as being not guilty – it was just another plot to bring down someone famous – someone who had come from an obscure background. Not much was known about him prior to his first single at the age of twenty. He was much loved by his supporters. Over time, and once the trial commenced the support level had waned.

A key piece of evidence produced in the trial was the identification of the dental records of Kathleen Macey by Dr. Webster. The doctor did not mention the plan that Tony had told him of the day that he came in to have his chipped tooth repaired. No one knew about the conversation so why should he mention it. He owed his friend at least that. He had no choice but to testify at the trial.

It took several months for the trial to commence and then another two months to complete. During all of this time, Tony's lawyer kept confirming, "My client is innocent – he did not beat or kill his wife."

No one really believed him.

"Have you reached a verdict?" The judge asked the Forman.

"We have your Honor."

"Will the defendant please rise."

"In the charge of First Degree Murder how do you find?"

"We find the defendant guilty."

"So say ye one, so say ye all?"

"We do."

"In the charge of assault how do you find?"

"We find the defendant not guilty."

"So say ye one, so say ye all?"

"We do."

The following week the judge delivered her verdict.

"Will the defendant please rise."

"Anthony McKinzie you have been found not guilty of the charge of assault by a jury of your peers.

You were found guilty of the barbaric burning of your wife in her vehicle. For this crime you be will sentenced to twenty- five years in prison without parole."

Tony's lawyers lodged an appeal on the sentence but they lost.

At the age of thirty-four Anthony McKinzie faced the next twenty-five years in prison.

Those convicted of murder enter the various correction services venues every day. Murder will never be eradicated from society. Punishing the guilty will always be required.

New arrivals hardly raise an eyebrow. With celebrities, it always seems different. Prison Services strive to be equal-handed in processing celebrities but it is never easy. Many of the guards were their fans.

It did not take long for the jibes by the other cellmates to start.

"Hey, pretty boy, you burnt your wife – coward!"

Anthony ignored the comment.

"Hey, pretty boy, it's rude not to answer when someone speaks to you."

"Leave me alone." He could not see the person talking with him as the voice came from the cell next to his.

"Pretty boy you are never alone in here." Laughter could be heard coming from the other cells.

Standing in line for meals the taunting continued.

"Should we make way for the pop star?" More laughter.

"Thinks that he can just get rid of his woman – what were you tired of her!"

"Your weenie too small for her and she found a real man!" Laughter.

"I could have helped her!" More laughter.

Anthony swung around and looked at the men standing behind him.

"I did not kill my wife – just leave me alone." He should have stopped there but he continued, "And what are you in for? Baking cookies! You murdered someone – what does that make you? Dickhead!"

He did not see the blow coming but it felt like a hammer hitting him in his kidneys. He fell to the ground in pain. The voice above him said,

"Yeah, I killed someone – I killed a man in a knife fight – one-on-one, best man won – you ...you're a coward ...couldn't face someone when you killed them!"

The guards arrived and broke it up but the dye was cast. Anthony was a marked man.

The jibes did not stop.

He tried to focus on getting into a routine. He signed up for the carpentry shop and went to the library in the prison to read up on the subject. He took out books of poetry and of US history. He really did not know much about his own country. Most likely many people in the country did not either. Twenty-five years is a lifetime to be locked away so he thought that he needed to keep busy and educate himself. The carpentry would teach him a trade and keep his mind on making things and being creative.

He was about two months into his term when the trouble really started.

"Hey sweetie, when you gonna tell us the truth about how you fried your wife?"

Anthony tried to avoid the man standing in front of him. He attempted to walk pass him but his path was blocked. "Let me through!"

"What you gonna do? Set me alight!" It was not only the laughter that he heard around him, but he could feel the presence of those that were standing behind him - right behind him.

"Please! Leave me alone!"

"No, we decided that today you should meet *Knuckles!*"

"Who?"

"Knuckles" why don't you introduce yourself to our pop star!"

The group of men opened up and a man walked through and stood in front of Anthony. He was no more than five foot six but he was almost as wide as he was tall. He looked like a pocket battleship.

"Leave me alone! Let me go! Please, I do not want any trouble." Anthony feared what might be in store for him.

As "Knuckles" walked towards Tony he screamed for help. Even if the guards heard him, they were not going to react. It was just a bit of sport.

In total he was hit no more than five or six times. The first one exploded into his stomach knocking the wind out and doubling him over in agonizing pain. Then there was the upper cut that almost lifted him off his feet. As he straightened up he took a few more punches to the face. Then he fell unconscious to the floor. The group of men cracked up with laughter. By the time the guards walked into the recreation room, the group had dispersed.

Anthony suffered a cracked rib, a broken nose and a split lip. He spent three days in the Infirmary before being let back into his cell. He was given light duties for another two weeks.

When he asked if any action would be taken against those that had set up the beating – and against the guy known as "Knuckles" the answer was "We will investigate the incident". And "there is no one here known as

Knuckles." He knew that they were lying. He was on his own and would be the subject of further incidents.

The last thing that Tony wanted now was for the deep burning in his soul to be reawakened yet again.

The routine was the same. Each day was the same as the last. It was difficult to recall what day of the week it was. One knew when it was Sunday because they were permitted to sleep an hour longer. It was a day to spend several hours in the outside yard or to sit in the recreation room.

Another optional activity was to attend a church service. A local pastor would come in and deliver a service at 3 p.m. The inmates had to sign-up to attend the service. Tony put his name down, as it was something to do.

"Son, are you Tony Macey?" asked the pastor.

"Yes." He replied.

"I'm sorry to see you in here. I used to be a fan of yours!"

Tony looked at him. The pastor did not seem to be more than forty years old – not much older than him. So it was possible that the man knew his music.

"Thank you sir!"

"I liked your ballads most of all. I enjoy being able to hear the words and not have them drowned out by the music." The pastor smiled at him.

A guard was standing next to them as they spoke.

"Ok Macey move along and take a seat."

He heard the pastor say, "Bless you my son and may you be forgiven your sins!" as he walked away. He thought to himself,

"Yeah I have many sins – there are many things to be forgiven for!"

He hardly heard a word of the sermon. His memory came back to life again. There was his life in Vale. Then there was his living in a camper at the diner.

His few years as journeyman singing in pubs, on the beachfront or anywhere where he could get a gig to bring in some money. Then his mind drifted to the few years that he was famous and wealthy. On a shelf at home he had awards for singing – from platinum records to People's Choice Awards.

He had photographs of the rich and famous with whom he had hung out...It seemed like a lifetime ago – but he was only now just over 36 years old. His last birthday had gone unnoticed. Not even one card from a fan anywhere in the world. At one time he used to receive over ten thousand cards a year for his birthday and his fan mail exceeded a hundred thousand letters.

He tried not to think of the fires but he could not avoid it. He briefly thought of Bill McKinzie, of Snake and of Big Gus - the only man who had ever loved him – and the man that he loved back. He thought of Kat and wondered if he really did love her. Maybe they were just two dysfunctional souls that needed each other. Maybe she only loved him for his money. And then they said that he had murdered her.

"Hey Macey! The service is over. Time to move to the dining hall."

As the pastor walked by him he thought that he noticed a small nod of the head in greeting. He could not be sure.

"All those wanting to go to church must sign up after breakfast." The week had flown by. He stood in line to sign up.

"Macey! The pastor wants to see you."

He was walked forward with a guard at each arm.

"Good morning! May I call you Tony?" asked the pastor.

"Sure, whatever you want to call me is fine!"

"Son, I have something to ask of you. Would you be interested in singing at our Christmas service that is coming up? I thought that you might like to do that."

Tony had not expected this. It had been several years since he had performed in public – a lifetime ago.

"I'm not sure Father. Can I think about it?"

"Yes of course. Let me know in a week or two as we will start rehearsing soon after that."

Again Tony hardly heard the sermon. This time he thought about the songs that he had sung and where he had sung them. He could think of at least fifty venues in the States and Canada, venues in South America, across the UK, Ireland and across Europe. He had sung in South Africa, Australia, in Japan and even in Moscow.

"Everyone up!" He heard the guards yelling at the end of the service. Maybe it was not the service itself that was important, rather the time to begin reflecting on what he had achieved in life – and where he had failed.

He looked forward to the next week in church. He still did not know what he was going to tell the pastor about singing at the Christmas service. That was a more difficult decision to be made.

Before he could decide what to do about the Christmas service, he had another encounter with the inmates who kept jibing at him.

"Not seen you in a while – we missed you!" There was always that animal-like laughter from the members of the "gang".

Tony looked at them.

"Guys please tell me what you want? What do you want?"

"Did you forget that we don't like wife killers? You got a bad memory."

He was surrounded and he could not see any guards near him. Most likely they had walked away so not to spoil the bit of sport.

"Tell me what you want. Just leave me alone!"

"He wants us to leave him alone – that's not good manners. Maybe we got to teach him to be polite around us!"

"Knuckles! He needs a lesson again. The yellow-bellied wife killer needs another lesson!"

"Oh No! Please! PLEASE!" no one heard him – or wanted to hear him.

This time Knuckles came at him from behind. The first punch caught him square in the small of his spine. The pain was excruciating. The pain short up and down his back as if he had been attached to an electric pole. He collapsed to the ground. He had no time to protect himself before he was rolled over by the pocket battleship and then kicked in the ribs.

When the guards came out they thought that he was paralyzed, as he could not feel his back or his legs. The medical staff was called and he was put into a neck brace and taken to the Infirmary. It took over an hour for the sting effect on his back to wear off.

He was in an induced coma for two days. Besides the injury to his spine he also had a cracked rib.

This time Tony made contact with his lawyer who lodged a complaint with the Correctional Services Authority. Little action was taken.

He was the victim here and no one cared. There seemed to be two levels in the justice system – the courts and the decision that was made to punish the guilty and then the life within the prison walls. Within the prison walls, punishment was worse because it never stopped.

"I hate them! Shit, I hate them!" He kept saying to himself. He knew that the beatings would not stop. His eyes seemed to change color as he felt his personality changing.

Tony missed the next two Sunday services. When he returned, he asked if he could speak with the pastor.

"What happened to you my son?"

"I had an accident Father." The pastor did not believe him.

"Father, I am not sure if I can sing with my injury. Can you give me two more weeks to recover and then I can decide?'

"Yes of course we have another six weeks to Christmas. I am sure that we could wait and see if you recover in time."

Chapter 38

Tony was on light duties again. He visited the carpentry shop and tried to do a few things but his back and chest still hurt. He seemed to find an inner peace when working with wood.

"Hey! Watch where you are walking!" the inmate said as he walked past him. He had slammed his shoulder into Tony.

"Sorry!" was all that Tony said. When he looked up he thought that is was one of the gang members that used to jibe at him. He could not be sure.

He was sitting on the bunk in his cell that night when he put his hand into his prison jump suit pocket. He felt something. He pulled out a small piece of paper. He unfolded it. He read the note.

"They are planning to beat you to death on Christmas Eve."

He read the note several times. Why would he receive a warning from someone who was part of the gang that used to jibe at him and have him beaten up? Was it a trap?

He stuffed the note into a crack in the wall of his cell. He did not want to be found with it on his clothing.

Over the next few days he kept a look out for the inmate who had slipped the note into his pocket. He saw the gang and the same inmate once or twice but there was no sign of acknowledgement from the man.

Sunday came around and Tony asked to see the pastor.

"Father, I would like to be part of your service for Christmas."

"Thank you my son. That is good news. I will speak with the Warden to change your duty roster in order that you can practice with us."

The Warden approved the request from the pastor.

He had just returned to his cellblock after his first practice session when he was surrounded again. He just looked at them – looking without making direct eye contact!

He expected another beating.

"Hey pretty boy we just wanted to wish you a Merry Christmas!" He hated that laughter from the clowns who surrounded him.

"It is not yet Christmas." he answered.

The group burst into laughter again. Then the leader stepped forward and placed his mouth close to Tony's ear. "We will have a special gift for you for Christmas!" and then he turned and walked away with the others.

Tony found a bench in the mess hall and sat down. His legs were shaking and he was sweating as if he had run a marathon. As he tried to calm himself down.

He hardly slept that night. He needed a plan. He needed to find a way of satisfying the demon.

There were always odd jobs needing doing in the prisons. Inmates could offer their services and be paid a very small amount for their time. Monies earned could be used to buy a number of items from the outside world – as long as the warden's office approved.

Although Tony was still very wealthy, his money had been placed in trust until he was released from prison – or died – whichever came first. His home in the mountains had been sold. His fifty percent ownership of a gas stop, diner and bar in Oregon was leased to a management company. Tony had access to funds from outside of the prison but he was afraid of what image it might project if he lived too well while behind bars.

He also needed no excuse to have the gang that had attacked him twice, to do so again just because he was wealthy. They seemed possessed with the fact that he had murdered his wife in a cowardly fashion by setting her alight – any further excuse could make things worse. If the note that had been placed in his jump suit was anything to go by, the gang had already decided to up the stakes.

"They are planning to beat you to death on Christmas Eve!"

The chilling message had been forefront in his mind since he had received it.

After dinner, the inmates had some free time before they were herded back to their cells for the night. Tony walked up to the Notice Board. There was never really much to read. He glanced at some items and then he walked on. He caught himself in mid-step and turned back to read the posting.

CAR WASH

Four inmates required for washing vehicles for three days.

Standard hourly rate. Sign up at the office.

He must have seen the posting many times before but somehow this time it caught his attention. An opportunity in the indoor vehicle-parking garage – the money was not the attraction.

He immediately walked over to the screened off office booth.

"That car washing position still available?"

"Fill out your name." The guard on duty pushed a pad through the small slot in the window to him. He filled it out.

"When will I know?"

"The Chief Officer will review the list and post the names tomorrow. You just made the close off – it shuts in a few minutes."

In his cell that night he thought through a plan that was developing in his mind. If the parking garage had gasoline then how would he get it back to his cell?

He had to find a way of protecting himself from being assaulted – or worse, being beaten to death – if the note that he had received was to be believed.

As he lay in his bunk he thought of his previous attempts with fire. He had replayed these thoughts in his mind so many times.

Sometimes – when he was happier with life, the demons inside of him were silent. Maybe they were contained to some extent. He had experienced years at a time when he was more stable and did not think of setting someone alight. When he felt cheated or unloved then the demons were awakened inside of him.

He lay for hours not even contemplating sleep. And then a thought struck him. He sat up on his bunk and blinked his eyes to ensure that he was awake. He thought that he had a solution to the threat posed to him by the gang. Fire! He needed to start a fire! But this one would be different.

After roll call and breakfast, he hurried over to the notice board. He found the posting for the car wash detail. His name was on the list!

All of the inmates who were participating in the Christmas service had their daily assignments re-allocated. It was the same for the car wash detail. He attended the practice for the service and would then be taken across to the garage. At the service he was going to sing three Christmas carols. His voice was rusty but it still had that smooth and gentle texture to it. The biggest problem was finding harmony with the organist who was untalented. For Tony this was very different from playing with world-class musicians.

On the first day of the car wash detail, Tony tried to check out the facility without appearing to be too interested. He made mental notes of where the gasoline supply was kept. He looked for small containers – something that he could use in his plan. His plan would depend on finding something smaller to use. He also needed to find access to something to use to start his fire.

The answer to the second question presented itself much easier than what he thought it would. On a break from washing cars, a group of guards decided to step to one side and have a cigarette. This was against regulations but many other things were also ignored in the prison – including the protection of some inmates from being beaten up.

Inmates were allowed to smoke on their breaks.

"You got a light?" he asked one of the guards.

The guard took out his book of matches and threw them to Tony who was standing about two feet away. The guard most probably did not remember that Tony did not smoke. Tony caught the booklet and turned to walk away – as he did so he slid the matches into the front of his jump suit and into his underpants. Mission accomplished!

The next day was December 23rd. One day until the gang had planned to beat him to death. Tony attended the final practice for the Christmas service. In a way he would miss the practices as it had given him the opportunity to sing again.

After lunch he was taken to the garage for the car wash detail. He still needed to try to locate a smaller container for the gas. Without it the plan might not work.

He was almost half way through his shift when he looked up and saw one of the mechanics from the garage walk across the room with what looked like two empty containers. He placed them up against the wall not five paces from where the gasoline was stored. If Tony had really believed in God he would have looked up and said, "Thank you!"

With about five minutes to go before the end of the shift he began to sweat and shake. He knew that his objective was the gasoline. He had prepped and set fires before but this felt different. He thought of quitting his mission but the voice inside of him kept saying, "You need to do this! You have to do this!"

His hands were trembling as he stood up from washing the wheels of a prison truck. His movement would not appear to be suspicious as it was getting towards the end of the shift. He slowly walked towards where the gasoline was located. He carried some rags that he had been using on the vehicle. No one paid any attention to him.

When he reached the wall, he glanced around and still no one seemed to be interested in what he was doing. He quickly grabbed the one smaller can that the mechanic had placed up against the wall. He walked to the larger container.

In an instant he had put it down and started pouring gasoline into it from the heavier container – he had to tip it, as it was heavy.

The noise caught the attention of one guard. He looked up and said, "Hey, Macey what are you doing?" He started to move towards where Tony stood. Tony ignored him – he almost had enough gasoline in the small container.

"Set that down immediately!" The guard no more than twenty feet away when Tony lifted the can over his head, poured it over himself and struck the match. He looked at the guard and said, "Too late – it's better this way!" Then he dropped the match onto himself.

In an instant he was engulfed in flames. He screamed the scream of the dying. He stood there as a human torch as the flames burnt his head and shoulders and spread to his legs. By taking his own life, he was depriving the gang of beating him to death on Christmas Eve.

This fire was different. He was the target.

Chapter 39

The guards ran for hand-held fire extinguishers and sprinted towards Tony. Within minutes they were spraying him. Blankets were brought in to wrap around him to smother the fire.

The alarm was set off and the prison was shut down as a precaution. Only the other inmates working in the garage knew what had happened but they were taken to one corner and chained to a rail. They were not going anywhere until the situation was stabilized.

In just the few minutes that Tony was ablaze, the damage was extensive. He was alive but in great pain. His face in particular was a gruesome sight. The guards administered morphine to him from the emergency kit that was in the garage. It did not take long for Tony to stop convulsing and pass out.

"What the hell happened here", yelled the Warden when he arrived.

"Sir, he just walked over to where the gasoline is stored, dumped it into a container and then poured it over himself. It all happened so fast!"

"And where did he get matches to set himself on fire?"

That and many other questions would be addressed and answered during the investigation that was launched by the Department of Correctional Services.

Tony was taken by ambulance to a nearby city hospital. Several hours later he was airlifted to a hospital that had a special Critical Burns Unit. He was placed into an induced coma and his condition was described as "serious but stable."

An extensive search was conducted of Tony's cell. The note that he had hidden in a crack in the wall was found. The handwriting could not be identified as the words had been written in a strange manner – a precaution if the note was ever found. The tipster's life would be worth nothing if he were exposed. Those that beat Tony were eventually identified. The gang was broken up and each member was sent to a different prison location. The Department of Correctional Services did not make the findings from their internal investigation known to the public.

It appeared as if Tony believed that his life was in danger and instead of reporting the threat – and having the good chance that the threat would have been discounted – he decided that he could not bear the pain of a slow death and so he attempted to take his own life.

Because Tony Macey was a former celebrity the Head of Correctional Services made a statement to the media.

"Ladies and gentlemen on the afternoon of December 23, Tony Macey was involved in a fire accident at the prison where he is serving his sentence. The circumstances surrounding the fire are being investigated. Once complete the findings of the investigation will be presented to the Director of Correctional Services.

Mr Macey's condition is described as stable but he has sustained severe burns to his head and upper body. He is in an undisclosed medical facility that specializes in burns caused by combustible fluids.

The Department of Correctional Services will release future updates on the condition of the prisoner as we receive them from the hospital. We have no further comment to make at this time. Thank you."

Many of Tony's former fans saw the news casts around the world. Some felt great pain for the star while others thought burning was doing justice - justice for burning his wife.

Tony spent several months in hospital. He had some burns to his legs but nothing too serious. His torso also had burns – more so than his legs but nothing that would inhibit his life.

His shoulders had been badly burned. There was significant tissue damage to the right shoulder in particular.

His neck was even worse. He would have visible discoloring of the skin and a skin graft was required.

The most damaged was his head and face. Both ears had been severely burned and the tops had to be removed because the skin was charred and dead. The tip of his nose was disfigured and he required plastic surgery to reshape it. Both of his eyebrows were completely burned away as was the top of the upper lip. This injury combined with the fact that he had inhaled the burning gasoline, had slightly changed the pitch of his voice. It was now more throaty and raw.

His head was covered with red blotches where the tissue had been damaged. He was not a pretty sight to see. He could not hide his face. Over the years it did become more acceptable but was always a shock to people who saw him for the first time. The prison authorities permitted him to wear a hoody that covered most of his face and his head.

In total he underwent eleven surgeries. His mission to take his own life with fire had also failed.

For the next seventeen years, Tony Macey was held in a new location. He graduated with a diploma in Carpentry Science and with a BA degree in History. He hardly ever sang – not even in Christmas services. He earned money by making wooden trays, fruit holders and other items. Life was routine but safe. The demons seemed to have gone.

Chapter 40

Michelle Loren was born after the heyday of Tony Macey. Like the other greats of his era, she missed out on his music and the soft tone of his voice. Every so often she would hear an "oldie" on her car radio – a song by Andy Williams, Johnny Mathis and Nat King Cole. The music was pleasant to listen to but seemed dated by today's standards and tastes in music.

Michelle had obtained her bachelor's degree in psychology with a sub major in criminology. In her master's degree, she focused on the function of the criminal mind. Now she was intent on completing her doctorate but as yet could not find a topic that she would want to research and write about.

She was in her late twenties and already had developed an excellent reputation with those that she had worked with in her field. During her master's degree she had spent many hours in the District Attorney's office in Los Angeles reading up on old cases as part of her research.

She had obtained her master's degree *cum laude.*

She had a junior lecturer position and assisted law practices on providing an analysis of medical information on clients that had been charged with violent crimes. It was not the career that she wanted but it paid the rent.

One night she was curled up on her coach watching TV. The host of the program featured ballads sung by up-and-coming artists.

The host said how the voice reminded him of Tony Macey, who had his prime years earlier. "It is a real pity that Tony's life fell off the rails in the 1980s. This clip is from an appearance that Tony made on the Frank Sinatra show when he was in his early twenties. Tony, wherever you are this song is a salute to you!"

Michelle sat up and watched the clip. She became totally captivated by the soft almost tender voice of a young Tony Macey. At the end of the song she turned down the volume on the TV and walked over to her desk and switched on her computer. She then spent the next two hours researching Tony Macey – his achievements, which were many, the fortune that he had made – his problems with addiction and alcohol – and then his trial and sentencing to life in prison.

Michelle made notes as she read more and more about the man. She sat back and sucked on her pencil. *"Is there enough here to develop a doctoral thesis?"*

The next day she spent finding out even more about Tony. She visited library sources and established a list of police officers, lawyers and other persons who were mentioned in the various archives that she could access under public domain availability.

It took her several days to put together a comprehensive dossier on Tony Macey. It was a research topic that she sincerely hoped would be acceptable to her professor, and compelling enough to persuade the authorities to make available the case file. If those hurdles were overcome she would press for an interview with Macey, to which she hoped he would agree.

Tony had now served almost eighteen years of his sentence. Would he even be interested in granting interviews now after all of these years? No one else had shown an interest in him over this long period of time.

Michelle approached her professor almost a month later with the topic "Celebrity crime: Justice or Injustice – Is the Criminal Code Applied Equally to Those of Privileged Status? – The Tony Macey case."

"Why do you think that there is a research topic here?" he asked.

"My feeling is that there is so much sensationalism attached to celebrities – actors, singers, business executives – that it could be difficult for the law to be applied equally when there is so much external pressure. The pressure could be both for an acquittal and for conviction."

Michelle continued, "I think that there are three lines of logic that I would like to pursue...equal application of the law, leniency of the law and excessive application of the law."

She paused.

"It will take a great deal of effort to obtain the approval of the DA to permit access to the case files, and access to Tony Macey or to his financial records, which could be held in trust right now."

The wheels turned slowly and it took another three months for the faculty to approve the subject proposed. Thereafter, it took another two months for the DA's office to grant access to the files and to other documents pertaining to the case. A letter had been sent to Tony Macey's lawyer requesting the co-operation of his client in this research topic. Once confirmation was received, Michelle Loren commenced her research.

Chapter 41

Michelle divided her research into different projects. These included a comprehensive understanding of the law pertaining to murder, investigation into the background of Tony Macey, and his mental health record. She would research if any studies had been conducted into the field of sudden changes in financial and popularity status - say coming from an under privileged background and becoming very wealthy very quickly – and how this impacts behavior. She would research the impact of "fan club" status and the impact on self-esteem and behavior patterns of the famous. Another category was the impact on those serving in the police force and judicial system when the rich and famous were charged with murder.

She was not sure as yet as to when she would make the request to visit Tony in prison. She was sure that she would require several sessions with him. It was not a set of meetings that she was looking forward to, as after all, he was a convicted murder.

The initial plan was to take about eighteen months to complete her doctoral thesis and then to wait for it to be accepted. In the meantime she still worked. The bills did not stop coming just because she was so busy!

Michelle was permitted to take trial and other files home for her research. Many an evening was spent reading the documents.

Once she stared working through the actual trial material then her interest level increased. She began drawing a timeline of the events that led up to the death of Kathleen Macey and the subsequent arrest of her husband for her murder.

The description of the remains of Kathleen Macey was very disturbing. She was almost completely devoid of flesh and her organs were also burnt beyond recognition. The gasoline fire had totally consumed her body. It was not only the gasoline of the fire that had exploded but also the additional cans that had been placed under the driver's seat. The propane gas added dramatically to the inferno.

Small pieces of clothing had been recovered and these were confirmed as being what Kathleen was known to have owned. Her wedding ring and melted jewelry were as also recovered. The skeleton was charred beyond recognition – it could not even be described as a corpse. After reading the coroner's report Michelle went to the washroom and threw up.

Page after page of information lay scattered over Michelle's large bed.

Michelle was in the kitchen making tea when she remembered two dates in her timeline of events. She left the tea and returned to her bedroom. "*What am I looking for?*" she asked herself. "*Something ...something...what am I looking for?*"

She picked up the death certificate. It was dated for a Friday.

"OK, got that but what else am I looking for?"

It took her another few minutes to find it. She located the x-ray of Kathleen's mouth that had been used to identify her body. The date on the x-ray was a Thursday. The day before Kathleen had died. This did not seem that odd but Michelle made a note – she needed to follow up on something the following morning. Her tea was calling for her attention.

The next morning Michelle telephoned the number that was on the x-ray.

"Dentist's office – how may I assist you?"

"Hello, I am conducting some research – could I please speak with Doctor Webster."

"I am sorry but Doctor Webster sold his practice many years ago. Doctor George Mendez purchased the practice – could I maybe assist you? I was with Doctor Webster for many years."

"If you could it would be great! Thank you. It is just a small matter but it goes back to the death of Kathleen Macey."

"Oh yes, I remember it well. She was a lovely person. What do you need to know?"

"I am tidying up some case files and I saw that Kathleen Macey had a dental appointment with Doctor Webster the day before she died. I was wondering if there was anything wrong that had to be corrected that day."

"Oh, that I can't remember." Michelle was about to say something when the receptionist spoke again, "I can't give you confidential information about what the doctor did on Kathleen but maybe if I check our boxes of stuff that I keep of our old appointment books I could find something for you. What was the date that you were looking for? Can I telephone you back if I find anything?"

Michelle was still sitting thinking about the call when her telephone rang. "Hello, this is Mary from the dentist's office. I found the book. It was from many years ago now – but I found it right away – I never throw things away!

No, Kathleen Macey did not have an appointment with Doctor Webster on the date that you gave me. I checked for her last appointment before she died and it was two months before. Does this help you?"

"Are you sure about this?"

"Oh yes, I have the book opened right in front of me. The doctor's last appointment that day would have been just as I was leaving. I remember that a young lady came in – just as we were about to close the office that afternoon. But it was not Kathleen Macey."

Michelle did not know what to make of this discrepancy. It was not an error by a day or two as Kathleen had been in two months before.

Michelle placed a big star next to her notes.

Michelle's large bed now only provided her with a narrow section to sleep on. The rest of the bed was covered with copies of items from the trial and other information.

The previous night she had looked at the x-ray Kathleen's face. After dinner she sat on her bed and crossed her legs and recommenced her research on the case. She picked up sections of the complete body x-ray taken of Kathleen. All in all there were about twenty x-rays to look at. There was nothing of interest so she moved on.

Then she picked up the one x-ray again and looked at it. She made another note on her pad and added a large star next to it.

In the morning she made a telephone call to a hospital in Vale, Oregon.

She introduced herself and asked to speak with the Director of Hospital Services. It took some convincing but he finally agreed to look into the matter. Michelle was not sure if he would telephone her back. It took three days before she received the information.

Her next step was to call in a favor from one of the senior police officers, which she had previously worked with. The information that she required was a little obscure but he would see what he could do for her. This time the wait was even longer. About a week later he telephoned her with some information. She owed him one!

She pulled up outside a small motel. The building had seen better days. She walked into the reception area. This was not a great place to hang around!

A very large man was sitting behind the desk and watching sport on TV. It looked like re-runs of professional wrestling – but who could tell the difference! Although she stood right in front of the desk, the man ignored her. The wrestling was far more important. Michelle rang the bell and he raised his eyebrows at her.

"You want a room?"

"No thank you. I was hoping to see the owner."

"That would be me."

"My name is Michelle – I am following up on old unpaid hotel bills and I have a case that I would like to ask you about."

Maybe it was the thought of making some money that aroused the beast. He turned down the volume on the TV – turning it off would have been asking too much!

"Lots of people try to skip paying. Now we take payment up front – we take no chances anymore!"

"So you have had a number of incidents of people not paying and skipping the motel?"

"Yes lady. You gonna pay up on an old bill?"

She had to keep him interested or he would ignore her – then the volume on the TV would be turned up again.

"That depends if you can help me. I am looking into a case of about eighteen or more years ago. Were you the owner then?"

He just nodded. Good, he is still engaged!

"You reported to the police that a young woman checked into the motel. She booked in for three nights and according to your statement on the fourth morning when it came time to check out, you entered the room and it had been cleaned out. She had skipped without paying. Do you remember that incident?"

"Yeah I do. She seemed ok. She arrived by cab if I remember – said that she wanted to stay a few nights" Before he finished his sentence he yelled and Michelle almost fell over with fright.

"Hey, Barb..." He turned towards the back office.

"Hey Barb you there?"

"Yeah, what you want?"

"Come out here."

"This is my wife...she remembers everything!"

Michelle recovered from the yelling and recomposed herself.

"Do you remember that women who skipped on us ...maybe mid 1980s...cute young woman...she just left without paying?"

"Yeah, I remember, I filed the police report. What they caught her?"

"Do you remember her name?" asked Michelle.

"No, but I could find it somewhere in the junk back there." The woman pointed at the back office.

"Could you maybe check that out for me and I will come back in a few days."

"We gonna get paid?"

"I'll see what I can do". Michelle was pleased to leave the motel.

The waiting was always the worst part. Michelle did not know what news she wanted to receive. Either way there could be ramifications.

It took two days before she received a telephone call from Barb at the motel. She drove down immediately and remembered the stale smell as soon as she walked into the reception area. The big man was sitting there watching football. Most likely it was re-runs, as it was not football season.

"Hello, you have some news for me?"

"Hey Barb that woman is here!" he yelled.

Barb came out from the back office.

"Do you have any information for me?"

"Well, it took time to go through all of the stuff. There were so many boxes to go through." Michelle was not surprised that some trading was about to take place.

"Oh, before I forget I have some money for you to cover the room rent that you lost a few years ago." Two can play at this game she thought!

"How much?"

"Well, I checked your room rates from the time that the person stayed here. I then added up for three nights and came to a total. We were then able to add something extra onto that for your troubles." She hesitated then said, "I would have to check if your information matches mine before I can hand over any funds to you."

"Sounds fair!" said Barb.

Barb opened up an old guest registration book. She had tagged a particular page. She turned the book around so that Michelle could see the information. She could hardly control herself as she looked down on the page.

GUEST NAME DATE IN DATE OUT ROOM NUMBER

Connie Warner Sept 21 Sept 24 Room 3

Michelle could not take her eyes off of the page. She swallowed hard and clenched her hands in order to stop them from shaking.

"Is this what you wanted?"

"Yes. Are you sure about this?"

"The book doesn't tell lies lady!"

"Is there anything else that you remember about the woman? Was she tall, short, what was her build like?"

Every question she asked would increase the amount of money that she would have to pay to the owners of the motel. This information was after all extra from what she had asked them for.

"Not sure – can't recall the details so well anymore." This was another way of forcing the price up!

"Anything would help. It's really important. You see she went missing and her family is also trying to trace her – it has taken time but now we might also be able to assist them. Anything would really help!"

"Well, she was nothing special. She had medium build, light red hair, if I recall. She might have had a slight limp. I'm not sure. Anymore."

Michelle was struggling to keep herself under control. Her fingernails would soon draw blood.

"Thank you this has been very helpful. Please keep the guest book safe – I am sure that her family would like to see this entry."

Michelle took a photograph of the entry in the guest book.

"I hope that this covers the cost of the unpaid room and other expenses that you might have incurred," Michelle handed them $300 dollars – she could not spare more out of her own bank account.

The beast looked up from the TV and his hand tried to grab the money. He was not fast enough. Barb took it first.

"Thank you very much for your assistance. Good bye!"

As she was walking out Barb said, "There is one more thing that I remember."

Michelle listened, said thank you again and then just made it back to her car. She felt like passing out. She drove directly to a coffee shop not five minutes away. Before she walked into the shop for a large black coffee with two sugars she took another photograph.

Chapter 42

Michelle spent two days preparing her notes and compiling a dossier. She kept checking and rechecking her information. It had to be correct before she shared it with anyone. She was delayed in doing so by two days because she had prior arrangements with the law firm that she was assisting. Besides, she needed to make back the $300 that she had just spent.

"Hello Professor Lombardi speaking."

"Hello professor, Michelle Loren here."

"Oh, hello Michelle. How are you?"

"Good." She did not ask him how he was. She was too much on edge to waste time. "I need to see you as soon as possible."

"Is anything wrong? Do you want to come over this afternoon?"

"No now – can I come over now?"

Within thirty minutes she walked to Professor Lombardi's office.

"Michelle, are you alright? You sounded upset!"

For the next hour she slowly walked the professor through her initial research and how she had stumbled upon the discrepancies in the x-ray dates for Kathleen

Macey. Then she built her case further on the information about another x-ray of the remains of Kathleen. The x-ray had shown a small plate that had been inserted into the ankle of the deceased. Upon investigation, it appeared as if the ankle might have been weak at birth. The surgery was most likely conducted before the child turned five years old.

"Professor, Kathleen Macey never had surgery to her ankle as a child!"

"How do you know this?"

"I traced her back to the town of Vale in Oregon where she was born. I spoke with the Administrators at the hospital. Being a small town, they knew of Kathleen. They confirmed that she had never had issues with her ankles and had not required surgery as a child – not in Vale or anywhere else."

"Are you sure?"

"Absolutely!"

"So what are you saying?"

Michelle then informed the professor of her discovery of an unpaid bill at a local motel. The dates were a match to the date that Kathleen was burnt to death.

"I confirmed the information with the owners of the motel who had lodged the complaint with the police. Here's a photograph that I took of the motel guest book." She handed the photograph to the professor.

"There's more. The guest was Connie Warner. I traced her back to her hometown in Georgia. She had set off to hitchhike across the west coast of the States. She kept in regular contact with her family. She telephoned them the morning that she went missing. They told me that Connie always used to call from a Pay Phone and then quickly say "hi" to confirm that she was fine. She told them that she must have eaten something hard the night before and that she was in some pain in her mouth. They suggested that she have it seen to.

"They never heard from her again. She was reported missing. She had given her family the name of the motel where she was staying in LA but when the police checked it out, the owners said that she had skipped without paying. The case went cold."

"You found out all of this?"

"Yes, but there is more – Connie broke her ankle as a child and she had surgery to insert a small plate to correct the break. The surgery was not a complete success and she had a slight limp."

If the professor had thought that he had heard everything, he was very wrong, there was still more to come.

"Sir, I believe that Tony Macey was set up. It was not his wife that died in the fire, it was Connie Warner."

"Wait! Before you jump to that conclusion you told me that Kathleen's personal journal mentioned that Tony had beaten her on several occasions and that he had treated her badly in public and said that he wanted to burn her alive. How do you explain that?"

"I'm not too sure – I have an idea but before I put it forward let me say this – when she had a black eye she went out in public – to her hairdresser – so that people could see her damaged face. The entry about her injured arm tied in with her going to see her bank manager – witnesses to her injuries. And with the case of her damaged arm – well, no one could actually see if there was in fact any injury at all. I believe that they were staged to build up evidence against her husband."

Professor Lombardi sat and looked at her. He was dumbfounded but he did not want to further interrupt the case that was being laid before him.

"Professor, I believe that Kathleen must have had an accomplice. It is obvious – someone either assisted her capture Connie or the accomplice abducted Connie. I believe that Kathleen placed the gasoline and gas cylinder in her own car. I believe that she met her partner on the road where she quickly changed Connie into her clothes and jewelry and then set the vehicle on fire. They escaped but not before Kathleen dressed as Connie went to the motel and removed all of the items from the room. This would make it appear as if Connie had skipped without paying her bill. It worked perfectly. Connie simply disappeared. But there was no way for the killers to know that Connie had a plate inserted in her foot."

"Ok, then tell me about the ring and jewelry found on Kathleen's body?"

"Simple. Kathleen took off her ring and necklace and placed them on the body of Connie. It was just another way of confirming that it was the remains of Kathleen in the car."

"You said that she must have had an accomplice. I agree with that completely – the evidence points to it. But how did they track down someone like Connie so that they could swap out the bodies?"

"They didn't find Connie – she found the accomplice!"

"What? Connie wanted to die!"

"No! That I could not work out either. But the Barb – the wife from the motel – said something as I was walking out of the motel. She said that Connie had said to them that she must have eaten something the night before and her mouth was sore. She asked where she could get some medical attention. They gave her the address and called a cab for her. I was very lucky in that the cab drivers in that area have worked there for years. I found the cabbie that took her there – I was amazed that after all these years that he remembered the ride. She paid and asked him to wait. After thirty minutes or so he was called for a pick up so he drove away."

"Away from where?"

"Connie went to see a doctor. I believe that he is the accomplice. I believe that he saw Connie and realized just how much she looked like Kathleen Macey. I believe that he drugged her and kept her alive until he and Kathleen placed her inside of the vehicle before they set it on fire.

When I left the motel I asked Barb where the nearest coffee shop was. It was just a short ride away. When I stopped and was about to walk into the coffee shop I looked up at the signs on the big board outside. There was a sign, which read "Doctor Webster Family Dentist."

"Tony Macey had been a patient of Doctor Webster since before he became a star. That is why they had a dentist in not such a great part of town".

Michelle looked at the professor and said.

"Doctor Dick Webster was the family dentist to both Tony and Kathleen."

"What! I can't keep up. What are you saying – that the dentist and Kathleen set the whole thing up? Can we get to the dentist to have him detained while we check this out? – And, wait! Kathleen was identified from her dental records – how does that add up?"

"I believe that when Connie came into the dental office with her sore mouth that Doctor Webster saw the opportunity that maybe he and Kathleen had been looking for. Connie had almost the same build as Kathleen and similar colored hair. I believe that he made contact with Kathleen while Connie was still waiting for treatment. If Doctor Webster and Kathleen were formulating a plan for her to disappear, then one had just presented itself. They must have agreed to carry it out right away. The dentist then told his staff that it was late and that they could go home – he would treat Connie.

I believe that he put her to sleep and took an x-ray of her mouth but he put Kathleen's name onto the title of the x-ray – the x-ray that would be used as evidence in the trial of Tony Macey.

As for contacting Doctor Webster well, unfortunately we can't right now. Doctor Webster sold his practice a year later and moved. Mary, the receptionist at the dental office told me that she was surprised when he announced that he was selling and moving out of the State. I believe that he moved and linked up with Kathleen Macey."

"Ok, before we make that assumption how would Kathleen benefit from her own death? Would she not want the payout from any life policies that Tony Macey might have held?"

"I thought about that too – but I think that it might have raised too many suspicions if Tony Macey – a celebrity – had died. No, I believe that with Tony's known addictions and threatening of his wife that Kathleen had to stage her own death. She would be rid of her husband and could move on."

"Without any funds of her own? And even assuming that she linked up with Doctor Webster after the staged murder?"

"But she did have funds! She was previously married. When her first husband died he left her a small amount of money – about $40,000 at the time if my research proves to be accurate. But that is obviously not enough money to stage a murder for or to start again. I discovered that there was some rumblings about the funds held in the Fan Club that Kathleen operated on behalf of her husband. I believe that further audit of these accounts might prove that she was draining cash out of this portion of Tony's empire. Kathleen basically operated the Fan Club by herself.

I also had an informal discussion with – well, let's say some contacts that I know" Michelle just smiled at the professor.

She continued.

"Kathleen was a spender. She spent Tony's money like water. I believe that we might find that she was drawing the sums that she was from their accounts and hoarding the funds somewhere. My suspicion is that it would be in cash so as not to raise any eyebrows from her bank or other financial intuitions regarding large deposits that she might make from time to time.

I think that she had hoarded enough funds in order to walk away with several hundred thousand dollars in cash – not a fortune, but enough to start a new life with the dentist."

Professor Lombardi sat with his hands held across his chest. He was deeply considering what to do with the information, facts, evidence and conjecture that had been laid before him. Michelle had trusted him with this information. The question was what to do with it. He knew that if he did not take action on it then Michelle would anyway.

"I'm not sure how to handle this. I don't want the university to become involved in a case such as this – by you coming to see me I suppose that the university is involved. I can't pretend that I do not know anything about this."

For an instant Michelle thought that he was going to ask her to drop the investigation and maybe even to change the topic of her dissertation for her PhD.

It took the professor another minute or so to sit in silence and then he said, "You are absolutely sure about the facts – not the conjecture – just the facts that you have?"

"Yes professor, I am."

"You know that this could blow up in your face if it is proven to be wrong?"

"Yes." Then she smiled at him, "but I still would have a long life trying to redeem myself if the evidence did collapse! And I would also know that I did the right thing."

Professor Lombardi picked up the telephone. He arranged for a meeting to take place with the Dean of the Faculty and the university

President. It was not an easy meeting to arrange when people are busy with their university lives. The meeting did take place.

Another meeting then followed it with the District Attorney and his senior staff and then with members of the police department. Very confidential investigations took place – including the seizing of the guest book from the motel and medical records of Kathleen and Connie. At the same time the police tried to track down the whereabouts of Kathleen and Doctor Webster but that was proving to be difficult. The FBI was briefed on the case.

It took over a year before the decision was made to release Tony Macey from prison. When he was released he was whisked away to a private location where he would spend time re-acclimatizing to life outside of prison. He spent time in a rented house in the mountains that he loved. He loved to be near trees. His bank accounts were unfrozen.

He had spent over eighteen years in prison for a crime that he did not commit. During the years that he had spent in his second prison location, he had sat and written dozens, if not hundreds of songs. It had kept his mind active. His passion for carpentry, history and song writing had really been the three pillars that had kept him interested in life. Unfortunately his facial features had deteriorated over the years. The beatings to his face that he had taken at the hands of Snake and then Knuckles had weakened his one cheekbone. With the effects of his self-inflicted burns the facial structure on the one side of his face had begun to slide. He had undergone surgery and a steel plate was inserted into his right cheekbone. He was not a pretty sight to look at.

He had always pleaded that he had not murdered his wife. Does one forgive over such a long time period or does one seek revenge?

Chapter 43

Tony Macey had never met privately with Michelle Loren. His release from prison was a direct result of her investigation. It was about three months after his release that, through his lawyer, contact was made with Michelle and he invited her to dinner in LA. He was coming into the city for a TV interview and he thought that he would like to thank her personally. They had met just before his release from prison but they had not really spoken at length.

"Thank you for meeting with me." He said as she sat down at the table in the restaurant.

"My pleasure Mr. Macey – thank you for inviting me!"

Tony wore a fashionable hoody, which hid his ears, his neck and part of his face.

"Please excuse my appearance. I'm not a work of art!"

Michelle just nodded.

Tony asked her about the progress with her doctorate.

"I should get it done within a year or two – I'm slightly changing the topic of my dissertation."

"Not because of me I hope!"

"Well, actually yes. I had to sanitize some of the information. I could not put that information into the public domain – I thought it best – and the police department strongly advised me to!"

"To protect those that provided you with the information."

"Yes. We did not want any possible retribution."

Tony asked her to repeat the information that had led her to believe that he had been set up. She spoke almost non-stop throughout dinner, only being interrupted when they ordered their meal and dessert and coffee afterwards. She had red wine and he ordered mineral water.

When she was finished he said, "The thing that I could not remember was how Kathleen almost copied exactly the plan that I had to murder her."

Michelle had warmed to Tony over dinner, but this comment sent chills up and down her spine. She might not be sitting in front of a murderer but she was listening to a man saying that he had planned to set his wife on fire and see her die in agony. Her opinion of Tony changed from warm to cold in a second. She could not leave the dinner table – she would have to hear him out.

"I thought that I wanted to get rid of my wife. I think that deep down I have always had a fetish with fire. I was a falling star, addicted to booze and pills – and not a very nice person to be around – in fact I was a complete piece of crap – excuse the language – at thirty-something I was throwing my life away – as you most likely know." His smile was weak – almost an acknowledgement of his failings.

"I suspected that she was cheating on me – I really didn't care – but I was beginning to hate her. Maybe "hate" turned me to fire. That was my way of taming the demons inside of me. But the point is that I did plan to burn her to death – I cannot deny that.

As I said, I could not understand that the way that Kathleen actually died was just how I had planned for it to happen – well, not exactly the same but my idea was the same. I was going to make sure that a fire started in her car while she was driving. I purchased small cans and put gasoline in them. I stored them in the garage. In my blurred state of mind I thought that I would wait for an opportunity and then I would act. Most likely I would have fallen over trying to do it!"

Tony's attempt at humor had failed. Michelle just looked back at him.

He continued.

"Then it happened – she burnt to death in her car – in the sports car that I bought for her. When the police came to tell me what had happened I remember that I was sad – sad but I also felt cheated. I never got to carry out my plan."

Michelle was turning very pale. She really did not want to be seated across from someone – anyone – who was telling you how that wanted to murder his or her partner.

"I'm sorry if I'm making you uncomfortable but I have a point to my story."

Michelle nodded – very reluctantly.

"I kept the plan to myself. I could never understand the co-incidence of my plan and then of the events of Kathleen's death. Your investigation finally brought my memory back."

"How?"

"When I read the report that was based on your investigation I remembered, after all these years, I remembered. I had gone to my dentist to have a chip on my tooth fixed. I was drunk again. I then told my old buddy Dick Webster about my plan to murder my wife – and how I was going to do it. Maybe I was just babbling at the time but only one other person now knew of my plan. He was the only one that I told – and now, after all of this time, I realized that he was the one that my wife was seeing behind my back. I shared my plan to kill my wife with her lover!

He must have shared the information with Kathleen. They then plotted against me. Their plan fell into place when Connie walked into Dick's surgery. They then had to act quickly. Kathleen must have checked if there was gasoline in my garage at home – and she took the gas cylinder. We know what happened. I would then be out of the way and they could be together – even if she was technically dead!"

Tony remembered, too, the day that he had left home at the age of sixteen. Bill McKinzie had told him that he knew of Anthony's plan to try to kill him with fire. Anthony had told the guy at the gas station that his Dad's truck had run out of gas. Bill had found out about this when he was next at the gas station. Bill had warned him that day not to share his plans with anyone – he had not learned his lesson. By sharing his plan with Dick Webster, he had given away many years of his adult life.

"Michelle I wanted to thank you personally for getting me out of prison. I have made many mistakes in my life."

As the evening wound down Tony asked, "Any news on the FBI tracking down Dick and Kathleen?"

"I really don't know. I would assume that they are working on the case but I have no idea what they are doing. My investigation for my doctorate ended with you." She smiled at him.

"What are you going to do now?" she asked him.

"I completed a BA in history while in prison. I would like to travel across the States and see things that I studied during my degree."

The evening ended on a better note by talking about the era when Tony was so famous and some of his experiences from around the world. At the end of the evening she called a cab and he shook her hand.

He thanked her again for the work that she had done which lead to his release from prison.

He then walked back to his rented car and drove to his hotel.

Many things happened over the next two years but they did see each other again. Michelle obtained her doctorate.

Chapter 44

"What are you telling me? I'm almost broke?"

Tony's accountant responded, "No, you are not broke – you just do not have the amount of money that you had thought."

"And what is that supposed to mean?"

"Let me try to explain. When you went to prison your net worth was down to $500,000 – you had spent well over 1 million in the two years prior to your conviction. Your home was sold and your 50% interest in the bar and grill place in Oregon was put under a management team. There have been small profits or losses from that place each year – personally I think that they have been ripping you blind but we could never prove it."

"That place has got a name you know!"

"Yes, of course, I'm sorry. Anyway there has not been any real income from that source over the last fifteen years. If you recall, the other joint owners offered to buy you out some years ago – a minimal offer that you turned down.

Your cash and other liquid assets were placed in safe interest- bearing accounts. So they have not moved by much each year."

"Then what's the issue?"

"Both our firm of accountants and your lawyers were permitted – as per your written approval and standard practice – to draw a management fee off the interest and dividends earned each year. For us this covered your annual returns to the IRS and for the lawyers their fees in holding your investments in trust."

Tony thought for a while. *"So these bastards were slowly bleeding me dry!"*

"Tony, if you are thinking that we stole from you then you are incorrect – we only took fees due to us – nothing more".

"You read my thoughts!"

"No, just your facial expression!"

"OK, so what do I have in cash?"

"You still have about $400,000 – then on top of that you will be receiving compensation from the State for wrongful arrest and imprisonment. You will be entitled to $100 per day for wrongful imprisonment. If that should come through then it would amount to about $650,000 – not a great sum!"

"I thought that my lawyer was going to sue them and others for several million dollars – what happened to that amount?"

"Yes, that's correct. Fred is asking for a large sum - but I doubt if he will get anything near that amount."

"So, let's say that I get the $650,000 which would mean that I would have about a million to start a new life in my early fifties! How long would that last?"

"It's not a small sum but you would still have to be careful. Once you've purchased a house, furniture and a vehicle you would have to keep a tight budget for the rest of your life!"

Tony Macey had money in the bank but not enough that he could spend like he used to in the young, wild days!

SUV's had become the fashionable vehicle to drive since Tony had been sent to prison and he decided that he wanted just such a vehicle. First he had to apply for a new driver's license and that was delayed until it was confirmed that he was legitimately released from jail. As if the authorities did not know – the whole episode had been extensively covered in the California media.

The day that he test drove and decided upon a Ford SUV he came face-to-face with the reality of being an ex-convict.

"And how will you be paying for the vehicle Mr. Macey?"

He toned downed the sarcasm, "Certified check! Give me the total cost and I will come into tomorrow and pay the amount! I'm sure that would suit you!"

"You will need to give us a deposit today so that we hold the vehicle for you and do the required paperwork – that would be $500." Tony opened up his wallet and counted out the five hundred. "Now be a good man and give me a receipt!"

The following day the salesperson was friendlier as a sale had now been made. "Thank you for your business Mr. Macey! There is a box on the back seat of your vehicle with car polish, touch-up paint, clothes and a bottle of champagne. The tank is also full. Your first two services for the vehicle are free – let us know if there is anything else that we can do for you!"

Tony drove away in his blue Ford. He could have got a discount on a red one but that would have constantly reminded him of Kathleen's red Audi A4 that he purchased for her. Some memories will not go away.

Instead of buying a house, Tony rented an apartment. He liked the fact that it was furnished and that the building had front desk security.

Besides, he wanted to travel the country. Once some of his plans were in place he could give notice on the apartment and drive away.

There were a number of places in the USA that Tony genuinely wanted to visit. Until recently he had thought that he might only be able to visit some of them at the end of his prison sentence. He had less than seven years to go before the twenty-five year sentence would have been over. He would have been in his late fifty's by then and he did not know what his health would be like. The money that he earned in prison had primarily gone to reading materials. The cost of taking his degree in history had come out of his own funds.

While still making his plans and investigating where he wanted to go first, he heard the news about the settlement that his lawyer, had been seeking,

He sat in front of Fred and his senior staff.

"Tony, thank you for coming in. We have received notification of the settlement figure in your case. As you know, based on your length of stay in prison and applying the State's standard formulae of $100 per day, the baseline claim would have been approximately $650,000. We pursued other litigation avenues and in total the amount that we sought as compensation was $12,650,000."

Tony looked at Fred. He anticipated the minimum payout.

"We received an offer that combines all of the parties that we sued on your behalf." Fred opened up a letter that lay on the desk in the boardroom table.

Fred started reading the letter.

"Cut the crap – give the bad news?"

Fred looked at him and said, "Ok, I'll cut the legal crap!"

He smiled.

"Tony this letter offers you a total amount in full and final settlement of $12.65 million – exactly the amount that we asked for!"

It took Tony a few seconds to register what he had just heard.

"Tony do you understand what I just said – we got the whole amount – no argument! We did it!"

"Holy shit!" was about all that Tony Macey could say. "Holy shit!"

"Congratulations my friend – you deserve every penny!"

After everyone had shaken hands and hugged – which was very un-lawyer like – Tony asked, "What now?"

"If you accept the offer then you sign the letter confirming that this settlement is full and final. We then return it to the consortium of lawyers' that represent the various parties. If things then go according to plan we will have your check within the week."

"Crap!"

"What's wrong?" asked Fred.

"I have a brand new Ford – anyone want to buy it from me?"

Tony kept the vehicle. The following week he was handed a check.

Several weeks earlier, over dinner with Michelle Loren, he had casually asked her if the FBI had made any progress in locating the whereabouts of Dick Webster and

Kathleen. She had said that she did not know – which was the truth. The FBI would not make public any information that they might have. It had still been worthwhile asking the question. Tony wanted to travel and see places around the country. This is what he had told everyone and it was the truth. The other reason was that he was determined to track down his friend the dentist and his un-dead wife.

Chapter 45

The computer age had greatly accelerated during the time that Tony had been in prison. Prison services had some basic equipment but Tony had shunned it completely. Now he realized that not only did he have no knowledge of personal computers but also that he needed one. If he were to conduct his research into the potential whereabouts of Dick and Kathleen then he would need to learn about the Internet. He did not really know what the word meant or what it was.

"Can I be of any help?" asked the assistant in the computer store.

"I would like to buy a home computer."

"Any particular make or model?"

"No idea!"

"What size memory do you require for the computer?"

"What's that?"

The assistant looked at the man standing in front him – he was wearing a hoody and dark glasses. *"Where do you come from - the Middle Ages?"* He thought to himself.

"Why don't you tell us what your requirements are and then we can look at some different options for you?"

The selling process was a long one! The assistant had to either nurse Tony through the various concepts or repeat himself several times. Tony believed that she was speaking in a foreign language most of the time.

Finally Tony walked out of the store with a trolley filled with a desktop computer, a printer, photocopier, a scanner and various other items that he most likely did not require. The assistant made a good commission that day.

In the apartment Tony opened up the various boxes and then went into a middle-age stage fright, as he had absolutely no idea what to do next. Not even a coffee could settle him down. He then looked up computer support businesses in his area. The next morning a young man came by to connect everything up – "Sir, you have no Internet dial-up facility in your apartment!"

The young man looked at Tony with a blank expression on his face.

The placing of a one hundred dollar note in front of the technician helped resolve the issue with the young man making the necessary telephone calls and arranged for a service to be provided. The same young man then came back and connected everything and was about to leave when Tony asked him, "Any idea where I could get lessons on this thing and how to search things on the Internet?"

"Yes sir, we provide that service too."

Chapter 46

Tony was not trained in conducting any type of research. He was a simple man. He had completed his high school diploma in his mid-thirties while he was in prison. He then obtained his carpentry certification and his history degree while serving his sentence. But all that he had ever really done was to write songs and sing.

Nevertheless he broke down his search for Dick and Kathleen into a number of categories: what he knew about the two people in question, the research of Michelle Loren, further pursuing her leads and then a broad category of where they might have gone. Where to start was the million-dollar question.

He bought dozens of boxes and files and labeled them. As he worked with a piece of information he would decide which box it had to go into. He was smart enough to make a master list on which he noted all of the things that he examined. He would then photocopy and number label the item and place it into a box.

Once a week, when the cleaner came in he wondered what she thought of the guy that rented an upscale large apartment, lived alone, wore a hoody all of the time and was surrounded with boxes in every room. He told her that he was writing a book on the history of the USA. Whether she believed him or not did not really matter.

Several weeks into the project he was not really any further ahead.

He had speculated that Dick had linked up with Kathleen – but where?

Kathleen was from a small town and she had liked that life style. But in a small town people talk and maybe someone would ask the wrong questions of two new people coming to town – even if not at the same time. Tony thought that somewhere in a larger city might have been more appealing – somewhere where Dick could set up a practice.

But that could be in countless different places in the country.

Tony compiled a list of possible towns and cities. He put stars next to a number of places that were on the eastern and western coastlines. Kathleen loved open spaces and maybe that would be where she wanted to start her new life.

Even reading Michelle's research he found no obvious lead on where to focus his research.

The weeks passed by and he was beginning to fear that he could not even begin his journey – his quest. Was this just going to be a pointless exercise?

"The clues must lie with people and not places. If I could find a person then it could direct me towards a place. But which person could be the starting point? Dick said that he wanted to move away – take a break from a big city. He told people that he was not sure where he would settle – that could have just been a cover up – he knew exactly where he was going".

Tony would talk to himself often during his research.

Then a thought came to mind. Who was close to Dick and saw him every day? Only one name came to mind. Mary, Dick's long serving receptionist. But should he visit or telephone her and what if she knew where Dick really was and tipped him off. That could spoil everything for him. He decided to hold back on contacting Mary – the risk to his plan was too high.

Then he thought. *"If Dick wanted to set up a practice he would have to prove that he was a dentist in good standing. The only way that he could obtain a license and open a practice was if he received some documentation from the dental association that he was a member of in LA."*

Tony first searched online for a listing of dentists in California. Once he found a master list, he drilled down until he found the breakdown for southern California and LA in particular. Although Dick probably left the State there should still be a record of him on the site. As expected there was. "Doctor Richard G. Webster, Family dentist."

There was a notification that Doctor Webster was no longer a member of his professional association - whereabouts unknown after the practice had been sold. A dead-end!

Tony then looked up the telephone number for the dental association that Dick would have been a member of.

"Hello, my name is Anthony McKinzie, I have been out of the country for some time and I would like to try and find the dentist that I used to visit as a client. I visited his old office location but I was told that he had moved. Could anyone assist me?"

When he was asked to hold he expected that he would not receive an answer to his question.

"Yes sir, I see that Doctor Webster moved to Washington State. There is a notation on file that we provided information on his good standing with our association. Unfortunately I am not permitted to provide you with any further information. I hope that this helps you to locate your friend!"

Tony's hand was shaking as he put down the telephone. He had his first lead. Dick had moved to Washington State. As he sat and thought about it, the location made sense because he had suspected somewhere near open spaces – and this was close enough to Kathleen's northwest upbringing. Her family had mourned her loss in a car fire many years before so they would not even expect in their wildest dreams that she was living not that far from her birth home in Oregon.

He did an Internet search for dentists in Washington State. He had written up a list of towns and cities in descending order of population of towns and cities. First on the list was Seattle and then moving down.

"BINGO!"

"Doctor Richard G Webster, Family Dentist, Bellevue."

Tony wrote down the address and telephone number of the dental practice.

With a very shaky hand he telephoned the number of the dental office.

"Hello dental office, how may I assist you?"

"Is that the office of Doctor Richard Webster?"

"Yes it is, how may I help you?"

There was no reply. The caller had hung up.

Now that he had a location for Dick Webster, Tony did not know what to do. Did this mean that Kathleen was in Bellevue too?

Tony felt that sensation in his stomach again. He had not felt it for a very long time. He had a significant choice to make, to leave his search right here and now or to pursue those that had set him up for murder and ruined his life – and to take revenge.

He had no one to discuss this with.

He really had no one at all.

He walked to his bedroom. There was a small box on a shelf in his closet. He took it down and sat on his bed. He removed two photographs from the box. The one was of him holding the hand of his mother. He hardly paid any attention to the second photograph.

He could not remember his mother. He could remember Big Gus – who had loved him like a son. But even those memories of his brief nine months at the diner and bar were beginning to fade. He looked again at his wedding photograph.

The next morning he gave two weeks' notice on his apartment. He set off for Seattle.

Chapter 47

All of the way driving up highway 101 along the coast of California he thought of what he would do when he reached Seattle. Would he find Dick and Kathleen and confront them face-to-face about what they did to him? Would he find a way to hurt them? Would he see them together and then decide that he had enough and just turn around and drive back to LA?

Each of the options took up many hours of his thoughts as he travelled. Even when he stopped and overnighted twice on the way he did not think of anything else! He did remember people looking at him with his hoody on and thinking to themselves,

"Who is this weirdo? What a creepy looking person!"

It was these looks that finally pushed Tony on the path that he would follow. Dick and Kathleen would have to die before he could be released from this hell.

"This apartment will be fine. Could I rent it for a month?"

The furnished apartment building was north of the city near the intersection of highways 5 and the 520. The 520 led off to the east to the 405 and then south to Bellevue.

His first drive to Bellevue was on a Sunday. He thought that he could locate the dental office without too many people around. He also wanted to just generally check out the town and entry and exit roads. His only stop was to purchase a street map at a convenience store. The store attendant hardly looked up when he served Tony.

The security cameras in the store kept a watchful eye on regulars and strangers alike. Tony had lived many years with cameras watching him so he was aware of what the little black glass bulbs were on the ceiling. He never faced the cameras directly.

Once he was connected to the Internet again, he started a search – this time he was looking for marriage records in the town of Bellevue. It did not take him long to find what he was looking for – the marriage of Doctor Richard Webster to Catherine McKay. "She must have changed her name", he thought. Just a subtle change but that is all that is required to become someone else. There is not too much a difference between being called "Kathy" or "Cathy".

Locating where they lived proved to be more of a problem. They were not listed in the local telephone directory. Being a doctor, this was not unexpected. Tony would have to be careful in making any enquiries as to their home address. Any police investigation after an incident could bring in a number of leads if someone had been snooping around town.

In order to complete his mission he would have to strike them both at the same time and then disappear as quickly as possible. That would be difficult because as he could not skip out early on his apartment rental – even if he was based in Seattle, the police could possibly pick up on his moving out in the middle of a lease.

"You need a good plan! A plan that hits quickly, silently and is successful!"

Without finding a home location he could not even begin to devise a plan. What he did think through was that he wanted to act on the day that he moved out of his apartment. He would then drive to Bellevue and carry out whatever plan he had and then turn and start driving somewhere south.

But he still had nothing to work on.

Twice he drove in Bellevue and parked in a variety of parking lots at malls hoping that he might see Kathleen. But he did not. He decided not to hang around the dental office in case Dick saw him first. Time was running out and he had nothing to work with.

On his third visit he was sitting in his SUV outside of a strip mall when two women walked towards him with their fully loaded trolleys of groceries. Tony's quick glance at them confirmed that neither one was Kathleen. The windows of the SUV were open and, as the women started to offload their groceries into the car that was parked next to him he overheard the conversation.

"Can you believe that it is fifteen years since he died? My husband was commenting on it last night. What a terrible thing to have happened."

"Yes. We read the article in The Mirror on the weekend. It seems like yesterday that it happened. What a freak thing – dying while out camping with your wife."

"He was our dentist. Fairly new to town and just married for a few years when he died so suddenly."

Tony's ears pricked up *"He was our dentist. Fairly new to town and just married a few years when he died while out camping with his wife."*

The one woman was about to climb into the car next to his SUV. Without thinking he asked, "Excuse me, I overheard you talking of someone dying. Do you mind if I ask who that was?"

She turned and looked at him. "Oh you must be new to town. Everyone from here knows what happened. It was Doctor Dick Webster. He died when he was out camping with his wife. It was such a shock to us all.

She left town soon after it happened." The women got into the car and drove away.

Tony had severe chills running up and down his spine.

Dick Webster was dead.

It happened fifteen years ago.

When Kathleen had come to his concert all of those years ago she had casually mentioned that she had married the son of the man in Vale who owned the hardware store. When he had asked her what had happened to her husband she said that they were out camping and he died in an accident.

This was too much of a coincidence to believe. Could it be Kathleen? Married three times and numbers one and three both died while they were out camping with her! And she had set up number two to go to jail for twenty-five years.

He sat for some time in his SUV just thinking back as far as he could remember about Kathleen. He thought of their meeting up all of those years after he had left home. He now no longer thought that she just wanted to say "hello" again. Now he believed that she had planned the whole thing – even their marriage.

Now he believed that she could be a multiple murderer. Had she used Dick just as she had used him?

It was early afternoon and he asked directions to the offices of The Mirror – the local town newspaper. He asked if he could check on some old records.

There he found a number of interesting articles.

There was the announcement of the opening of a new dental practice in town.

Sometime later he found the engagement announcement of Doctor Dick Webster to Catherine McKay. He also saw their wedding photo.

Then he found the death notice of Doctor Webster.

However, there was something that he could not understand. When he had telephoned the dental practice while he was still in LA, the receptionist had confirmed that it was the office of Doctor Dick Webster.

His next stop was at the dental office.

"Hello, sorry to worry you. A few weeks back I telephoned and asked if these were the offices of Doctor Webster – and you said "yes" – unfortunately the call was disconnected and we never did complete our conversation." He lied.

"Oh, I remember that. You asked if this was Doctor Webster's office. When I said, "Yes" I was going to add that Doctor Webster was no longer with us – he passed away you know – but he had a partner, Doctor Ristow. The name of the practice was Doctors Webster and Ristow, but before I could provide you with the information the line went dead."

"Did you know Doctor Webster?"

"Yes. He was my dentist many years ago and I just wanted to make contact with him. I did not know that he had passed away."

"He met his wife here. She came in one day asking if the doctor was taking new patients. It was just after he had arrived in town. They seemed to hit it off right away – not long after that they became engaged and were married. It was so sad that he died just a few years after they were married."

Chapter 48

"Every time that I make plans, I get screwed!" Tony was thinking aloud. "The only thing that you ever were good at was singing – and then you screwed that up too".

He had driven back to his apartment near Seattle and ordered in a large pizza. That was two days ago. He had hardly eaten since. He had drifted in and out of self-remorse, failure, and thoughts of being cheated of his kill – on more than one occasion.

He had not shaved or washed in several days. When the door opened in the afternoon and the cleaner walked in, she stopped dead and looked at him sitting on the armchair. He did not have his hoody on and his disfigured head and face was fully exposed. She took one look at him and screamed and ran out of the apartment. He never saw her again. Tony broke out into uncontrollable laughter. He laughed so hard that he began to cry. Then the laughter stopped and he just cried.

He awoke as the sun was streaming through the window. He had fallen asleep in an upright position in the chair and as he stood up his back and neck hurt. He looked at the mess in the living room. He cleaned up the room and then the kitchen. He telephoned the service cleaning company and apologized for scaring the cleaner. He told them to pay her for the visit. He also gave notice to stop the service.

He then went to the bathroom, shaved and took a long hot shower. Dressed only in a towel he made himself breakfast. He could not recall when last he had eaten – maybe two nights ago. He was not a great cook but the taste did not matter. The smell of burnt toast soon was expelled from the apartment when he opened a window.

"What now? What are you going to do now?"

He poured himself another cup of coffee and went to stand at the living room window. He seemed set apart from everyone outside. Maybe he was different.

"Time to take stock old buddy!" he said to himself.

He sat at the desk in the bedroom and started doodling. There was no purpose; he was just trying to think.

When next he realized it, his coffee was cold.

"Oh Kathleen." He corrected himself, "Kathy or Cathy – whatever your name is now – where are you now?"

Then he had another thought.

"I wonder what the FBI knows? Are they on top of this? Or are they not even showing any interest? Would I be alone if I continued to pursue her?

Where did you run to this time? Where would you go? And most of all, do I still want to catch up with you?"

He dressed and covered up his head again. He needed some fresh air. He stood for a short while outside of the apartment block. There was a grocery store and deli not too far from where the apartment was located. A walk would do him good.

He entered the store and was walking around looking if there was anything that he wanted to buy for dinner. He walked up and down the aisles looking at various things. He did not really pay any attention to the fact that there was no one around him. He was absorbed in shopping. After the confines of prison, seeing so many different things on the shelves was always of interest to him. He also thought back to when he used to pick up the money left for him by Bill McKinzie and how he used to shop for himself.

He did not see the two police officers slowly walking towards him. Nor did he notice that the other end of the aisle had been blocked with a shopping cart.

"OK, put the basket down and put your hands above your head!"

He looked up and saw a firearm pointed directly at his head.

"What the hell is this?"

"Put your arms above you head."

"I have not done anything. What is going on?"

He felt strong arms grab his hands and force them behind his back. He was turned around to face the police officers.

"What the hell is going on? Let me go!"

The one police officer took Tony's dark hoody and removed it. Tony stood there with his head and face showing.

"Sorry – we were called in because you looked suspicious."

He looked at them. "You stupid people – are you afraid of something? What sort of world do you live in?"

He walked out of the store and back to his apartment. He slammed the door shut behind him. In his rage he said, "Kathleen you did this to me! I'll never be accepted as a normal person. You bitch – I am going to find you and take my revenge – even if it takes me all of my life and even if it kills me! And I hope that it does!"

Chapter 49

Without any idea or leads on the whereabouts of Kathleen, Tony decided that he should also fulfill his desire to see parts of the States. His Ford was heavily packed with his baggage in the large trunk and his computer safely packed in boxes on the back seat of the SUV. There was no such thing as packing light when you have decided to be on the road for a while. He had packed up many of the boxes that he had used in his research and sent them back to a storage facility in Los Angeles.

After exploring some of the areas of Washington, he bypassed Oregon and drove to Montana. He spent a very relaxing month in the mountains. Then he headed down into Wyoming and cut back west to Utah. From Utah he decided to drive down to Las Vegas. He was sure that the city had changed dramatically since he performed there well over twenty-five years before. Ten shows a week and very little sleep. He was undecided if he would try to look up any old friends that might still be around.

When he reached Las Vegas, he booked into an Embassy Suite Hotel. No one at the front desk recognized the name, Anthony McKinzie.

Once based in the hotel, he took two days of just walking and exploring the Strip. With his hoody up and his dark glasses on no one even thought that he was more than another weird tourist.

His trip to the Grand Canyon was one of the items on his Bucket List. He was not sorry that he had put it onto his list – the vista was spectacular.

He tried to remember the suburb that he had visited when he had performed on the Strip. He could not remember the name. That is not until he purchased a newspaper one day and flicked through the house prices. Then he remembered – when he saw the name he remembered it well. Summerlin.

The next afternoon he drove to Summerlin. It had developed substantially since his visit there in his heyday. Where there were once open spaces, now stood shopping centers. Streets were lined with lovely homes. Although much more highly populated than before, the suburb still looked rural and peaceful. There were restaurants everywhere on the main street. Although people drove wherever they went he thought that things were close enough to walk.

He parked his SUV in an open-air parking lot. The price surprised him. Nothing in Las Vegas was cheap.

He walked around from the parking area to the front of the shopping center. After meandering for a few minutes, he took shelter from the sun in an air-conditioned coffee shop. He was sitting with his hoody up and sunglasses on and was sipping his second cup of coffee when the small tinkle chime on the door of the coffee shop sounded. Tony looked up.

He looked straight into the face of his former wife!

There was no doubt about it at all. She was a little fuller around the waist and in her face and her hair was darker than before, but it was Kathleen.

He froze in his seat. She stood facing him, not ten feet away. He could not move – even if he wanted to – his heart was racing at an abnormal rate. Then she started to walk towards him.

He tried to look away. Had she found him?

Kathleen walked right passed him and sat down just two tables away. “Same as usual?” “Yes please Sam - that would be great!”
Not even her voice had changed.

Tony decided not to move. He had waited so many years to catch up with her and now she casually walked into a coffee shop in Las Vegas and sat down near him.

The server brought her a large iced tea and a muffin.

She sat and sipped on her drink while she glanced through a magazine that was lying on the table.

Tony could not take his eyes off of her. “Thank god for my dark glasses and hoody.” He said to himself.

“Sir, another coffee?” He nodded, as he did not want to speak.

It was difficult to believe that in front of him sat a murderer.

He motioned for his check and paid while he was still sipping his coffee. He was going to follow her as soon as she left the restaurant. He had to be ready.

He was beginning to feel uncomfortable by just sitting there. Would she begin to suspect something? She clearly did not recognize him – or had she? Just then she called for Sam and asked for her check. Tony started to get ready to walk out of the coffee shop behind her. His vehicle was two minutes away and he was afraid that he might lose her once they exited the shop.

His worst fear came true. Kathleen's car was parked in the street not more than twenty feet from the coffee shop door. She walked over and in a flash drove away. Tony had no chance to follow her. In seconds she was roaring down the road in her red Audi A4 convertible.

"I have a fix on her and I am not going to let her go!"

Back in his hotel suite he checked the telephone directory but could not find a Cathy Webster listed. He telephoned the operator and was told that it was an unlisted number. They could not provide him with an address.

With his odd appearance he would be noticed if he hung around the coffee shop too often – or even in Summerlin too much. His dilemma was to try to find Kathleen without raising any suspicions.

Twice more he visited the village. He drove around the business area in the hope of seeing her red vehicle parked somewhere. He came away empty handed. Once more he went into the coffee shop – had a quick cup and then left. He did not want to leave the impression that he was loitering or waiting for someone. Again he came away empty handed. He knew that she must live in the area as he had noticed the license plate of her car as she drove away the day that he had seen her.

Tony then decided to stay away from the neighborhood for a week. It was the longest week of his life. Trying to keep busy in Las Vegas without going to shows or walking the streets is very difficult. With his appearance he also did not want to be seen and then later recognized as being in town when a major crime had been committed. He therefore also decided not to try to locate any of the people that might still be around from when he performed on the Strip.

Sometimes a break from looking for something pays dividends.

Tony had purchased a street map of the neighborhood and had decided to drive down every street in order to try to locate a red convertible. He memorized the streets that he wanted to cover on each day. He had made no notations on the map itself – just in case he was ever apprehended – the marking of streets could have looked like a detailed search pattern – which indeed it was!

Tony started down the older section of the village. That part that he and Kathleen would have visited together all those years ago. Surely it would make sense that she would try to be in an area that she liked.

As he turned his SUV into the street that led to the older part of the village, he saw a large signboard that advertised a new housing development on the opposite side from his planned route.

He decided to turn right instead of left.

His first impression of the new part of the village was just how beautifully it had been landscaped. Modern homes lined the street that he was on. Some homes were already built and occupied while other lots were still empty. He was taking in the new area and almost missed seeing Kathleen.

As he drove past a house, he saw two women standing outside talking. It was only as he drew level with them that he saw a red Audi standing in the one drive way. He forced himself to look straight ahead and keep driving. About two hundred yards up the road the development came to an end and he had no choice but to turn the vehicle around and drive past the two women again – a risk that he did not want to take. He turned the SUV around and parked. Just as he did so, he saw the women walk towards their respective homes. Kathleen's home was on a corner lot and separated from that of her neighbor by two empty lots.

Tony drove past the homes and took a mental note of the address of the home on the corner. This was a major breakthrough in the surveillance of his target.

Back in his hotel suite he studied the map of Summerlin and liked what he saw. Not only were there two empty lots next to Kathleen's corner property but also the one directly behind her was also empty.

"This is where I will get her. All alone in her home! All I need now is a plan!"

Tony purchased a number of different colored baseball caps and hoodies. It would not alter his overall appearance but it might just make him look a little different each time that he drove down into the village.

He rented a car for two days in order to avoid having his SUV spotted too often as he drove around.

Kathleen proved to be a creature of habit. By the time she pulled into the driveway and entered her home, it was pretty much dark. She lived alone and no one ever came to visit her. Tony's surveillance was very detailed. It took him three weeks to put together. Sometimes he would avoid the village for days on end and then he would drive another rental car through the streets at night.

Several weeks earlier, while on a day trip out of Vegas, he had purchased a plastic jerry can at a garage sale. It would prove to be a good investment.

He selected a Thursday evening to execute his plan. Fridays were always busy in Las Vegas and he might not be noticed if he checked out of his hotel and just slipped away.

He had rented another small car that day. He drove away from his hotel wearing a light colored hoody. Once he was away from the hotel he changed into a black hoody and black pants. He drove to Summerlin.

Within fifteen minutes he had parked the rental car behind the empty lot at the rear of Kathleen's home. He changed his shoes. He then walked up between the small trees to the empty lot and stood to check that he could not be seen in the failing light. Then he moved very quickly across the lot and onto Kathleen's property. When he reached her rear sliding door of the house, he removed his shoes. He did not want to leave any prints inside of the home - even if the prints were not from his regular shoes.

He carefully maneuvered the handle on the sliding doors and then, with a heavy push and lift of the door, it opened. He stepped inside of the house and slid the door closed behind him. He stood still while his eyes acclimatized to the half-light inside of the home. Then he moved into a position where Kathleen would not see him when she came in. He did not have long to wait – he heard the car pull into the driveway and he waited for the side door to open.

Kathleen entered her home and put a light on. After putting the parcel on the kitchen table she walked back to the front door, removed the light jacket that she was wearing and hung it up in the closet.

Then she walked through to the living room.

She did not see the blow coming. It hit her on the back of the head and she fell unconscious to the ground. Tony hit her at the back of her head with an old baseball bat that he had found on one of his drives out of town. Tony walked to the windows and drew the blinds shut. He then turned on several lights – just as Kathleen would have done. He then walked to the kitchen and carried a chair through to the living room. He lifted the still unconscious Kathleen onto the chair and tightly bound her arms and legs to the chair. He gagged her. Her head was hanging forward – she would not wake up for a while yet.

While he waited for his former wife to wake up he walked into the kitchen and unpacked the parcel that she had carried in with her. He found were everything was stored in the kitchen and packed the items away. He folded the bag and placed it in the recycling bin. No one would ever query why Kathleen had left an unopened parcel on the kitchen table. He walked into the living room and turned on the TV in order to provide some background noise.

Slowly she began to stir. Tony walked forward and placed his gloved hand over her gagged mouth.

"If you scream I will kill you now. Do you understand?"

Kathleen tried to struggle but she could not move.

"If you scream or struggle you will die now. If you co-operate, you will live."

Kathleen tried to bite the hand that was covering her mouth but he held her tightly in his grip. "I mean you no harm. If you co-operate I will not harm you. Do you understand?"

Kathleen nodded.

"Right, I am going to remove my hand from your mouth and untie the gag but if you scream you will die – do you understand?"

Kathleen nodded again.

He slowly uncovered her mouth – he then took two steps back away from her. In the darkened room she could not see who the man was.

"What do you want?" she asked.

"Information."

"Information? Who are you?"

"Kat do you not recognize your husband?"

There was silence in the room. Tony expected that she might scream but she did not. If she had he would have hit her with the bat again.

"Tony?"

"The very one! Are you glad to see me?"

"What are you doing in my home? What do you want?"

Then she said, "I had heard that you were released from prison."

"What do you want with me?", she asked.

"Do I call you "Kat", Kathy", Kathleen" or "Cathy? I'm not sure which name you go by these days!"

She ignored his question.

"What do you want?' she repeated.

"Just some answers to questions and then I will leave – you'll be rid of me!"

"Step forward so that I can be sure that it is you."

Tony stepped forward and stood right in front of her. He pulled the hoody away from his head. Even in the shallow light in the room she could see the disfigurement to his face.

"Oh yes, this is the new me. Actually I have had this new look for many years now! Do you like it? It was caused when I tried to burn myself to death in prison. You know the place that you condemned me to when you set me up for your murder."

Kathleen tried not to look at him.

"What do you want from me?"

"I told you – information. Answers to my questions! And then I will leave you alone. It is very simple, I ask you a question and you tell me the truth, then when we are done I untie you and I walk away. You will never see me again."

"What you want to know."

"That is what I wanted to hear - but if you lie you die!" The smile on his face was full of evil.

"Let's get started. You murdered your first husband – correct?"

"Are you wired?"

"No", he lifted his hoody and showed her his chest, "No wires just you and me!"

"What is it to you?"

"Well, let's just say that I have an interest in your career with men. Now answer the question. Did you murder Daniel?"

"Yes."

"Why?"

Kathleen hesitated before she answered. "You want the truth?"

"Only the truth!"

"It was because of you!"

"ME! You murdered someone for me!"

She was silent for a moment then said, "I really liked you in high school. You seemed odd – moody, even sad. I felt that you and I did not fit in with the other kids. The kids used to call us both very ugly names. I tried to talk with you several times but I couldn't get a word out of you. Do you remember our school musical?"

"Yes."

"I pushed you to try out. Do you remember?"

"Yes, I remember."

"You were really good! I could have listened to you sing all day. I tried hard to let you know that I liked you. Then you just went away. You didn't even say goodbye!"

"I left very suddenly."

"I know. It was just after you tried to burn down the fire hall – with your father inside. You tried to murder him!"

Tony had not expected to hear this. No one knew that he had planned to murder Bill McKinzie that night.

"No one knew that. How do you know?"

"I saw you set the fire hall on fire."

"You did what? No one was there – just me."

"Our musical had the last performance that night. When I got home I couldn't sleep. I was standing at my bedroom window when I saw you come out of the back door of your house – although my house was around the corner from yours I could see into your back yard – I often used to watch you just sitting out on the back step by yourself.

I thought that it was strange that you were going out so late so I decided to follow you. I tiptoed down the steps so that I didn't wake my parents. Then I grabbed a jacket and shoes and slipped out of the house. I thought that I had lost you then I saw you a block ahead of me.

I followed you to the high school and then across to the back lane. Then I saw you under the wall of the fire hall. I almost gave myself away – I stood on a branch and it broke under my foot."

Tony remembered that he had heard a loud crack, as he was getting ready to light the gasoline. He had stopped to listen but had heard no further noise.

"It was you that caused the crack?"

"Yes, I thought that you could see me as I was between the cars in the parking lot. But I pushed back into the shadow. Then I saw you start the fire and run. You ran down between the cars – if you had run just one car over you would have fallen over me."

"I saw the building catch on fire and then I ran home too."

"How does this tie in with Daniel?"

"You wanted the truth so I'll tell you."

"I didn't understand why you had set the fire. I was going to ask you – the day that I suggested that we have a soda sometime over the summer. I thought that you might want to talk about it. I wanted to help."

"Do you remember that I asked you about getting a soda?'

"Yes, that's what I took you for when we met here in Vegas."

"Go on." He asked her.

"The next week I heard your dad yelling at you. I couldn't hear what he was saying but I didn't like it when he did that. I wanted to come over and see if you were ok. I did go over the next day. Your dad came to the door – he was very drunk and used some awful language at me! I was very angry that you had gone away."

"I never knew that you cared for me!"

"You asked me if I murdered Daniel. Before I answer that question let me tell you that I knew that I needed to pick myself up out of borderline poverty. After school I tried a few things but there was not much work. I then started to see Daniel."

"You married him for money?"

"Yes. For money and security."

"Why then did you murder him?"

"I told you. I killed Daniel for you."

"I don't understand."

"I married for money – I admit that. Then one day I saw a national TV interview that you had given. You were in your mid-twenties and heading to becoming a millionaire."

"You murdered Daniel so that you could be free to come after my money!"

"Yes. At first I thought that I wanted you but I realized that it was really your money."

Neither of them spoke for a minute and then Tony said, "It was never about me – you came to Vegas to meet me and have me fall for you – you planned the whole thing. You set me up right from the beginning! You bitch!"

Kathleen did not answer. Finally she said, "I wanted you in high school – and I wanted you back after you left town. I thought that if I did something in town that it might get you to come back – and then we could get together."

"What did you do for me? What could have tempted me back to Vale?"

"I realized that you'd tried to murder your father that night at the fire hall. You failed. So I did it for you – I hated your father for your leaving town - I thought that if he was gone that you might come back.

I waited one day until your father was drunk at home – through the front window I saw him lying out cold in the living room. I then set his house on fire – I thought that you might love me for getting him out of the way – but you never came back and I hated you for it."

"You were the one who burnt my house down and murdered Bill? IT WAS YOU?"

"Yes. I did it!"

She paused. "So you see I had killed twice before I tracked you down in Las Vegas."

Then before Tony could answer she said, "Daniel left me about $40,000 in his will. Not a great deal today but a good amount of money then. I kept it mostly in cash – you thought that I was almost broke when we met in Vegas. I had some backup money."

There was another long pause then Tony asked, "How did you kill Daniel?"

"We used to go camping. I hated it but he loved camping in the middle of nowhere. I had seen your TV interview and was thinking about moving out from Daniel - but I had no money – so he would have to die."

"You say it as if it was a cold business decision."

"It was, I suppose."

She continued, "We were out camping about twenty yards from the edge of the cliff. Daniel thought that it gave us a great view of the sunsets. I was terrified. He always used to get up during the night to go pee. That night when he came back, he woke me up and said that I should check out the full moon. The more I protested the more he kept at me to see it before the clouds rolled in.

Finally I got out of my sleeping bag and followed him out. I took the flashlight. He walked in front of me and stood near the edge of the ledge. By now the clouds were covering the moon. I saw an opportunity and came up behind him and pushed him really hard. I heard him screaming as he fell to his death. I put the flashlight back inside the tent and drove to the main campgrounds. I woke the park warden and told him that Daniel must have walked out of the tent without the flashlight and misjudged the edge of this cliff in the dark. The incident was declared an accident – a very tragic accident!"

"You're evil!"

Kathleen did not answer him.

"When did you start seeing Dick Webster?"

"I can't remember – sometime around when you really were hitting the booze and pills. I went in to see Dick for a check-up and he saw that I was very upset. He suggested that if I needed a shoulder to cry on, we could talk privately. I telephoned him a few weeks later and we met. Things soon developed between us."

"You were going to use Dick to find a way to get rid of me?"

"At first he thought that we were just having a fling. I had to convince him that I loved him and that I wanted to be with him. It took a long time to persuade him that I was really in love with him."

"Were you?"

"No. I needed him – and he provided me with the love-making that you could not."

"How long had you been stealing from me?"

"You know a lot of things!"

"Now I do – then I was too drunk half of the time!"

"You admit it?"

"Yes – it took me a long time to understand that."

"So how much did you take?"

"That was a long time ago."

"I told you to tell me the truth – I have no problem in slitting your throat right now if you do not tell me the truth!"

"I took about $500,000 out of our joint account. I drew cash to buy things every month – but I was building up a nest egg. That is what I tempted Dick with – the chance to be together and have big money."

"That's not the full amount. What about the Fan Club funds that you were taking?"

"That was easy money – I ran the entire show and you trusted me! I had taken over a million dollars over the time that we were married."

"So – about 1.5 from me – you stole about 1.5 million from me."

"Close enough. Yes."

Tony was thoughtful for a while and then said, "Why did you not just murder me and get the insurance money as well?"

The answer was simple and clinical.

"That would have raised too many suspicions. Any celebrity that dies attracts the media vultures. The insurance money would have added to my stash but the risks were too high. It was better if I died."

"Very smart!"

Kathleen did not answer him.

"But you didn't know how to disappear – and then I gave Dick a plan – my plan to get rid of you!"

"Yes. But your plan was only an idea. You told Dick what you wanted to do but there was nothing behind it – just a plan to burn me alive in my car. Just a simple idea – nothing more! We had to find a way of making it not only work for us but to implicate you in my gruesome death."

"You hated me that much! You could have run away with Dick - you had the money – and you could have started over. But you had to destroy me in the process."

Kathleen looked him straight in the eye – even in the half-light he could see her face glaring at him. "You had already destroyed yourself."

He slapped her.

He thought that she would start screaming but she did not. There was blood forming on her lip where he had hit her.

She spat the blood out at him. "Coward! Hitting me while I'm tied up! You haven't changed – no guts, no backbone – you are just a weak broken man!"

For the next minute neither of them spoke.

"Why don't you kill me now - or don't you have the balls to do it?"

He looked at her, "There are more questions – and then we'll see what to do with you."

"Your plan came together when Connie Warner came to see Dick. She was a perfect match?"

"Yes. Dick phoned me and we had to make up our minds quickly."

"He drugged her?"

"Yes. He kept her drugged in the trunk of his car overnight and the next day – until we could swop out her clothes and mine – and my jewelry - and then set the car on fire."

"So you murdered an innocent young woman just to set me up?"

"Yes. The plan worked."

Tony stepped even closer to Kathy and looked her in the eye. "That makes Daniel, Connie and then Dick that you murdered."

"And Bill McKinzie." She added.

"Oh right, let's not forget Bill! So that makes four that you have killed."

Kathy did not answer.

Then rather matter-of-factly she asked,

"I have a question?"

"Go ahead."

"When we fought you asked me if I was seeing someone – I said that I was – do you remember that?"

"Yes."

"You said that you were seeing someone and you said that you were seeing a man – who was it?"

"First I want to know what happened to Dick. I believe that it was another camping accident – another push off of a cliff?"

"No, that would have been foolish – Dick died as a result of an acute asthma attack."

"Do you expect me to believe that? What bullshit!"

"You can believe what you want – his official cause of death was from an asthma attack." She paused, "Dick used to have bad attacks and he lost his breath several times – there was my opportunity. I told him that I loved to camp – which I did not - Dick was afraid of the pollen. Eventually I convinced him that if he took his puffer with him on the trip that he would be fine.

When he packed his gear for the trip he made sure that he had his puffer in his backpack. Once he had checked that it was packed, I then removed it and put it back in the bathroom. I took an empty puffer and placed it in the backpack. We drove out to a beautiful spot. He had a massive asthma attack and when he tried to use his puffer it would not work. I went for a walk – when I came back he was dead."

"And the police didn't expect any foul play?"

"None at all. Dick had tried to use his puffer but it was empty. The police assumed that Dick had packed an empty puffer by mistake."

Again there was a long pause.

Then Tony asked another question.

"One thing that I could never understand was your black eye. I never did hit you – so where did it come from?"

Kathleen answered in a very clinical tone, "We did not have a plan to start with but we needed to begin to set you up. It took a while but I finally convinced Dick that he had to hit me. He didn't want to but he would do anything that I wanted him to. So, he hit me and then people thought that it was you!"

"You are pure evil. You deserve to die."

"So you lied to me when you said that if I told you the truth that you would let me live...what does that make you - a monster too?"

While Kathleen was talking to him he walked back to the sliding doors where he had entered the house. He bent down next to his shoes and picked up a jerry can. He then slid the door closed again.

"I never should have believed you! You're still playing with fire – but this time to make it work you need to tie me to a chair for your plan to work – you're a coward!"

"Before I send you away I'll answer your question about who I was seeing. It was a man – I told you the truth then. I was seeing was Victor Gomes – one of the best hypnotic experts in L.A. I had been seeing him for several months – he was trying to cure me of my addictions. If you had paid any attention at the time, you would have noticed that although I was still drinking I was on the path to recovery. He thought that I could be booze and drug free within a year. I was hoping to get my life back together – he had great hopes for me.

Who knows, maybe if I had started my treatment earlier, then none of all of this would have happened – maybe if we shared more things together we could have made things work out."

Tony unscrewed the cap on the can. He looked at Kathleen. He could not understand why she didn't scream for help.

"You're going to kill both of us? Is this your only way out? Are you still playing with gasoline and matches? When are you going to grow up?"

He ignored her.

He started pouring the liquid onto the floor where Kathleen sat tied to the chair.

Maybe she had resigned herself to the fact that she was going to die. Kathleen just sat and looked at him.

Tony took the empty jerry can back to the sliding door and put it down outside of the house.

He walked back and stood in front of her. He then lit a match.

It burst into life.

Half way down he blew the match out.

"You don't have the balls to set anyone on fire and see them die!"

Tony did not answer.

He took out another match. He lit it – and when half way through, he looked at Kathy and then dropped the match into the liquid.

Instead of igniting the liquid it went out.

"What the hell are you playing at?" she yelled at him.

All he said was, "What do you smell?"

"What do you mean? What do I smell?"

"Answer me – what do you smell?"

"Nothing – I smell nothing!"

"It was water that I poured over the floor."

"Why? What the hell are you up to?"

"It was water. I had no intention of setting you – or me – on fire. Those days are gone. Sometime over the last few years the demons went away. I no longer need fire to vent my hate."

"Then why have you pursued me since you got out of jail? Why not just leave that to the FBI to find me?"

"I just wanted to hear it from you what happened and how you had plotted to set me up." He paused, "I didn't know that you killed Bill – maybe I should thank you – you did the job that I had failed to do. When I was released from jail I needed to find out what happened the night that you died – that night that poor innocent Connie died in your car. Initially I couldn't remember that I had babbled to Dick that I wanted to murder you – and how I was going to do it. I think that I just needed to bring things to a close – I knew some things but I had to track you down and fill in the missing pieces."

"And now what are you going to do?"

"I am going to untie you and then walk out of here. I never want to see you again. I will walk out and you will be free to live your life."

"Just like that!"

"Yes, just like that."

He walked up behind Kathleen and started to cut the ropes free. He did one arm and then one leg. He did not want her to do anything stupid while he was untying her. As her one wrist and arm became free she began to move it to try to get the blood circulating again.

Once she was completely free Tony stepped away from her.

He picked up the burnt out match on the carpet.

"Good bye Kathleen!"

He turned and walked towards the sliding door.

"Tony!"

As he turned around, she hit him with the baseball bat that he had struck her with not an hour before. He had forgotten to pick it up as he turned to walk out of the house. The blow hit him across the front of his face and he dropped limp to the ground.

"You stupid naïve man, if you thought that I would let you just leave. You were going to leave and not tell anyone! You pathetic fool! You could never do anything right!"

As the life returned to her limbs she had to think quickly.

"Kathleen – it's time for you to run again. Bid farewell to your new home and fly into the night again!"

She walked through to her bedroom and pulled out a set of suitcases. She quickly filled all of the suitcases and then took them through to the garage and put them into the trunk of her car.

Then came the important part.

Kathleen kept detailed records of the cash that she had hidden. She had used the money from Dick's will to buy her first house in Summerlin years before. She needed to appear legitimate if ever she was audited. The money from her late third husband had set her up in the community.

She always knew just how much cash she had hidden away – and where. She opened the safe behind the painting in her bedroom. She had just over $400,000 in cash. Then from a variety of hiding places in the house she retrieved four more envelopes. Each one contained about $50,000 cash. That gave her $600,000 from her home. She placed the cash into a duffle bag and took it through to the garage. She stuffed the bag under the driver's seat of her car.

She then went back into her bedroom and changed her clothes. She would have to drive all night in order to try to get away. She did not know in which direction she would head but she wanted to be warm in the car.

She grabbed a scarf and walked out of her home.

Seated in the car she closed the roof of the convertible.

Kathleen had two more stops to make before she sped off into the night. Her first stop was at the Greyhound station in town. Not a great place to visit at night but she had no choice.

She walked into the station with a grocery bag in her hand. At the lockers she checked that she was not being watched before opening her locker. She quickly removed the parcel and placed it into her grocery bag. She then walked back to her car as quickly as she could. The convertible sped off hard as she accelerated away.

In the bag was $100,000 in cash.

While she was waiting for a light to turn green she stuffed the bag under the passenger seat.

The second stop at the railway station was equally well executed.

This time the envelope recovered contained $150,000.

The combination to her home safe and the two lockers were numbers that she would never forget. They were the dates that she had murdered three men.

She had another $ 100,000 in a bank vault in Washington. She would keep that in reserve. The combination of the bank vault was the date that young Connie Wagner had died.

She had a cash hoard of just on $850,000 – excluding the money in Washington. She wrote off the value of the house – she could not have everything.

Earlier in the afternoon she had filled the tank of her car with gas. That had been fortuitous, as now she did not have to stop. She could drive for several hours before having to refill the tank.

"Where to go? Which direction? Not too many options from Vegas!"

She was driving with one hand. The other hand was rubbing the lump on her neck where Tony had hit her with the baseball bat.

Her mind was so full of the decision that she had to make that she did not see that the traffic light had turned red. She drove straight through the intersection doing about 60 miles per hour. All she heard was the horn and the sketching of heavy brakes. Then came the impact, as she was t-boned.

Her car was crushed under the front of the thirty-ton fuel tanker.

The Audi was being crushed under the front of the tanker. The sound of tearing metal was drowned out by the explosion of the car's fuel tank. Not thirty seconds later the gas tank of the tanker exploded and then that was followed, a minute later, by the entire rig being ripped apart. The explosion could be heard ten miles away. Store windows were blown out by the shock waves of the gigantic blast. The damage scene was a nightmare.

The driver of the rig had jumped from the cab just after the impact and he had struck the curb with such force that he had broken his hip and leg. He was found barely alive with his clothes on fire when the First Responders arrived on the scene. Casualties were found up to a hundred yards away from the blast. Several did not make it.

Kathleen had no chance.

This time she actually died in an inferno that took everything with it – including taking $850,000 in cash burnt to a cinder.

The police identified her car from a scorched license plate. The body was unrecognizable.

Chapter 50

Tony was brought back to semi consciousness by a booming noise in his head and the house vibrating. He had no idea where he was or what the gigantic boom was that had brought him back. He tried to sit up. He felt a severe pain in his face. He could hardly move his head it was so painful. He touched his cheek and there was blood on his hand. He could feel the lump on his cheek.

Slowly as his vision returned, he looked around and realized where he was. A kitchen chair was lying on its side in the living room. Kathleen was gone.

He stood up and his head began to spin. He placed his gloved hands on a table to steady himself. After minute or so he slowly let go of the table. He took out a piece of cloth from his pocket and wiped away the prints from his glove. He did not wish the blood on his gloved hands to be traced back to him.

He walked through the house to check that Kathleen was indeed gone. Nothing seemed disturbed – she had closed the wall safe and replaced the painting before she had left the house. All of her bedroom closets were closed. Everything seemed neat and tidy.

Tony walked through to the garage. The car was gone.

He returned to the living room and carefully lifted and carried the chair back to the kitchen. He placed the cut ropes and the baseball into the bag that he carried. Then he double-checked everything.

There was no trace that he – or anyone else – had ever been there – except for the large pool of water that was now soaking into the carpet. At the sliding door he picked up the jerry can. He put on his shoes outside of the house. He slid the door closed behind him. He moved quickly across the empty lot between the shrubs and small trees.

When he reached his rental car, he took off his shoes and socks and placed the four items into four separate old grocery bags – these he would dispose of one at a time in garbage cans as he drove back towards his hotel. The pieces of rope were cut up into smaller portions and also disposed of at various places as he drove back to his hotel. He changed his hoody and pants and put on clean socks and his shoes before he stepped behind the wheel of the car. He just hoped that no one could see him in the darkness. He disposed of the bat in a garbage can behind a shopping center.

His norm was to enter the hotel through the front lobby and that is what he did again that evening. He made sure that he covered his face with his hoody as he walked casually across the lobby of the hotel to the elevators.

Upstairs in his room, he stripped down and took a long shower. The shower water hurt his face where Kathy had hit him. He had a significant swelling and bruising on his one cheekbone. He lay down on the bed with an ice pack on his face.

He did not know where Kathleen had gone, and he did not care.

While he had been driving around town dropping off the evidence that he had been in Kathleen's home he saw many emergency vehicles speeding towards the road that led to the interstate.

As soon as the police department was able to approach the completely burnt out shell of what was once a red convertible and had seen the license plate, a number of squad cars were sent to Kathleen's house.

After knocking on the front door of the home and receiving no reply, they broke the door in an entered the home. While inspecting the home all that they found was that the sliding door had been picked open and that the carpet in the living room was wet.

There were no other clues. It appeared as if Cathy Webster had packed up and left her home – but they did not know why.

Most of the cash that was in the car was completely burnt but some notes survived the inferno. The Las Vegas police department would conduct an investigation into the late Cathy Webster.

The next morning Tony had a massive headache from the blow that he had taken the night before. He made breakfast in his suite and turned on the TV. The weather forecast was being delivered – he thought, "Hey this is Vegas; is the weather not the same every day?"

Then he almost gagged on his toast as the news anchor returned to the story of the collision the previous night between a fully loaded fuel tanker and a car on the outskirts of town.

"From what we understand the vehicle, owned by a Cathy Webster of Summerlin, ran a red light at high speed – a fuel tanker could not stop in time and rammed into the side of the car. Both vehicles exploded in the collision. It has been confirmed that Cathy Webster owned the vehicle – we still need to confirm that it was her who was in the vehicle at the time of the collision. The driver of the rig jumped from his vehicle as the collision occurred. He suffered a broken hip and leg and has burns to his body. Four pedestrians died as a result of the explosion and twelve other people were injured in the blast – all are in hospital with burns – they are reported to be in a stable condition. There is extensive damage to property in the area. At this time we have no further update from the police or from the hospital.

"Holy shit! She must have been in a hurry to get away after she hit me! Where was she going?"

He rubbed the broken skin on his cheekbone. He had been saved from major damage to his face by the steel plate that had been inserted while he was still in prison. Without the plate the blow might well have killed him.

He did not know how to feel about the death of the woman that he pursued all over the northwest. She had encouraged him to sing, she had murdered for him while still a teenager. She had then murdered again in order that she could run after his money. She had set up the death of young Connie. She had set him up to go to prison. She had set up Dick to die too.

Then on a more sober note he thought, "*So, what am I? I tried to kill by fire – so many times I tried to kill by fire. What does that make me?*"

He sat very still for a long time and then he had a very chilling thought. "*What if it wasn't Kat in the car last night! What if she had done the same thing again?*"

When the police department confirmed that the remains found in the car were those of Cathy Webster, there was still doubt in Tony's mind. Four days after the inferno Tony checked out of the hotel and returned the car rental.

"Mr. McKinzie, we hope that you enjoyed your stay. We hope to see you again sometime." He thanked the receptionist and drove away from the city.

Part 3

Chapter 51

"We hope that you will be happy here Mr. Macey!"

"Thank you! I'm sure that I will."

Tony Macey had taken out a six-month lease on a beautiful fully furnished home on Zuma Beach, just off of the Pacific highway in Malibu. He looked forward to enjoying sitting outside under the large retractable canopy that ran along the entire back of the house that faced the ocean.

He had returned to California after his visit to Las Vegas. After spending more time in the confines of an apartment suite, he decided to try something different and to live by the ocean.

A few old friends had made contact with him again. It had almost seemed as if they were unsure if they wanted to be seen with an ex- convict, but eventually a small – very small – group formed around him. They all lived in the Malibu area so it was convenient. He had not seen them often since his return but that suited him just fine. In truth, it most likely suited them just fine too.

He recruited the services of a house cleaner. On the three days a week that she came in, he would try to be away.

He still spent a great deal of time alone.

All of the boxes that he had stored in other locations were delivered to his new home. He spent time going through the content of the boxes and shredded many bags full of his research concerning the whereabouts of Dick and Cathy Webster. There was no need to keep this information any more. And he did not need to be implicated in her death in any way.

There were two boxes that he did keep. The first was full of the songs that he had written while he was in prison. The second box contained the photographs of Tony with his mother and some other documents.

He had hardly touched a guitar in twenty years. He found a guitar store on Sunset Boulevard and purchased the same model that he used to play on stage. He was not very good at playing then and now he was even worse. He used to sit outside of his home under the canopy and try to put music to his lyrics. The sessions were mostly fruitless but it passed the time.

He could not believe just how many potential songs he had written while he had been in prison. Then it kept him sane. Now it kept him occupied.

There was no desire to sing again but his time sitting and singing softly to himself was very calming. He also had to get used to the change in the pitch of his voice. His speaking voice had become squeakier as a result of the gasoline that he had swallowed when he had tried to kill himself.

He would drive up and down the Pacific highway and stop at small coffee shops and read magazines or buy books to read in the evenings. He would read at least one book a week. He found books to be another form of improving himself. He would read anything.

He was in a bookstore in Santa Monica when he saw a promotion for a new book release. He read the front and back covers of the book and, thinking it sounded interesting, decided to buy it.

After dinner he started to read the book. It was slow to get going but then he became more intrigued with the story. Early the next afternoon he picked up the book again. This time he could not put the book down. Dinner was a quick sandwich, eaten while sitting with the book in hand. He read through until well after midnight.

When he had completed the book he could not believe the time - he had read for almost eleven hours straight! It was one of the best books that he had ever read.

He slept late the following morning. After brunch, he picked up the book again. He read the authors bio. Something sounded familiar but he could not place it. He looked up the author but still he could not make a connection.

He enjoyed the settings and his walks on the beach but after a while he felt himself becoming restless. The setting was so beautiful and yet he felt as if his heart was not committed to living full-time by the ocean. He had thought that it would be soothing – and it had been – but now he was bored.

While watching the TV news one day he saw that some areas of Nevada, which normally did not have much rain, had been hit with storms that had caused road closures. The damage was excessive – in particular in the town of ...Tony looked at the screen but more so at the name of the town that had incurred most of the damage. Somewhere deep inside of him a memory cell came back to life. He had heard or seen that name twice before but he could not connect the two thoughts.

Then all of a sudden he thought that he knew. He walked through to the bedroom and picked up the book that he had just completed reading. He read the piece written about the author.

He then took out the box that contained his personal effects. He quickly found the second photograph that was in the box.

The name of the town mentioned in the biography of the author and the name of the town on the photograph was the same! The photograph had been in his possession for almost forty years. It was dated 1952 – long before he had been given the photograph.

Tony booted up his computer and waited impatiently for it to come to life. Once logged in he searched for the town and soon found it.

He sat in a semi-trance for several minutes. He was trying to comprehend the co-incidence. *"The same town! The same town! What are the chances that it would be the same town?"*

He then looked up the distance from Malibu to the town and then from that town to another one further north that he had also intended to visit. It made sense to make one long trip out of it.

It was just on a week before he was ready to drive off and visit the two places that were now fully the center of his attention.

Chapter 52

The drive to Reno in Nevada is slated to take eight hours depending on the traffic. It took Tony just on eleven hours to reach it. At one stage the traffic on the road to Sacramento had been blocked for two hours because of a collision. By the time Tony reached the hotel that he had booked, he was stiff, sore and very tired. He ordered room service and was in bed and asleep early.

The next morning he had a short drive to his first destination.

He checked into the hotel under the name of Anthony McKinzie.

"Is there a coffee shop or diner in town – some place that isn't part of a national chain?" The hotel receptionist told him of the well-known diner which was only a five-minute walk away. Tony was not wearing a hoody but a baseball cap so the scars on his neck and ears were showing. Although it was only a short walk to his first destination, Tony decided to drive. The air still had a damp feeling to it from the heavy rainstorm that had hit the town.

Tony entered the diner and picked a booth near the back. He sat in a position facing the entrance. He ordered a coffee and doughnut – his breakfast was an hour before but he still felt hungry.

When his coffee and doughnut was brought to his table he asked, "Do you know Elizabeth McKenzie - the author – I believe that she lives in Alpine Meadows?"

"Yes Sir. She is one of our newer residents – you know her?"

"No I don't but I recently read her novel The Solar Murder and the information indicated that she lived here. I was hoping to get to meet her and ask her to sign my copy of her book."

"We're really proud of her book. She has travelled the country promoting it. She is a very smart professional-looking lady – she used to work for a law practice in San Francisco before she settled here."

"Has she been here long?"

"No – most folk here were born in town. She must be here about two and half years now. She married our local sheriff last summer."

"What's his name?"

"Sheriff Norman Wilson – he's been sheriff here for a long time.

I've known him and his family since we were kids at school. This is a small community."

"Well, it would be great if I could meet Elizabeth McKenzie and ask her to sign my book! How can I make contact with her?"

"I'll give the sheriff a call – he might know where she is today."

"Sheriff Wilson."

"Hello sheriff, it is Ted here from the diner."

"Oh hello Ted. How are you?"

"I am good thank you sheriff."

"Is anything the matter?" asked Norman Wilson.

"Not really. I have a guy at the diner who says that he would like your wife to sign a copy of her book – he said that he really liked it and was passing through town and wanted to check if she was around."

"Did he say who he was?"

"No, actually I forgot to ask him his name. He does look kinda weird though."

"What do you mean?"

"Well, he must be in his mid-50s. He is wearing a baseball cap and a scarf around his neck. He has large dark glasses on – he just looks odd – weird looking!"

"And you say that he would like to have Elizabeth sign a copy of her book?"

"Yes sheriff."

"Ok, let me come down. I'll check him out before I call Elizabeth."

Ted did not return to the table where Tony was sitting. He busied himself behind the serving counter until

Sheriff Wilson walked into the diner about five minutes later. In a small town everything is nearby.

As Sheriff Wilson walked into the diner he glanced at Ted and followed his glance towards the table where Tony was sitting. Behind his dark glasses Tony watched the exchange of looks between them.

Sherriff Wilson walked to the booth where Tony was sitting.

"Good morning Sir, my name is Sheriff Wilson – I'm Chief of Police in Alpine Meadows. I believe that you were asking about my wife."

"Hello sheriff – yes, I was asking about your wife. No offense meant – I just wanted to check if she was in town and if she could sign a copy of book – I really enjoyed it."

"Are you from around these parts?"

"No, I'm from Malibu in California – I am just passing through town."

Tony had taken a copy of Elizabeth's book out of the small bag that was on the table. "It would be great if your wife could sign a copy of her book for me".

Norman Wilson thought for a moment then said, "Let me check if my wife is available."

He walked away from the booth and stopped at the entrance of the diner telephoning Elizabeth on his cell phone.

"Hello, this is Elizabeth Wilson speaking." She had not changed her professional demeanor when answering the telephone!

"Hi, it's Norman." He sounded a little edgy.

"Are you alright?"

"Yes, I'm fine. I'm at the diner and there's a guy here from California. He has read your novel. He has asked if he could meet you and for you to sign a copy of your book."

"Oh, that's very nice!" she paused, "But you sound a little uncertain about it?"

"I think so – he just looks weird, middle-aged, baseball cap, big dark glasses and a scarf around his neck."

"Are you just being a policeman again? I am sure that he's fine. Should I come down to the diner?"

"Yes, if you're ok to come down."

"I'd like to meet him. Don't have any pie while you're waiting for me!"

Norman walked back to the table where Tony was sitting.

"My wife is on her way. She should be here in about ten minutes."

"Thank you sheriff! That's great. Can I get you a coffee while you wait?"

"Thank you – I'll have a tea." Norman took off his hat and sat down at the booth with Tony.

All Ted needed was to see Sheriff Wilson remove his hat and he knew to bring over the tea.

"Thank you, Ted." As his tea was brought out, Tony took a refill of his coffee.

"So you say that you are from California?"

"Yes. I've lived there for over thirty five years." Tony did not elaborate on the fact that over eighteen of those years had been in prison.

"Have you ever been to California sheriff?"

"Only to San Francisco – nothing further south than that. We didn't travel much as kids and then after I became a police officer I never really had time to travel much. I would like to go back someday."

"You done much traveling?"

"Yes. At one time I travelled all over the world but that stopped many years ago. Lately I was just in one spot." "*Being in prison does eliminate the ability to travel!* , he said to himself.

Norman did not really know what more to say to the weird looking man sitting opposite him. The bell saved him! The bell on the door of the diner came to life as Elizabeth walked in. Tony looked up as Elizabeth approached them.

"She looks more like a city girl than one I would have expected in a small town." He thought to himself.

As Elizabeth reached the booth where the two men were seated, they both stood up. "Elizabeth, I would like you to meet...", then he remembered that he had not as yet asked the stranger what his name was. "Pardon me, I forgot to ask your name!"

"Tony. Just call me Tony!"

Elizabeth shook his hand. She thought that he looked scary with his baseball cap and scarf around his neck. Norman shifted across the seat so that Elizabeth could sit next to him.

"Tony, I believe that you enjoyed my novel!"

"Yes, I did. But there is one thing that I didn't like about the book."

Elizabeth was not sure what the criticism would be so she just waited to hear what Tony had to say. "I sat up all night reading the book – it kept me glued to the story. I couldn't put it down!"

"Oh, I'm sorry to hear that!" She answered smiling.

"I believe that you would like me to sign the book for you?"

"If you wouldn't mind!"

"What name should I write on the book?"

"My name is Tony Macey."

Sheriff Wilson looked at Tony and said, "Tony Macey – the singer!"

"Yes, sheriff that's me – I look a little different these days!"

"Elizabeth, do you remember Tony Macey? He had all of those songs in the charts ...it must be 25 years ago! This is Tony Macey!"

Tony sat and watched the two people sitting with him in the booth.

"Yes, I remember Tony Macey! I loved your soft ballads – they were so sincere!"

"Thank you! I actually brought out my first record over thirty years ago, I was in my early 20s at the time."

"Is it that long ago? – I don't believe it!" Sheriff Wilson was so excited to be sitting with Tony Macey.

"You were such a big star!" he said.

"I had a string of hits and platinum records while still in my 20s – and I appeared on all of the TV specials – do you remember those?" he asked.

"Yes, I watched them all – I think – I tried not to miss one of them!"

Norman called over to Ted, "Ted come on over here – this is Tony Macey!"

Ted was in the same age group as Norman and Elizabeth so he had also grown up listening to the gentle sound of Tony Macey.

"Gosh! I remember you on the Dean Martin Show!" It would not take long before everyone in the town knew that Tony Macey was in the diner! Ted would make sure of that. In a small town where most of the population has lived all of their lives it would not take too long for the grapevine to spread the news.

"What happened to your career?"

Elizabeth was surprised that Norman had asked such a direct question. Maybe he had forgotten that Tony had been convicted for the murder of his wife. At the time Norman had followed the trial closely. Every police officer on the west coast of the States seemed to have followed the trial. Tony was a superstar of his day and when a star falls everyone follows it. Particularly police officers!

"Norman – how can you ask such a question!" Elizabeth felt embarrassed that the chief of police – and her husband – had been so direct with someone – and with a star like Tony Macey.

Tony answered very directly, "I fell into the trap of booze and pills – not an easy thing to say but I was falling off a cliff – maybe I could not handle the pressure – I was stoned half of the time. My wife died and I was arrested for her murder…" he paused, "I got twenty-five years. For a crime that I didn't commit."

"Oh, I remember that now." said Norman.

"My life was in a mess at the time but I kept saying that I didn't murder my wife – I couldn't remember much that was going on around me! I was a real bastard – excuse my language!"

"If I remember you were recently released from prison?"

"Yes, that was last year – a review of the evidence against me proved that I had been framed – I spent over eighteen years in jail."

He paused and then continued, "And that is when I got burned - I tried to kill myself – but all I got was a disfigured face and neck."

Elizabeth changed the subject.

"So, let me sign your book for you. Do you want me to sign *"To Tony Macey, from Elizabeth McKenzie?"*

"No, I'd like you to use my real name – Tony Macey is only my professional name."

"Sure, what is your real name?"

"My name is Anthony James McKinzie."

He paused.

"When I was 16, my dad me told me that he wasn't my father. He gave me proof that McKinzie was not my real name.

"My full real name is Anthony James Wilson.

"My real father was John Charles Wilson – he was known as *Big John."*

He waited for the bombshell to hit home.

"What! What sort of game are you playing? Is this a con game?"

Tony thought that the police officer was going to grab him from across the table.

Tony put his hand up in front of his face – not to protect himself but to try to request that he could get a chance to speak.

"What is happening?" Elizabeth was trying to hold Norman back as he was attempting to rise out of the booth. Then she turned her attention to Tony, "What are you playing at?" The tone was from her old days in a law firm when she was known as Sergeant Major!

"PLEASE! Please let me explain!"

"It had better be good!" Norman was glaring at him.

"Sheriff, the man I grew up with – Bill McKinzie – told me that he had been injured during the war. While he was in hospital he discovered that he could never have children. He married my mother but years later when she fell pregnant he knew that he could not be the father. Bill then found out that my mother was seeing someone else. But he didn't know who it was – in a small town he might have worked it out – but he couldn't.

After I left home he sent me a box that contained some photographs of my mother and me. I still have the photograph. Also in the box was another photograph –it was of my mother and another man. At the back of the photograph is a date and name and address. It seems that my mother met the man when she worked part-time in the town of Ontario - which was not too far from Vale, my hometown. She was working shifts at a diner to boost our family income.

It seems as if they were meeting up at a motel near Ontario. The man was a traveling salesman. He was in town every month – and he would see my mother at the motel."

"Sheriff, I have a photograph." Tony took out the photograph and handed it to Norman.

Reluctantly Sheriff Wilson took the photograph from Tony.

He looked at it.

It was of a man and a woman. The man had his arm around her waist. Norman didn't recognize the woman but saw that she was pregnant. He recognized the man. It was his father. Norman turned the photograph over – at the back was written: *"From Big John Wilson, December 1952."* Underneath the message was an address.

"202 First Avenue, Alpine Meadows NV."

"Sheriff, is that your address – the home where your father lived?"

Sheriff Wilson only nodded his head. Elizabeth took his hand and squeezed it.

"I don't know if you are who you say you are. Why did you come here? What do you want from me?"

Norman asked,

"You have not answered my questions."

"Sheriff I'll answer your questions. What do I want from you? The answer is nothing. I don't want anything – nothing at all. The second question was why did I come here? I always had the photograph of my mother with another man – but I never paid any attention to his name or the address that was on the photo. The name Alpine Meadows meant nothing to me – but it was buried way back in my mind.

Then by chance I was in a bookstore and saw Elizabeth's book. I purchased the book and read the bio where Elizabeth lived. At first the name didn't bring my memory back. I was watching the TV news and the reporter was covering the floods in Alpine Meadows. Then I thought that I remembered where I had seen the name before. I pulled out my old photographs and saw my mother with Big John Wilson and the address.

I had some business in Oregon and I decided to drive here first. I wanted Elizabeth to sign my copy of her book – and then I researched and found out that she was married to the police chief – Sheriff Norman Wilson - and lived at 202 First Avenue, Alpine Meadows. So I came here to meet you both.

As for your first question. No, I can't prove who I am – we have photographs but you don't know if I was the child born to John Wilson and my mother. I was hoping that you would agree to a DNA and a blood test. Either way let me be clear – I don't want anything from you or your wife."

Norman had been taking in deep breaths and now he felt that he had to say something.

"If we have the tests done then what will you do with the information?"

"I give you both my word that I won't do anything until we discuss what is best. If you decide that you want nothing to do with me then all it will be is another closed chapter in my life. All I seem to be doing now is closing chapters – anyways you have my word."

Norman looked at Elizabeth – he knew her answer.

"Where are you staying?"

"I've checked into a hotel for two nights."

Norman agreed to the tests – so long as they were discreet.

Tony paid the tab on the way out of the diner. Norman and Elizabeth sat alone.

"What do you think?" she asked.

"I don't know. I just don't know. My dad was such a stern and strict man. I know that he was a salesman and he traveled all over Nevada – and if I recall, he used to go to Ontario to train the staff. Could he have found someone there? It's possible but just so difficult to believe. I wish that Maddy were still alive – she would remember more than me."

And then he thought, "Even if Maddy suspected anything she would not have told me!"

The following morning the two men went for blood tests. Tony checked out a day early from the hotel and drove north.

Chapter 53

Tony tried to empty his mind as he drove north to Oregon. It wasn't easy. He kept thinking if it had been the right thing to do to invade the privacy of a local sheriff and his wife. What was there to gain from sharing his findings with them? Maybe there was more to lose than to gain. If anything, it would just close another chapter – if only he could stop closing chapters and could concentrate on opening new ones.

He was just sixteen years old when he had stepped off a Greyhound bus. Officer Gellis had seen him off at Hood River. Now, as he turned into the parking lot in front of the trucker stop, diner and bar he was a very different man. He was nervous.

He had returned only once when Big Gus had asked to see him just before he died. He was twenty at the time. With the money that Gus had left him in his will, he had established his own small music label. Gus had also left him half of the property and business. He had been approached several times if he was interested in selling his 50% share. He had always turned down those offers.

One thing was for sure – no one that he knew all those years ago was still working in the diner or the bar.

He walked up the steps and into the bar. It looked old. There was a funny smell. He walked over to the bar. "Get you anything sir?"

He ordered a sandwich and coffee. "You know that you can get that in the diner next door". It was no so much of an insulting comment but rather a statement. "I know, but I'll have it here." Tony knew that the kitchens were connected!

"Not seen you here before."

"No, I'm from California."

"I'd love to visit there. Maybe when my winning ticket comes in!"

The barman left him alone to eat his sandwich.

"Everything OK here – more coffee?"

Tony decided not to be rude. "Yes, I'll have another cup."

The barman looked to be in his early forties. "You worked here long?" asked Tony. "About eight years – tough to make a living – not great pay but it keeps the family fed!" He smiled but there was no humor.

Tony looked around the bar. The stage had been removed and the paint was a different color. The tables and chairs looked to be a hundred years old.

"Do you get much business passing through?"

"Lunch times are pretty good – nights are so-so."

"Mind if I look around? I'm writing a book on old diners."

"Sure! What would you like to see?"

"How about the kitchen?"

"Follow me!"

The kitchen needed a redo!

"Where does that door go?" he asked

"Oh, just to the back. Nothing special there."

"Could I look anyway?"

"Sure! If you want."

Tony stepped outside. There was no camper. Later he found out that it had been removed when Gus passed away. Without asking permission from the barman he started to walk around the corner of the building. "Oh, I hear the bell, I've a customer. Wander around if you like."

When Tony walked around the corner, he felt a tingle. There was still a strong memory of Snake lying dying in front of him. He walked away.

He went down the side of the bar and up towards where Gus had his cabin just up in the forest. It was not a long walk but he found it tough going. His heart was beating double. When he saw the cabin, his heart slowed to half its normal pace. The cabin stood in ruins.

He imagined he could smell hot cakes on the grill and see a plateful being placed in front of him. He could visualize the Thanksgiving turkey in 1969 – now the smell was one of a rotting log cabin. He walked further up the hill and stood and looked out over the valley. This is where he had stood with Gus after the Thanksgiving dinner in 1969.

"Did you see what you wanted to?" asked the barman.

"Yes, thank you – I saw plenty." He paid his bill and left a large tip.

In one way he was disappointed with what he had seen. In another way he was rather pleased.

His next destination was town, just a few miles down the road.

He used the name Anthony McKinzie when he checked into the hotel. He spent most of the next two days on the telephone.

He did not want to be seen around town too much. While he waited for the information that he sought, he took day drives in the area.

He ate in his room in the evenings.

On the third morning he received a telephone call from his lawyer.

"Tony we've identified the owners of the other 50% of the property – we're trying to make a deal. It could take a while because there are five other owners."

"How long?"

"Not sure. It could take weeks or months – I don't know. Let's see what value the accountants provide. Do not worry about that just now – they will try to push the price up now that they know that there is a potential buyer – and of course they don't know that it is you. Are you sure that you want to do this?"

Tony answered honestly, "No, I'm not sure!" He hung up.

At the end of the week it was time to place a telephone call to a sheriff Wilson.

They agreed to meet the following day. Tony checked out of the hotel after breakfast and headed south.

Chapter 54

Tony checked back into the hotel. As arranged, he met with Sheriff Wilson in Tony's room.

"Did you have a good trip down from Oregon?"

"Yes, thank you. It went by quickly."

He did not want to spend time on idle chatter, "What news do you have?"

Norman Wilson had sat down on a couch in Tony's room. He looked uncomfortable. How was he going to break the news to Tony?

"I got the lab tests back yesterday." He hesitated, "The two blood samples are a match."

Tony bit his bottom lip. How does one respond to this? He could not even begin to think what had gone through Norman's mind since he had received the news.

"No doubts at all?"

"No. It's a complete match."

"What now sheriff?"

"I don't know. I can't believe that my father was having an affair. It was just not in his personality – not in his profile – not his attitude towards life. I don't know what to think!"

"If it's any consolation, I don't know what to think either." Tony paused then continued, "I do know that what I said to you when we first met is true - I don't want anything from you.

That isn't why I decided to visit. Maybe I just needed to know the answer."

Norman seemed to stare into the distance almost unaware of Tony sitting in a chair near the window. His mind was not racing; rather it was functioning very slowly.

Tony sat out the silence. He did not know what to say.

The next thing that Norman said surprised him.

"Elizabeth and I would like you to come for dinner at our home this evening. Maybe we could talk about a few things together."

Tony had not expected this.

"Are you sure?"

"Yes we are – and besides you need to see where your father lived."

At 6:30 p.m. that evening Tony rang the doorbell of 202 First Avenue.

As was the custom they sat outside on the front porch –just as when Elizabeth had met Maddy for the first time.

"Thank you for coming." Elizabeth said, guiding Tony to a chair.

Tony accepted the offer of lemonade. He had not touched alcohol in many years.

The evening was very difficult for Norman and Elizabeth could feel his discomfort. She had been surprised when Norman suggested that Tony come over for dinner.

He was not a super star – or even a fallen super star sitting in front of them that evening – he was Norman's family. But it was still a very difficult thing to acknowledge and to accept.

The evening began awkwardly. After all they were really complete strangers.

When Elizabeth looked at Norman he seemed ill at ease. She then engaged Tony on his career.

He briefly discussed his rise to fame in his early 20's and his double platinum records. His fall from grace was touched on by, "I could not handle the pressure of being wealthy and famous and I started drinking and popping pills – from there everything just seemed to fall apart."

His response to Elizabeth's questions had taken only a few minutes. He was not ready to discuss his life with anyone, nor was Norman and Elizabeth really open to hearing about it now.

Elizabeth excused herself in order to get the dinner ready. Norman and Tony were left alone. They both seemed very ill at ease.

"I hope that your trip to Oregon was successful."

"I'm not sure if I would use the word *successful*." He paused.

"A long time ago I was given a leg up by a man who gave me a chance in life. He owned a truck stop and diner and bar. I washed dishes for him – worked my butt off!" It was the first time that he smiled. "I sang my first song in the bar while I was there." He smiled again.

"The man left me a large sum of money and a half share of his business when he died – that was well over 30 years ago now. I wanted to go back and see the place."

Over dinner Norman spoke about growing up in Alpine Meadows and then joining the local police department. There was little discussion about his father.

Tony declined coffee after dinner and thanked Norman and Elizabeth for inviting him over. "I think that this is the first time that I have eaten in someone's home in – well, in a very, very long time. Thank you!"

As Tony was about to leave Norman asked, "What are your plans now?"

"If the local sheriff does not mind I would like to stay in town for a few days. I need to talk with my lawyers about the property in Oregon and I may as well do it from my hotel room."

"I don't think that the sheriff would mind – maybe he could even buy you a coffee while you are in town!"

Chapter 55

Word had spread around town that the once-famous Tony Macey was back at the hotel. If Tony stepped out of the hotel lobby, he soon had people greeting him – or not – his appearance kept some of them away. But he was a little guarded about the attention he attracted.

On Friday – Tony was walking through town when he heard a voice behind him, “Tony!” He turned around and Norman was trying to catch up with him.

“Good morning sheriff.”

“I was going to stop by the hotel and ask you if you wanted to join me for that coffee.” Tony was surprised by the invitation. “Sure, I think that it’s better coffee there than at the hotel!”

“Elizabeth mentioned to you that the late Greg Winters left her a cabin about seven miles out of town. It’s a great location with its own small lake and forest. We go there on most weekends. We are going up this afternoon after I come off duty and were wondering if you would like to join us for the weekend.”

Tony did not know what to say.

As the wheels in his brain were still turning Norman said, “Please join us! We are sure that you will enjoy being away from town.”

“Are you sure?”

"Yes, we are sure – both of us would like you to come."

"And what if I turn out to be a real pain in the..." He stopped himself before he said the word.

"Tell you what, why not drive out in your car and then if we don't get along then you can drive back to town!"

That afternoon, Tony checked out of the hotel – with his reservation on hold. His blue Ford followed the car driven by Norman Wilson out into the country.

Like most people who visited the cabin for the first time, the beauty of the location surprised Tony. As the dirt road turned to the right and then left, the lake, the cabin and forest came into view. Greg and Mary Winters had chosen well when they had acquired the land and built on it.

Elizabeth showed Tony through to the guest bedroom. "The room is small but comfortable – and the private bathroom is just through that door."

Once they had settled in, Elizabeth suggested that they sit outside for drinks.

"I can't believe how beautiful this place is. It is so close to the main road and yet it's tucked away."

"We love it here – it is very quiet – which has its disadvantages – but it gives us time away from town." Elizabeth could not imagine herself living in a big city again.

Once they had refills of their drinks, Elizabeth excused herself to prepare the salads. As was their ritual, she would make the salads and Norman would take care of the BBQ.

The tightness between the two men seemed to return once Elizabeth had gone into the cabin. Finally Norman said, "Tony, there is something that puzzles me about the photograph that you showed me – the one of my father with your mother."

"What was that?"

"Well, my dad was a very quiet man so even to think that he was seeing someone else is still almost too much for me to believe. But what puzzles me is that surely he would keep the affair quiet – why draw attention to it or try to expose it.

What I don't understand is why he would write the address on the back of the photo? It's almost a roadmap to get caught. All that it would have taken was your mother to come to Alpine Meadows and the game would have been up!"

"I never really thought of that. It does sound strange. I wonder why he did it?"

"Do you have the photograph with you – could I look at it again – if you don't mind?"

"Yes, I carry it with me wherever I go. It's in my bag – I will go and get it."

Tony handed the photograph to Norman. He looked at the front of the photograph and then turned it over. After he had done this a few times, Tony said, "What are you looking for?"

"I'm not sure. The light isn't good outside. Let's take a look in the kitchen – the lights are bright there." The two men walked into the house.

Norman sat down at the kitchen table and looked carefully at the photograph again. He kept turning it over. "What are you looking for?" asked Elizabeth.

"I need the magnifying glass – is it still in the drawer?"

With the magnifying glass in hand he continued his review.

"See anything?" asked Tony.

"Tony, could I look at the photograph of you and your mother?"

With both photographs in hand he looked again.

"Tony, take a look at the handwriting on them. At first glance it looks alike but the curves of the letters are different. Also the one on the photograph of your mom and Big John was written by a man – the strokes are bolder but it's not my dad's writing either. Also look at the photograph and see how it is faded – it has "1952" written on it – but then look at the ink on the other photograph, it hasn't faded anywhere near as much as the photo itself."

Tony looked and then said, "I do not understand."

"I think that the first photograph is from 1952 and the handwriting is female – most likely your mother's. The second one is much newer - you said that you received a box of items from Bill McKinzie after you left home – is that correct?"

"Yes. That was in 1969."

"Tony, I believe that Bill McKinzie wrote our address on the photo, not your mother – I think that he wrote it about the time that he sent you the box of items in 1969."

"Maybe he had found some information after you had left home – possibly a letter with my father's address - and then wrote it on the back of the photograph for you. I wonder if he was trying to give you a roadmap to go and find your real father. I think that maybe he was trying to point you towards a new beginning in your life."

There was silence in the kitchen. If Norman was right then Bill had tried to do a good thing after Anthony had left home. If Anthony had decided to travel to Alpine Meadows in 1969 then what would his life have been like? Maybe no fame, no wealth, no seeing the world, no booze or pills, no bad wife, no prison, no scars, both physical and emotional.

Would he have embarrassed or even ruined John Wilson? Or would he been accepted into the Wilson home – and finally had a family life.

Norman and Tony spent the weekend either walking through the forest or around the lake. They shared a great deal that weekend.

Chapter 56

"I'll see you in a few weeks – there are some things I need to attend to in LA." Tony set off on his long drive to southern California.

Three days later he met with his lawyer.

"The news is not good. The other owners are not willing to sell their shares to you – they would rather buy you out."

"That does change things!" Tony was smiling.

"You look happy about it. I thought that you were dead set on owning the business."

"Yes, I was. But things have changed. I'm willing to sell to them – with several conditions."

"Why the change of heart?"

"I finally realized that it was an old chapter in my life. I tried walking back through that door but it didn't feel right."

Tony sold his 50% of the truck stop, diner and the bar.

Tony's condition that he insisted on was that the stage be rebuilt in the bar, and that Tony could book bands to perform there. He also insisted that the cabin where Big Gus had lived for so many years be renovated. The artists coming to perform at the bar would be accommodated there for free.

With his settlement after his release from prison and now the sale of the diner, Tony was well set for the rest of his life.

When he returned to Alpine Meadows, he met Norman and Elizabeth at the diner. "I have something that I need your opinion on.

When I was at your cabin for the weekend I loved the place. The surroundings were so peaceful. The lake and forest seem like a million miles from any town – and yet it is just a few miles away."

I had wanted to buy out the other owners of the bar in Oregon. I thought that I wanted to go back and live in the cabin that Big Gus owned. I think that I could visit but I couldn't live there – and running a bar and diner eighteen hours a day doesn't interest me".

So, I'm thinking of making an offer on the piece of land that is next to a small lake just outside of Alpine Meadows. The land next to your cabin is for sale – but I wanted to ask you guys before I made an offer."

The three of them went to the property the day that Tony took ownership.

From the main road the dirt track turned left to the cabin that Greg Winters had built. Tony decided he would lay down a dirt track that went slightly to the right. Greg's cabin would have the lake on the left hand side and the new construction would have the lake on the right.

Once built the new cabin would only be about fifty yards from Greg's cabin.

It, too, had solar panels, which would produce most of the electricity required for the house. At night he could hear the trees talking to him – and he remembered standing next to Big Gus on a hill overlooking a valley and a forest – it was Thanksgiving 1969. Maybe it was Big Gus talking with him.

The two men spent a great deal of time talking to each other about their lives. Norman listened to every word that Tony had to say about his life – a life full of loneliness, hate and revenge.

His new cabin contained a special room. It was a state-of-the-art recording studio.

It was about six months later when the stage was ready in the bar in Oregon. The first show booked was *Tony Macey* In the sell-out audience sat a number of important people.

Tony had made contact with Michelle Loren and he had flown her and her new husband in for the show. Also present was the widow of the late Officer Gellis. Next to her sat long retired trooper James Williams and his wife. In the front row was an old friend – a man who he had invited to help him prepare for the concert. It was Mike, who had walked out on Tony after countless arguments with Kathleen. Now they were together again.

Then there were Norman and Elizabeth. His new family!

One guest that not too many people knew was Doris Leveson. She was a singing teacher who had been working with Tony in Reno over the past few months. She had to retrain his damaged vocal cords. The voice was more rustic than in his heyday but now maybe even more soulful and sincere.

Tony drove up to Oregon several times a year for concerts. The evening business at the bar greatly increased when he was there. He was also actively involved in finding new talent around the country. Many a rising star got their true break on a stage in a small town in Oregon. Some signed contracts on Tony's new label, owned by him and Mike.

When he performed at the bar, he never walked outside of the building near the kitchen. He did not want to chance his luck that there was a ghost of a snake lying on the ground.

Tony released a new album. It was his first release in over twenty-five years. The album went gold. When Tony was asked if he was disappointed that the album "only" went gold he responded, "I'm thankful that I sold one copy!"

He sponsored a child-feeding program in Alpine Meadows and named it in honor of the late Ruth Kempster, who fed him as a young child. Without her he would have died. He finally said thank you.

The lyrics to the title song of the album spoke about his life.

"I knew where I came from but it was not a home,
Just a place where I grew up before I started to roam
I remembered her smile so sweet and kind,
She held my hand so briefly – but never out of my mind!

The need for attention turned me to fire
It possessed me and was my desire!
I tried and failed at my quest
In the long-term it was the best!

There was pain going away
Cold hungry nights and lonely days
At sixteen he hurt me deep inside,
And there was nowhere to hide!

I was trying to rise up because of the flames,
The hatred tore at me but I had no shame!
I could not see that there was nothing to gain,
Disappointed at trying and failing again.

I stopped at the diner and stayed a while,
I worked hard and was welcomed inside!
Then the beast arrived and died by the blade,
I moved on and my memory of Gus will never fade!

Success came too quickly and brought me fame,
With it came booze, pills and a bad dame!
The judge sentenced me for the crime,
Singing was over and no need to rhyme!

The system does not care for those in pain,
No guards to protect and nowhere to hide!
The burning disfigured and twisted my soul,
I wish I were dead and in a black hole!

I was trying to rise up because of the flames,
The hatred tore at me but I had no shame!
I could not see that there was nothing to gain,
Disappointment at trying and failing again!

Then an angel set me free,
The door was opened and they threw away the key.
I burned with rage to find the firebird,
My logic was blurred – so very blurred!

Then finally the show down – would the she-devil win?
What would be required to remove her sin?
Would the fire of hate win or be put out?
Would I be left with only ashes after the bout?

I was trying to rise up because of the flames,
The hatred tore at me but I had no shame!
I could not see that there was nothing to gain,
Disappointed at trying and failing again!

Then the redemption – the pouring of water,
It cleansed my soul – but I could have fought her!
Then finding peace at a lake and the trees, and family true
I no longer needed the bar and bury my blues!

I built a new foundation – a solid platform,
I rose up with hope and was reborn!
To love and be loved was all I ever desired,
I no longer needed hate or was stimulated by fire!

Closing chapters, closing chapters,
Closing chapters, closing chapters.
I found new life soaring from my own ashes,
Phoenix rising, Phoenix rising.
Phoenix rising, Phoenix rising.

Phoenix ri-ri-sing!"